The Hunter's Paradox

by:
Garrett S Rawson

Dedicated to my mother for keeping my imagination alive; and to my father for being my own Hunter and keeping the monsters in the dark at bay.

Table of Contents

Chapter I. --- 3
Chapter II. --- 15
Chapter III. --- 30
Chapter IV. --- 43
Chapter V. --- 62
Chapter VI. --- 79
Chapter VII. --- 96
Chapter VIII. --- 108
Chapter IX. --- 123
Chapter X. --- 136
Chapter XI. --- 147
Chapter XII. --- 156
Chapter XIII. --- 168
Chapter XIV. --- 179
Chapter XV. --- 190
Chapter XVI. --- 202
Chapter XVII. --- 218
Chapter XVIII. --- 237
Chapter XIX. --- 253
Chapter XX. --- 265
Chapter XXI. --- 282
Chapter XXII. --- 294
Chapter XXIII. --- 308
Hunter's Notes. --- 320

Paradox

noun, par·a·dox, ˈper-ə-ˌdäks,

: a belief that is held to be true, but upon receiving outside opinion, instead proves to be false.

[I]

Eric Hahn walked down the streets of Pratertown towards the building he sought. The steel heels of his boots clicked along the cobblestone footpath as he took his steps. His right hand rested on the butt of his revolver. The other merely hung at his side, occasionally reaching out to brush his gloved fingertips against the sides of the worn stonework of the old buildings around him. The bell tower in the center of town rang out. One, two, three clangs of an ancient cast bronze bell atop the tall tower sounded for all to hear and know the current time. The young man didn't pay attention to it; he instead adjusted the dark gray hat he was wearing. He pulled the flat, wide brim downward to cover his eyes from the evening sun, which at times managed to shine brightly as it peeked from between the clouds.

A few passersby eyed him. One child excitedly pointed at Eric, yearning to get a closer look at the duster-wearing young man, but her mother pulled her back and made sure to give a wide berth for him to pass. The new attention he was getting was something he was not used to but was something he'd be force to deal with. Most people tended to get nervous at the sight of a duster like the one he now wore; the one he had earned. He curtly nodded at the mother and child as he walked by. The mother nodded back but did not smile. She stared at him until he was nearly ten meters away. Eric felt her glare the entire time and did not feel comfortable again until the feeling of the staring eyes dissipated.

The young man felt at the small bag that hung from his side. Through its rough leather material, he could feel two irregularly-shaped stones. He prodded at the stones with his fingers and counted them. *One, two...One, two.* He repeated the numbers in his head numerous times to be sure they were both there. The stones emitted a slight warmth that brought a small smile to his face.

They're still good in there. He thought to himself, letting the pouch resume hanging freely by its short length of braided rope just below his belt. Eric was nearing his destination. He finally looked up and placed his eyes on the building that sat in front of him.

It was a stone-walled building, as old as any next to it. To the normal pedestrian, it would seem like any other establishment in Pratertown. Yet, to assume such a thing was far beyond the truth. Hanging from a decorative wrought iron bracket on the face of the building was a carved wooden sign. Its paint was worn, and the wood itself was cracked and split in some areas as if it hung there for a millennium. The words displayed across the sign was still legible despite its weathered appearance.

'Order of the Arcane Hunt', it read in elegant, hand-painted cursive lettering. He was here. Eric had enlisted in the Order a few months ago. He had to go through rigorous training in both physical combat and firearms, as well as having to show proficiency in the arcane art of the Soul Stones. Since Eric's father had taught him everything he knew about the stones, that was easy. It helped he was a natural shot as well, so going through the training wasn't as bad as it was for most. He went through it with ten others; only him and one other person had passed. He was awarded with the Hunters' signature duster long coat and flat brimmed hat; any other equipment was up to him to purchase. He felt ready though and now stood in front of his new post.

Eric looked at the sign for a moment or two, then stepped up onto the chiseled stone steps. He climbed the small stairs to a heavy wooden door that served as the entryway into the Order. The door was as old as everything else. Its iron reinforcements were showing signs of surface rust and other neglect. On its face, about chest height, was a cast iron raven skull with a door knocker mounted beneath it. Eric reached out to grab the knocker and rapped it against the door several times. The knocks seemed to echo through the streets, and the young man at first felt as if it would attract more attention of the passing civilians, though the feeling quickly went away as he glanced around to see the streets were now eerily empty.

Several moments passed with no answer. Eric grabbed the knocker once more and banged it against the thick door. Another second passed, and he heard a familiar voice call out from the other side.

"I'm on my way, hang on dammit!" the voice yelled, causing a grin to spread across Eric's face. He knew that voice from anywhere.

Eric removed his hat and waited as the other person reached the door. Loud clanging could be heard as the door's locks were being disengaged. Once that was done, silence followed it. Eric sighed to himself, then straightened up his stance when he heard the door opening. It creaked loudly on its hinges as it swung open, revealing the person on the other side.

He was about Eric's age and height. He also wore a long, dark gray duster. The dark-skinned young man that stood before Eric instantly smiled upon recognizing him, revealing a set of perfect, white teeth. He opened his arms in greeting and pulled Eric in for a quick hug, happy to see him.

"Eric, buddy!" the young man happily exclaimed. "So, you finally joined up and became a Hunter, eh? That duster's looking good on you!"

Eric smiled as the man released him from the embrace. The man looked him over once more and sarcastically added to his previous sentence.

"Though I think it looks a little too new...don't worry, a few missions will fix that!"

The young man laughed out loud at his remarks, earning him a quick punch to the shoulder. It was true, Eric's coat was brand new, never having seen the dust of battle or even long roads. As for his friend's though, it was already slightly worn at the edges and sported a few stains here and there.

"Hey Joseph, long time no see, eh?" Eric replied.

Joseph's smile widened. He clasped Eric on the shoulder and beckoned him inside. Eric entered the old building, followed by Joseph closing the heavy door behind them. Eric watched his friend as he re-engaged the multiple locks that kept the commoners out, then the two made their way to the main room.

As Eric and Joseph wandered down the halls, they passed through several other rooms of interest. One was a library, lined with ancient oak bookcases that towered all the way to the vaulted ceiling. Various old wooden tables of different sizes laid about the library, many with tomes and novels resting upon them.

The next room they passed through was the dining room. A decorative chandelier hung from the ceiling and gave the room a dim, yet warm, glow with its small electric bulbs. The long dining table looked to be carved from a single redwood tree as its length and lack of splits gave the illusion that it was a single piece of wood. It was bare of any eating utensils or plates and had been freshly cleaned, unlike that of the rest of the room. The stone walls sported sculptures of various mythical beasts, their mouths widely agape as if in mid-scream. The sculptures would have been more appealing had they been dusted, which they had not been for what looked like several years.

Eric took in his surroundings as the two walked alongside the dining table and through the next doorway. The young man had wondered where any other people would be in here, as it had so far been empty of any other souls save for Joseph and himself. Once they wandered down the next hallway and into a cavernous room, his question was quickly answered.

This room was much like the library, only with fewer book cases. The walls were finished in a fine wood paneling, as was the floor. The stuffed heads of various animals and creatures had been mounted along the wall as well; though unlike the stone sculptures in the dining room, these stuffed heads had been well taken care of.

A large, ornate fireplace squatted against one wall with several padded chairs seated around it. Behind the arrangement of the comfortable-looking chairs was a small metal table. Three stools sat around the table and there appeared to be a card game going on atop its surface. Playing the card game were two men. One appeared to be in his early thirties and the other in his late twenties.

The two men looked over and noticed the stranger that Joseph had brought in with him. They immediately dropped their cards and stood, turning to the two young men. The first man, the older one, approached Eric with his hand extended. He was a bear of a man and seemed to tower over Eric's six-foot stature.

"Oy, the fresh blood, eh?" he said with a grin. Eric noticed the large scar going down his face and splitting his dark facial hair like a war stripe. The man pointed to himself with his thumb, jabbing his own chest with it. "The name's David McGowan."

Eric gave a friendly smile and shook David's hand. His grip was tight, and it felt as if the young man's hand was being crushed. David chuckled and let go, causing Eric to move his fingers to regain feeling in his hand. Eric quickly shook his head, regaining his train of thought and responded.

"I'm Eric Hahn, and yes I'm the new hunter."

David chuckled again and slammed an open palm against Eric's back, knocking the air out of him. He then turned and gestured to the other man.

"Come meet the greenhorn! Be friendly!" David exclaimed to his friend. The stranger let scorn show on his face as he turned back to the table and reclaimed his seat. David waved him off nonchalantly.

"Eric?" he asked, being sure of his name. Eric nodded. "Yes, Eric. Ignore him alright? His name's Ross Lancaster. He's just a bit sour that you're replacing Leon."

Eric seemed puzzled. He wasn't aware that he was 'replacing' anyone. His confusion seemed to show because Joseph noticed it and stepped up to speak.

"Eric don't worry about it. You're not replacing anyone. Leon...well, he betrayed us," Joseph said.

Across the room, Ross jumped back up off of his stool. It fell over and hit the wood floor with an audible bang as the hunter spun on his heels and met Joseph's stare with burning eyes. He stormed over to Eric's friend and got inches from his face.

"Leon didn't betray us dammit!" he yelled, banging his fist against the wall. He then pointed a finger at Joseph's face. "Don't you dare make another accusation like that...if I even hear another word about it, I swear I'll send you to Aedurus myself!"

Joseph didn't say a word, but he didn't back down either. The two Hunters glared at each other for several unspoken moments. After another second, David sighed to himself and stepped over to the two, placing his arms between them and splitting them up.

"No, there's no reason for such hostilities, especially in front of our new friend here," David said, nodding over to Eric. Ross glanced at the young hunter for a split second, then glared up at David as he shot past him and up to Eric, getting in his face as well.

"And you...you are not my *friend*..." Ross said. His voice was like venom as he mouthed that last word. "Stay the hell out of my way, and don't talk to me. Got it?"

Eric felt a flare of anger rise up in him. He gritted his teeth but otherwise kept his mouth shut. He wanted nothing but to punch Ross right at that moment, yet he resisted the urge knowing it would do nothing except upset things more. Instead he reached out and shoved Ross away, but he quickly recovered and reached for his revolver. He drew it from the holster and planted the gun's muzzle under Eric's chin, causing him to freeze up momentarily.

"Woah, hey!" Joseph yelled, drawing his revolver as well. David shoved Ross's arm down, pushing the gun away from the new hunter. Joseph glared daggers at the compatriot who just threatened his friend, but slowly lowered and re-holstered his gun.

"Ross, what has gotten into you?" David demanded to know. His voice boomed and echoed in the room. Ross looked from Eric to him.

"We don't need him!" Ross yelled, pointing viciously at Eric. "We need to be working on getting Leon back to us!"

David went to respond, but another presence was felt in the room. Everyone stopped and looked towards the person who had just stepped in from another doorway. Only Ross kept his back to the other person. He closed his eyes and sighed.

"What is going on in here?" The older man said. "Ross Lancaster, you are to treat all new recruits with respect. That is the Hunter's Code, is it not?"

Ross lowered his head and placed his revolver back into its holster. His voice shook slightly as he recited part of the Hunter's Code, "Always accept new arrivals into the Hunt, just as you had been accepted before, for they shall help bring forth the salvation of Man."

The older man pursed his lips and nodded. He stepped forward and slowly crossed the room towards the group. His steps rang out against the hard floor and echoed in the silence that had now permeated the room. He appeared to be in his forties and wore a gray duster much like that of any other hunter, only the coat was older than Eric himself. It was torn and patched at various places and was worn heavily at its edges. Sitting upon the man's head was a matching tricorn hat with a long, white feather sticking up from it. His black and graying facial hair was well-groomed and his face sported several scars. The old hunter reached the group and placed his hand on Ross's shoulder.

"You know the Code, but yet you seem to be having difficulties abiding by its terms. Do not fall down that path, Ross," he quietly said. Ross was shuddering slightly and hiding his face with his hand. The old hunter continued. "It was distraction from the Code that led Leon to his betrayal...you cannot deny that...The sooner you accept that he is now an enemy, the better off you'll be."

Ross didn't respond. He instead turned and walked away, leaving the room. Everyone watched him leave. After another moment of silence, Joseph spoke up.

"Sir?" he asked, getting the older man's attention. "This is our new recruit, the one I have told you about."

The man looked over at Eric and finally grinned. He shook Eric's hand gently and patted him on the arm.

"Yes, that is good," he said. "Joseph has told me quite a bit about you. Said you and him had been good friends since childhood."

Eric nodded and smiled back, "Yes sir, he helped talk me into joining your order. I wish to protect people from all threats."

The old man nodded as his smile grew larger. Eric could see several metal teeth that had replaced the original ones over the years in the man's otherwise clean smile.

"That's good to hear," he said. He then gestured to himself with a small bow. "I'm Jonathan Burke. Welcome to the Order of the Arcane Hunt."

On the island of Krehaul, a cage imbued with arcane magic to disable a creature's power was lowered to the ground. Inside it, a pair of frightened seraphs and their young cherub sat huddled together. The small, child-like sprite tightly held onto her mother. Her ruby red eyes were brimmed with tears and her blue hair was messy. Other cages containing various monsters was being lined up for examination. A few poachers watched over the captives as a few Black Sun disciples approached. The lead poacher jumped off a cage and walked up to the Black Sun commander.

"Here they are, as ordered. I'm sure your leader will be pleased with the specimens gathered here," the poacher said with a cruel smile.

The Black Sun leader, Mariah, looked around at the beasts, seemingly pleased.

"Alright then. Here's the money, as agreed," she replied. She pulled out an envelope and handed it to the man.

"Hang on now, see those seraphs over there?" the poacher said, pointing to the small family of creatures. "They gave us a bit of trouble trying to capture them alive. I lost some good men."

Mariah glared at him, "And? Your men are of no concern to me."

The poacher gritted his teeth, then responded, "Seraphs are among the deadliest beasts known to roam Plataea. I think we are due for a little more cash thrown our way."

The Black Sun commander chuckled and spun on her heels, walking away, "The money is in there, that's what was agreed and that is all you will be getting."

The poacher looked furious at what Mariah said. He motioned to the poachers behind him, then they all drew their revolvers. The lead poacher levelled the muzzle at Mariah.

"Bullshit, we demand more money. Otherwise your boss isn't getting anything," he said with a sneer.

Mariah smiled and glared at the brave grunt, "Fine then. Have it your way."

She snapped her fingers and the Black Sun members behind her pulled their own weapons and gunned down the poachers before they could react. Gunshots rang out for several seconds, the caged beasts ducked, trying to avoid being hit. The male seraph pulled his mate and the little cherub closer.

"It's okay, I have you, I won't let them hurt you," the male seraph told the female and child, though it failed to help the cherub from crying.

Once the firing stopped, the lead poacher that defied Mariah laid on the ground bleeding out. He coughed up some blood before saying, "You...c-can't do this! When Alexander finds out!-"

Another shot rang out. Mariah held a small derringer, having just shot the poacher dead. Satisfied with the dead man in front of her, she put the firearm away, laughing.

"That pathetic Alexander isn't going to do anything," she said with a grin. Mariah then looked over to the Black Sun members and yelled. "Well what are you waiting for! Clean up this mess and get those things to the camp!"

The others scrambled to do their thing; carriages drawn by scarred and beaten horses began to pull in to pick up the caged monsters. Mariah watched as her men worked, smiling to herself and looking up towards the sky. She knew these creatures would make good additions to the workforce. As for the seraphs and the little runt, they especially would be needed for what the Black Sun had planned.

[II]

Joseph escorted Eric into the building's armory. The new hunter gazed around at the room. It was modest in size and had nothing in the ways of decoration. The walls were simply barren bricks, and the floor was only covered with a simple and aged brown rug. A single electric bulb hung from a wire and suspended from the ceiling, giving the room a dim glow that turned to dark at the edges near the walls. Another small lamp was attached to a long wooden work bench. Atop the bench was a collection of various tools, likely for keeping the hunters' firearms in working order.

Joseph pointed to a wooden rifle rack that was bolted to the far wall, then said, "Just place your rifle over th-"

He stopped mid-sentence, looking over Eric's shoulder as if searching for something.

"Where's your rifle?" he then asked.

Eric shook his head, "...I don't have one. Just my revolver."

The new hunter placed his hand on the butt of his weapon, rocking it in its holster. Joseph let out a chuckle and shook his head. He then patted Eric on the shoulder and pulled him back out of the room and into the hallway.

"Eric, you gotta have a rifle," Joseph stated. "You can't go out on mission without a longarm."

Eric felt heat rise in his cheeks. It was something he honestly never thought about. The young man was just so used to only having his handgun, that the thought of a rifle never crossed his mind. He felt slightly ashamed for being unprepared.

"A hunter without his weapon is like a fisherman without his pole," a voice from behind Eric startled him. He spun around to see Jonathan Burke. The old hunter was leaning against the stonework walls and had the hint of a grin. "Without the tools of the trade, you will get to nowhere but failure."

Eric lowered his head, trying to hide his embarrassment. "Yessir. I will fix the problem immediately."

Burke nodded, then reached into his pocket. He retrieved a small cloth bag and held it out for Eric. The young man reached out and the old hunter dropped the pouch into his palm. It landed with the jingle of coins inside.

"Here is your base pay," Burke said with a chuckle. "Spend it wisely."

Eric nodded and thanked his superior. The new hunter then walked past Burke with Joseph in tow. The two left the building and made way towards the nearest arms shop. It was already beginning to get dark. The sky had turned an orange shade as the sun crept beneath the horizon.

The two hunters knew that most stores would be closing soon, so they quickened their pace to make time. As the two duster-clad men stepped along the cobblestone path, other pedestrians tended to stare at them. Some would pretend to ignore them and continue whatever it was that they were doing, but others would make obvious attempts to stay out of the way of the two hunters. Eric didn't like it. He even noticed that horse-drawn carriages and the automobiles would occasionally swerve as if there was an invisible barrier surrounding them.

"Do people still have issues with the Order?" Eric asked quietly, leaning slightly towards Joseph as he spoke.

Joseph glanced around at the civilians around them. He nodded politely at one as they passed.

"Intimidation I think," he responded. "People still aren't used to seeing hunters. A human that can control the souls and wills of beasts and kill a dozen draugr without a scratch? The idea is still insane to a lot. Hell, I still find it hard to believe myself...that...and the Order hasn't always been known for being a kind regime at times...that's something that I wished changed."

Eric thought about it for a moment, then responded.

"Yeah, I suppose that makes sense...You'd just think that people would be more warmed up to the idea of us being around and not scared."

Joseph just shrugged his shoulders and didn't immediately respond. They were passing a small candy sales cart. The wooden hand-drawn cart had various different homemade candies on display and for sale. Eric's friend paused and picked out a large lollipop and quickly paid for it. He then thanked the elderly man running the cart and they continued walking. Eric was confused as to why Joseph bought the sweet. On the busy street they walked down, Joseph stopped again and gifted the candy pop to a small boy, who enthusiastically took it with a smile.

"Thank you, mister!" the small boy said excitedly. His parents grinned at the boy and looked at the duster-wearing young man.

"Thank you, hunter," the father said, patting Joseph on the arm as him and Eric walked on.

After getting a few steps away from the family, Eric and his friend looked at each other. Joseph grinned.

"That's how we get people to like the Order more," he said. "Doing more friendly and human-like things. Let the public know that it's not all about the killing."

Eric chuckled; agreeing with him. The two continued walking to the arms shop. Once they were off of the more crowded streets, Eric reached towards the small leather pouch hanging from his side. He opened the pouch with his fingers and retrieved one of the stones from within it. He held the stone in front of him but kept it close. The hunter rolled the small stone around in his hand and stared at it.

It was a crystal more than it was a rock. The semi-translucent stone was a deep blue in color and had a haze of a lighter blue in its center. The blue swirled like a galaxy within the stone. It emanated a small warmth as he held it. Eric let a small smile crack at the corner of his mouth. While he was looking at the stone, Joseph was watching him, looking between the soul stone and his friend.

"How has Vesuvius been?" Joseph asked.

"He's been the usual," Eric responded. He then added with a chuckle, "I'm sure he'd rather be out of his stone though. He's never liked being confined for too long."

Joseph laughed. He adjusted the holster on his hip and then shoved his hands into his pockets.

"I'm sure he doesn't, but you know he can't just run around freely. This isn't Usora where we grew up," he said with a grin.

"I know," the new hunter stated. He went quiet for a moment, placing the soul stone back into his pouch. "Sometimes I miss Usora, you know?"

Joseph pursed his lips and nodded, understanding where Eric was coming from.

"I know. I miss it too sometimes," he said. He then smacked Eric on the back. "But don't worry about it! Avrush isn't a bad province! You'll be used to this place in no time!"

"Heh, yeah," Eric responded, elbowing Joseph for smacking him.

The hunters stepped around the next street corner. They passed several restaurants and bakeries as the arms shop came within view. Eric stared into the windows of the food establishments and remembered that he hadn't ate that day. The smell of freshly baked rolls and smoked meats wafted into his nostrils, making his stomach growl angrily in protest. He placed his hand on his gut, trying to suppress the feeling of hunger.

Eric watched through one of the windows as he passed. A server was delivering what looked to be roasted boar and a pan of hot gravy to a table. It looked amazing to the young hunter. He noted that he'd have to talk Joseph into stopping for a bite once they were done getting him a rifle.

The two friends reached the arms shop. The front of the business was covered in large glass pane windows. Wrought iron bars were stretched across the front of the glass, spaced only a hand's width apart. No doubt to keep thieves from breaking in. There was no special name to the establishment. Above the reinforced wood and steel door was a sign that read, 'Weapons and Ammo'. The sun had dropped below the buildings surrounding Eric and Joseph, leaving the streets darkened by the early night. Inside the store, gas lanterns were burning and giving off a warm glow through the windows.

Opening the door, Eric and Joseph walked in and removed their wide-brimmed hats. A small bell jingled, indicating the presence of customers. Eric looked around at the interior of the store. It was a small shop, only larger than that of a storage shed in size. Yet, the walls were lined with various long arms from outdated muzzleloaders to the most modern breechloaders. A few glass cabinets and a wooden one squatted along one side of the room with enough space for an employee to walk behind. Eric walked along the cases and looked down into them. The glass cabinets were full of revolvers, derringers and the like of every size and caliber, while the wooden one housed the locked register. Along the back wall was a series of wooden shelving stacked with boxes upon boxes of ammunition.

As Eric looked over the weapons in the shop, a man walked through an open doorway from the back to greet the two hunters. He was a well-built man, with a closely shaven head and facial hair. The shop owner looked from Eric to Joseph and formed a large grin.

"Hey, Joseph!" the man called out, his voice booming. "Didn't think I would see you this quickly between missions! How have you been?"

Joseph crossed the room and shook hands with the owner of the store. He smiled back.

"I've been fine, Mr. Walt," Joseph responded. "How's the missus?"

Mr. Walt waved his hand in an exaggerated fashion and let out a laugh.

"The ol' lady has been just how she's always been," he said, now looking back at Eric. "Who might you be? A new hunter?"

Eric nodded and shook the man's hand as well, bowing slightly in greeting.

"Yessir, and I am here to purchase a rifle. I need something worthy of a hunt."

Mr. Walt bit his lower lip in thought. His eyes squinted slightly and glanced around at the rifles stacked along the walls as he tapped his fingers against the glass tops of the display cases. After a moment, his face lit up as if he made a ground-breaking realization.

He quickly walked across the clean wooden floors and over to a stack of rifles. He grabbed one of them and opened its action to check and be sure it was clear. Once confirming it was empty, he turned on his heels and handed the weapon to Eric.

"Glenchester, Model 1873. Lever-action rifle chambered in the standard .45 caliber round," Mr. Walt said. "Good, robust design. Been around for over two decades and still top of the line when compared to even the newer bolt-action guns."

Eric was looking over the firearm like a priceless piece of art. He held the weapon by its grip and handguard, adoring its clean lines and checkered walnut stock. The metal was finished in a deep and rich polished black. He threw the rifle to his shoulder and aimed down the sights. It was a standard notch and post set-up, but easy to align. The fit of the metal parts of its action was perfect, making for a glass smooth slide as the lever was operated and the bolt was opened. It was also fitted with a nice leather sling, complete with small loops stitched in for carrying extra ammo.

Overall, the new hunter was happy with the piece in his hands.

"This weapon will do nicely," Eric said. "How much?"

The shop owner leaned against the glass cases for a moment. He placed his hand under his chin as if in thought, humming to himself for a second.

"Normal price is thirty dollars...but since you're a hunter, I'll knock off five," Mr. Walt said. He crossed his arms, "How's that sound?"

Eric thought about it for a split second, then nodded.

"That sounds good to me," he said, reaching into his pocket and pulling out the exact change. He flicked the coins through the air towards Mr. Walt, who caught them with a grin. Eric then added, "I'm going to need some ammunition as well. I need some .38's and .45's for my new rifle."

Mr. Walt quickly walked around the counters and to the ammo shelves. He pointed at each box, mumbling the caliber to himself as he searched for each of the requested rounds.

"Ah, here they are," he said, grabbing several boxes of each caliber and turning to set them down on the counter. "Here is what I call the 'hunter's special'. These rounds use a cast, pure silver projectile. Most monsters are burned by silver, so these nasty little things do extra damage. They're also only a dollar per box for .38's. A dollar and twenty-five cents for the .45's."

Eric gestured to the ammo shelf, bending one knee and resting the butt of his new rifle on his upper leg.

"Give me two boxes of the .38's, and several more of the .45's," he said, retrieving more coins to pay for the products.

Mr. Walt stacked the small cardstock boxes along the counter. Eric went through them one by one and opened them. He filled the magazine tube of his rifle to the brim, then filled the loops on the sling. With the rest, he slipped into the loops on the leather gun belt that Eric wore across his chest. He then slung the rifle and drew his revolver. Carefully so as not to possibly upset the store owner, he opened the loading gate and ejected the lead-headed rounds. He then loaded the new silver bullets, keeping one chamber empty, and spun the cylinder. The gun made a satisfying series of clicks as its cylinder spun. Eric then stopped it on the empty chamber and dropped the hammer slowly, then reholstered it.

"That's an interesting handgun you got there," Mr. Walt said, pointing at Eric's revolver. "Looks like a Richmond conversion gun."

"It is," Eric answered, rocking the old revolver in its holster. "It was my grandfather's. He gave it to my mother, who passed it to me when I left to become a hunter."

He stared down at the old, worn grips as he continued, "It was originally a cap and ball gun when my grandfather had it, but my mother had it converted to fire cartridges while I was still young...it's been a trusty piece."

The gun shop owner nodded.

"That's good. Very good," he said in agreement. "It's always nice to see an old weapon still being useful to someone. It's definitely not outdated yet."

A small cuckoo clock mounted on the wall next to the door to the backroom rang out. The ornately carved wooden clock struck the hour. Small wooden doors opened and closed as a little decorative bird shot in an out. It chirped each time it reached the apex of its travel on the scissor arm assembly it was attached to. The two hunters and Mr. Walt glanced at the clock for a moment, followed by the owner slamming his hand down onto the countertop.

"Well boys, closing time," he said. "Anything else you two need?"

Eric and Joseph both shook their heads.

"No sir, that is it," Eric said, shaking the owner's hand once more. "Thank you."

Joseph placed his hat back upon his head and flicked its brim.

"Thank you once again, Mr. Walt. You always seem to deliver," the friend stated.

Eric followed suit and replaced his hat onto his head. He gave a slight bow once more and the two hunters left the store, so Mr. Walt could close it down.

As they walked down the street and away from the shop, they could hear Mr. Walt call out to them.

"Thank you for your business, hunters! Stay safe and kill something big!"

With Eric's new rifle slung over his shoulder and his gun belts full of ammunition, the two hunters made their way back to the Order's building in Pratertown. The streets were dark and clear of any people walking as they reached the building's steps. Joseph banged his fist on the heavy front door a few times, ignoring the cast raven knocker. The two stood still for a moment, then straightened up as they heard the locks being disengaged.

The door opened, revealing Ross on the other side. He paid no mind to Joseph but gave Eric a slight look of scorn as soon as his eyes laid upon him. The new hunter ignored it.

"Come on," Ross said dismissively. "Burke has a mission that needs all of us tomorrow. We're to get some sleep for in the morning."

Eric perked up at the words. A mission? Already? He looked to Joseph as they entered the old building. His friend merely grinned and looked back at Eric.

"Hell, it's your first day and we already have a mission, lucky you, eh?" Joseph remarked. "Better get a good night's rest. Come on, I'll show you to your room."

Eric followed him to his new room, excited for his first mission.

The morning bells sounded, rousing Eric from his sleep. He looked over at the clock on the bedroom wall. It was only six in the morning. He hated waking up this early, but he knew he'd have to get used to it from now on.

Eric sat up in bed and stretched his arms with a yawn. The other hunters seemed like they were already milling about, so Eric quickly jumped up and started getting ready for the day. He collected a pan of water and sat back on his bed. He quickly shaved using a small hand mirror and razor blade. Once that was completed, he got into his usual clothing and threw on his gun belts and duster. The young hunter grabbed his revolver from the nightstand and lightly kissed its metal surface, saying a quiet prayer of protection. Holstering the gun, he grabbed his hat as well.

"Alright everyone get in the great room!" yelled out Jonathan Burke from the hallway. Eric left his room and followed the old hunter and the others.

"I'm sure some of you already have an idea of what we're going to be doing today, but I'm here to fill in any gaps," Burke began once they all were in the great room. "Today we're going over to Krehaul Island. There's rumors that a cult of freaks have hold themselves up in the mines and mountains there.

"If those rumors are true, then that cult can pose a major threat to the village of Krehaul and even some of the villages here on the mainland," Burke paused for a moment, looking around at his men. "We are to go in, investigate any possible presence and take them down if we find it. We know that whatever group this is, they are said to be necromancers, so that means wraiths and plenty of draugr. Now, I want everyone outside in five minutes for transport."

"Let's hunt!" the room yelled in unison.

Burke smiled, then spun on his heels and walked out of the room. Everyone began gathering their weapons and filling their canteens before heading out the door. Eric had just finished filling up his canteen when Joseph approached him.

"Ready for today?" Joseph smiled and smacked Eric on the back playfully. Eric smiled and punched his friend in the shoulder.

"You know it, let's get out there and make a difference," Eric said, checking the small leather pouch that always hung from his side. He felt for the two soul stones and acknowledged they were both there.

The two then both walked outside and onto the cobblestone path in front of the building. Parked in the street was a large wooden carriage being drawn by a team of clydesdale horses. The carriage had shutters covering the windows and the entire thing was painted charcoal black.

Burke and the others were waiting outside the carriage. The old hunter lit a cigar and took a puff. He watched the two young hunters approach. He felt a swell of pride; it was good to see youth still stepping up to protect others by joining the Order.

"Good to have you two show up," Burke chuckled, lightly chewing on the end of the cigar. "Get in the carriage, we're heading out now."

Everyone climbed into the transport, and the carriage doors were closed up. It was very dark inside the transport, and the seats were not the most comfortable, but Eric managed. The ride was long and bumpy, and within what felt like hours, they made it. They had arrived at a private dock where a paddle boat awaited them. The hunters wasted no time; they got onto the ship which made way to Krehaul Island in the distance.

Once out in open water, Eric leaned against the side of the ship and looked down into the water. Occasionally he'd see a shiny fish or two just beneath the water's surface. He let out a sigh and closed his eyes. He was a little nervous. Maybe it was because this was his first real mission, but he had a feeling deep in his gut that something really bad was going to happen. Joseph came over, sensing something was bothering his friend.

"You ok man? You look nervous," Joseph asked.

Eric looked at his friend and smiled, pushing the gut feeling away, "It's nothing. I'm fine, just a little worried about this being my first mission."

Joseph laughed, "That's it? Don't worry about a thing. You have all of us at your side, and you have your own beasts to help back you up."

Eric nodded, then said, "Thanks Joseph, I appreciate it."

A few moments passed without a word. Joseph pulled out a photo and stared at it. Eric glanced over and saw it was a photo of a girl.

"Your girl?" he asked.

Joseph looked at it for another second before putting it away, "Yeah, she's a great person. I miss her sometimes. She lives back in the Usora province," Eric smiled and nodded. Joseph added, "So when are you going to get a woman of your own, Eric?"

Eric chuckled, and his gaze dropped back to the water, "I don't know...I guess I'm just waiting for the right one to come along."

Joseph patted Eric on the shoulder, "Well, whoever she is, she's going to be very lucky. You're a good guy."

The ship's horn sounded, they were about to dock at Krehaul Island. Joseph nodded to Eric and walked away to join the others. Eric looked at the island, then unslung his rifle and began to join up with the others as well.

Let's do this. He thought to himself.

[III]

The hunters stepped off the ship and onto the rocky surface of Krehaul Island. High above them, the sun scorched down on the humans. Eric looked up at the mountainous hills ahead of them; realizing that if there was a cult here, that they could be hiding anywhere. Joseph came up beside him and playfully shoulder-checked the young man, knocking Eric out of his trance.

"Cheer up, this is going to be good! Even if there is nothing here, it sure as hell beats doing nothing back in town," Joseph said with a grin. "Maybe your monsters will get in a fight or two. Gods know it has been forever since they've been in a proper battle."

Eric chuckled. He shifted his rifle slightly in his hands, "Yeah, sure. It's just going to suck trying to search these hills, let alone the mines beneath this place."

"Eh, it ain't going to be too terrible. You need to raise your head up!" replied Joseph, still grinning. He turned and took off to catch up with the rest. Eric began running as well. He couldn't help but have a bad feeling about the entire thing.

The hunters gathered around Burke, who was chewing on the end of his burnt-out cigar. He spit it out onto the dirt and crushed it beneath his boot. He was looking at the hills, going over the plan in his head. The old hunter then looked over to the others; they seemed ready and determined. He just hoped that if things got bad that they would be prepared for it. He pushed his worry to the side for now, what was important was getting this mission started. He reached down and picked up the crushed cigar and shoved it in his pocket to throw away later.

"Alright hunters, everyone good?" he barked.

The hunters didn't respond. They all looked to him and nodded in silence.

Burke nodded himself. He said, "Good, because this is what we're going to do. The island has been temporarily evacuated until we deem it safe. Earlier yesterday the local fauna began to act odd and more hostile than normal. Be on the lookout and try not to piss off the wildlife. If we have to fight, take them down fast. We're not here for monsters, we're here for the cult."

The hunters nodded again, acknowledging their leader. Eric was glad he brought his beasts with him, they may prove useful in defending against local monsters.

Jonathan Burke continued, "Alright, we're going to begin by moving out along the west-side of the island. We'll clear along the hills there and eventually move into the mines. We'll do this by the books and get this done quick. After this, we'll enjoy a cold drink at Beck's. Any questions?"

The hunters all grinned and shook their heads. Burke felt a sense of pride swell in his throat.

"Alright, good. Let's hunt!" he waved them on.

The hunters quickly made their way around the first hill, weapons at the ready. Eric made sure his soul stones were within easy reach. He may need them fast if things go south.

As the hunters moved through the small village, two people stopped them at the gates leading out into the rest of the island. Burke rolled his eyes at the two strangers. They were wearing matching dark blue wool uniforms and carrying old and outdated Model 1864 single shot rifles. The first of the two men approached them.

"I'm Sergeant Hobbs, Krehaul militiamen. This is Private Oliver. We were told to join you on your hunt."

Burke scoffed at the militia members. The last thing they needed were two untrained civilians posing as hunters.

"We don't need militia getting involved with the Order's business. Step aside and let us handle this," the old hunter said.

The two militiamen glared at each other. The private, Oliver, pulled a piece of paper out of his knapsack and handed it to the sergeant. The senior militia member merely grinned and passed the wrinkled paper to Burke.

"I think you may wish to reconsider after seeing this. The Order requests that you take us on this mission," Hobbs said with a slightly-annoyed tone.

Burke snatched the paper from the sergeant's hand. He quickly unfolded the sheet and read it. After a moment, Burke cursed to himself and dropped the note. He then gave the rest of the hunters an irritated look and returned his gaze back to Oliver.

"Oh, how the high Order wishes to test me," the old hunter said. Annoyance crept into his voice, "Fine, but you and your soldier are to stay out of the way and preform as we say. Otherwise, you will die out here."

He then waved to the hunters to follow him. They all began moving once more, walking past the militiamen. As Eric passed Oliver, he noticed that his knapsack was a medical pack.

Something useful at least. Eric thought.

An hour had passed. It was about noon, and even with an overcast of clouds, it was hot. The heat reflected off the rocky ground made wearing the dusters miserable. Eric wiped the sweat off his forehead and took a drink from his tin canteen. They were crossing over another large hill.

Ross was leading the group through the ravines. He was on his stomach crawling up to see over the crest to make sure it was clear. They didn't want to get surprised by anything, so they had to take it safely. Eric looked around at the surroundings, keeping an eye out for anything moving. After a few moments, Ross looked back at the hunters and showed his hand to them. His index finger and thumb touched at their tips and curled to form a circle while his other fingers were outstretched. That was the okay sign. He then got up and went over the crest. The rest followed behind, making sure to stay evenly spaced. They kept this up for another hour without seeing anything, not even any local creatures.

Joseph fell back to Eric and leaned in to talk quietly, "This is weird. We haven't seen anything, you'd figure an island with a single village would be crawling with monsters."

"Yeah, it's odd," Eric replied, not looking at his friend directly, instead scanning the land around them. "Let's just keep an eye out, I hope whatever this is isn't anything bad."

"Maybe they're having a get-together and we just weren't invited," Joseph said with a grin like he just told the best joke ever. Eric shook his head and shoved his friend back up into formation. "Oh, come on it wasn't that bad!"

Eric smiled and couldn't help but laugh quietly at Joseph's bad joke. The hunters continued on, checking over every hill and in every canyon. This continued for another hour until Burke called them down into a small ravine for a quick break.

"Huddle up hunters! Drink water, rest, take a piss, whatever you gotta do. You got 10 minutes then we head out again," he said, pulling back his duster sleeve and checking his brass watch.

The men spread out to sit, relax and re-hydrate. A few did some quick stretches and others removed their dusters to cool off. Eric popped his back, then plopped down onto the dirt ground and took another swig from his canteen. He just started to get comfortable when the ground began to shake. Out of nowhere, a lapguis rose out of the ground. The large, stone-like serpent roared in anger at the intruding humans.

"Look alive!" yelled out Burke. The hunters all jumped up and leveled their rifles at the lapguis; preparing to fire if it didn't stand down.

Eric reached for a soul stone and retrieved it from his leather pouch. He squeezed the stone in his hand while muttering the ancient arcane words.

"Summone draco vocantem caeruleum," he whispered.

Blue smoke seeped out from the stone from between his fingers. The smoke turned into mist while taking the shape of a draconic beast.

"Vesuvius, take form!" Eric called out.

Vesuvius emerged from the blue mist, looking ready to fight. An Azure Dragon, Vesuvius was Eric's given name for the beast. Standing over eight-foot-tall and covered in dark blue scales with a red underbelly, the hammer-headed winged dragon let out a deafening roar.

"Let's make this quick, Vesuvius!" Eric said, aiming his rifle at the stone serpent.

Vesuvius nodded, then turned to face the lapguis. The giant serpent paid no attention to the dragon; choosing instead to focus on the hunters. It attacked by opening its mouth widely and unleashing a beam of bright energy. The humans it targeted narrowly jumped out of the way. They then opened fire on the monster. The soft, cast bullets proved to not be very effective against the armored monster, though it did make the rocky serpent flinch from the impacts. This provided a distraction for Eric.

"Vesuvius, take it out!" Eric ordered. His dragon burned in a dark fire-like aura and dashed forward. The lapguis turned its attention to Eric and let out a roar that was heard over the gun fire. Burke saw what Eric was doing and called for the hunters to hold their fire, so as to not accidently hit Eric's dragon.

"Hit it hard!" Eric yelled. Vesuvius flew into the lapguis at extremely high speeds, slamming into the hostile beast with enormous force. The attack sent the lapguis hurtling into the ravine wall and was hurt, but it regained its composure and attacked the dragon by swinging its tail at him.

Eric yelled out to his beast, "Dodge it Vesuvius!"

The dragon ducked and jumped back, narrowly missing the attack.

"Finish it off, now!" Eric ordered his monster.

Vesuvius charged the lapguis gain, slamming into it with full force. The lapguis slammed against the ravine wall once more. It fell to the ground and was near fainting. Before it could recover, Vesuvius jumped onto the back of its head and used his arms to grab at the serpent's jaws. He pulled the monster's mouth open and charged a torrent of blue flames in his gut. The dragon then unleashed the hellfire directly into the serpent's gullet, torching it from the inside out. While the smoke still poured from the interior of the monster's body, Vesuvius dropped its head limply to the ground.

The humans cheered for Vesuvius and Eric, who thanked his dragon before calling him back into his stone. Burke approached Eric, clapping him on the shoulder and giving him a proud grin.

"Good job hunter, and good job to your dragon," the old hunter said. "That was an excellent display of a hunter controlling his beast."

Eric smiled, "Thank you Burke."

The old hunter then turned to the others, "Alright, let's get moving. We may have just alerted any enemies to our presence if they don't already know that we are here."

The hunters nodded in agreement, then quickly got back together in formation and made their way to the next area. Soon after, a gunshot was heard in the distance. The hunters paused for a moment. Burke motioned them to continue. He could feel his instincts telling him to stay alert.

"Keep an eye out. Things are about to get very interesting."

The mother seraph held her cherub tight, ducking down behind a rock. The father joined her. The two were trying to keep the young cherub from crying. They just managed to escape their infernal cages less than an hour ago and were now trying to evade the Black Sun disciples that were giving chase. The father tried focusing hard to teleport his family to safety, yet whenever he tried his head began pounding. Earlier he had took a direct blow from the hardened fist of a Black Sun member's undead minotaur. It surely had caused a terrible head injury.

"What's wrong?" asked the mother seraph worriedly. Her mate rubbed his temples and shook his head from side to side.

"It is nothing, Grace. We just have to focus on getting to safety," he looked over the rock serving as their cover. He was looking to see if the disciples tracking them were close. It seemed clear for the moment, *"Come on, let us move. We don't have time to spare."*

They jumped up from behind the rock and made their way quickly around the hill. The male seraph tried to teleport once more, but his head began to pound worse. The pain caused him to wince greatly and drop to his knees.

"*Father!*" cried out the little cherub. The mother seraph stopped to help him up, but the mate gently pushed her away. He shook his head at her.

"*No, you two need to keep going. Leave me here and forget about me! I'll try to distract them while you find a safe haven,*" he said, panting heavily and holding his head in pain.

"*No! I refuse to leave you behind! I refuse to let you get yourself killed!*" The mother seraph demanded; tears were building up in her big red eyes.

"Check over there! They couldn't have gone far!" a voice was heard yelling. The father seraph looked behind them and then shoved the mother away.

"*Get out of here! Go!*" he ordered, using what little of his energy to push her away with his telekinetic powers.

The mother seraph stood still for a moment. She was trying to hold back her tears, but then remembered she had to get her daughter to safety. The mother leaned in and kissed her mate deeply, then pulled her lips away from his.

"*I love you,*" she said.

"*I love you too, Grace...now run...*" said the father, turning to face where the Black Sun disciples could be heard quickly approaching. He then quietly mouthed the next sentence, "*Until Aedurus, my dearest.*"

The mother seraph moved quickly; carrying her cherub around the next turn. She then stopped herself to try to teleport further away. She could barely focus; the fear of losing her mate was too much. She just hunkered down behind another rock to collect her thoughts before trying again to teleport. She held the cherub tight, the young creature shook in fear.

"Momma? Is Father going to be alright?" she asked. Her little voice seemed choked.

Her mom kissed her on the forehead, trying to reassure her, but she couldn't hide her own fears. Gunshots could be heard in the distance behind them, followed by a loud roar. They then heard yelling from around the corner; her mate had been found. She gathered the courage to look around the corner. The father seraph stood in a defensive position, his wings bursting from his back in a show of power. A short distance away stood several Black Sun disciples, and in front of them was a wraith.

"You disappoint the Black Sun, little seraph. I don't intend on letting you walk away from this," sneered the wraith, smiling wickedly at the psychic monster.

The seraph took a step forward. *"Leave my family alone! We just want to be free!"* he yelled back to the dark spirit.

"Wraith, don't waste any time, end this wretched being's life!" yelled one of the disciples. The wraith rushed forward, its fist covered in shadow. The seraph tried to dodge it, but to no avail. It connected, and it felt as if his insides got wrenched around.

The mother seraph gasped seeing her mate take a hard hit. She quickly noticed her daughter trying to see as well, but pulled her back. She didn't want her to watch. She herself did not want to see the events unfolding in front of her, but she couldn't look away. She continued to watch as the little cherub peeked back around the corner, worried about her father.

The father recoiled from the hit but regained his footing. He then grabbed the spirit and tried to crush it. Realizing he didn't have the strength left, he simply threw the beast away from him. The ghost was able to recover quickly, only being dazed for the moment.

"Spirit of the Damned, hit the unworthy beast with a ball of shadow!" ordered the disciple. The wraith moved forward, closing the distance and then threw an orb made of compacted shadow magic. It hit, knocking the seraph back and onto the ground. That attack felt as if it took everything out of him. He could barely move.

I must get up! I must keep fighting! The seraph thought in a panic. He could only picture his mate and child. **I must protect them!**

"Don't give that waste of life a chance!" called out the disciple again. The wraith released an aura of darkness that hit the seraph; stunning him and further incapacitating him.

"No! No! Get up now!" yelled the mother seraph, covering her mouth to keep her crying from being heard.

A red-headed Black Sun member then walked out from behind the other disciples. She smiled evilly to herself as she approached the wounded seraph. She was clearly in a sort of leadership position, judging from how quickly the other disciples cleared out of her way.

"Pathetic beast. You don't even deserve to live," said the human. Another disciple walked up with a lever-action rifle. He put the muzzle to the seraph's head. The creature braced for his death. The disciple then fired a single shot, ending the father's life.

The mother seraph couldn't handle seeing what she just saw. She broke down crying, pulling her and her cherub back around the corner. She collapsed to the ground, trying to regain her composure. The cherub just sat there, wide-eyed. Her young mind failed to think straight. Her father was just murdered.

Why does this have to happen to us? What did we do to deserve this hatred from humans? She thought to herself. Her mother stood back up, still holding her daughter.

"W-we have to go now, we have to get as far away as we can!" she told her young one.

As she turned to run, she blacked out and fell to the ground. She was hit in the back of the head by an ogre, which laughed at the mother's pain. The cherub panicked, seeing her mother lying unconscious. The ogre reached for her, but she cried out in protest. The monster glowed with a blue aura, having been grabbed by the cherub's psychic move. The young one slammed the ogre against the hill-side over and over before tossing his limp corpse away.

She heard the disciples yelling and running towards them, so she grabbed onto her mother and thought as hard as she could. Seeing into the fabrics of space around them, she teleported them both. Once they made the near-instant journey, she looked around to see they were away from the disciples; but still on the island.

The mother seraph regained consciousness and looked around, noticing they were in a different area. She hugged her daughter, thanking her for getting them somewhere safer. Both of the creatures knew they were not out of it yet, and that Black Sun would be searching every square inch of the island looking for them. They got up and started to run again.

"Ma'am! The cherub and mother seraph teleported!" a Black Sun disciple reported to Mariah, who smacked him. Her mouth curled into a sneer.

"Dammit! Find them! They couldn't have gone far! The mother seraph is too weak, and the cherub can't teleport that well," she said. The disciples then split up, searching the hills for the two creatures. Another disciple then approached her.

"Ma'am, did you hear those gunshots? We don't have anyone on that part of the island," he said.

"I'm aware of that," she replied, now grinning. "It sounds like we have some guests."

[IV]

The seraph's head still felt as if a thousand needles pierced her skull, but she put the pain aside. She glanced around at the canyons before them, trying to figure out where they were in relation to their captors. The mother then looked down at her daughter. The cherub held tight onto her leg; her small fingers gripping at the hems of her dress. The little one was shaking from fear after having just seen her father murdered. The loss of her father, and the seraph's mate, took a major toll on the both of them. Though despite it, the brave seraph was certain to protect her young one and get them both to safety. She knew she could not let her love's sacrifice be in vain.

The afternoon sun shone between the clouds, making the heat from the rocks beneath them even more miserable. The mother reached into the leather pouch she stole from the Black Sun before escaping and pulled out a bottle of water. She opened it, then handed the small glass vial to the little cherub.

"The heat must be wearing on you. Please drink and refresh yourself," the seraph said to her child.

The cherub reached for the bottle, her arms trembling. Once she took hold of it, she drank most of its cool, liquid contents. She handed it back to her mother, trying to put on a smile.

"Thanks momma," the cherub replied.

A faint smile appeared on the seraph's face; her young one was being brave given the circumstances. She put the bottle away and then took the cherub's hand, and the two began walking through the ravine and then up a tall hill. They had to get to a better vantage point in order to get an idea of their location. Once at the top, she noticed they could see for as far as the low-lying clouds would allow. She tried to keep her head low as to not attract too much attention, knowing the Black Sun could have their disciples anywhere. She knew that their enemies would be searching the area high and low for them.

The mother scanned the area for a few moments, moving her deep red eyes from as far left as she could see to her right. It only seemed like more and more hills and canyons in every direction. She knew the island where they were captive was fairly small; though from where she was at, it felt like the size of a continent.

"Momma, who are they?" the cherub asked, pointing at something off in the distance.

The seraph looked, squinting and shading her eyes from the sun with her hand to see more clearly past the glare of the blazing star above. In the distance below them, only another ravine away, was a line of humans moving along. About eight of them, all wearing dark gray long coats and wide-brimmed hats. They were carrying weapons not unsimilar to what was used to kill her mate. The one in the middle of the line stopped and let the others pass him. He appeared older than the others, and his clothing had seen much more wear than the identical coats of the humans that walked by him. The human looked up and around at the tops of the ravine walls; eventually resting his eyes in her direction.

The seraph panicked and dropped down behind the edge of their looking point. She pulled her daughter with her as to not be seen, but she couldn't be sure if he had spotted them.

Did they see us? She thought, worry creeping into her mind. She began to tremble as she slowly looked back over the top of the crest. The humans were moving away, not seeming to notice the two creatures only a hundred meters behind them.

Who are those humans? She wondered to herself. **Is this another group of their disciples trying to hunt us?**

The thought sent a shiver down her spine. These humans seemed better armed than their cloak-wearing counterparts.

Why do they want us? Why? She asked herself, feeling a lump form in her throat. She couldn't let her or her offspring be found. They needed to escape.

"Mom?" the cherub said again. A worried tone crept into her small voice as she tugged on her mother's white gown.

The seraph looked down at her daughter and held back her tears. She reminded herself that she needed to stay strong for her child.

"I do not know who those humans are, my sweet child, but we cannot allow them to see us. Understood?" she replied, answering her daughter's question from earlier. The cherub's gaze dropped to the barren ground. Her voice choked up.

"Momma...why do humans hate us? Why are they doing this?" she asked. A few tears left her eyes and fell to the ground, leaving small wet spots on the rocks.

The mother knelt to one knee and pulled the cherub into a tight embrace. She then kissed her on the cheek.

"I...do not know...But I do know we will make it out of here. We will make it through this and become free once again."

She looked into her young one's eyes, reaching out to wipe away her daughter's tears. After a second, the cherub finally smiled again.

"Now come along, we have to keep moving," she finished, standing once more and taking her child's hand once more.

The two continued on for a short while, passing through what felt to them like countless hills and ravines. Soon though, the seraph heard something in the distance behind them. It sounded like dense wings flapping in the wind. She quickly pulled herself and the cherub behind a rock and up against the hillside to obscure their position. Only a mere moment later, a massive Reaper Dragon soared directly over them. The black beast didn't seem to take notice to the two creatures below it, as it flew past them and to the next hill. She could hear the reaper give out a deafening roar, followed quickly by the sounds of humans yelling and the cracks of gunshots. The sounds of monsters being released from soul stones could then be heard. There was a battle going on close.

The seraph grabbed her cherub up and into her arms and began to run. Up ahead in the distance, she could see the mouth of a cave or mine tunnel. The mother figured that she and her child could hide there for the moment and gather their strength. She kept moving along, her feet hovering a few centimeters from the rocky ground as she neared the entrance to the cave. It was only another fifty meters ahead.

Almost there. The mother thought.

Her hopes were dashed though, as five Black Sun disciples came sprinting through an intersection that was also ahead. The disciples saw her and stopped in their tracks.

"There's the bitch and her runt!" one yelled.

"Let's kill these two quick and then we can finish off those heretics!" called out another.

Heretics? The seraph quickly wondered to herself before getting into a defensive stance. A set of blazing white feathered wings appeared as if from nowhere on her back and spread wide before stretching to wrap around her and her child.

The first disciple grabbed at a soul stone tied to his waist, releasing a wraith. The others leveled their weapons, taking aim at the seraph.

"Ready to die, seraph?" sneered the wraith, preparing to attack. Dark pools of energy surrounded the spirit.

"Quick, Spirit of the Damned! Attack the seraph!" ordered the Black Sun member.

The wraith released a large spray of dark powers. The seraph leapt out of the way as fast as she could while holding her daughter close, successfully dodging the attack. Her wings then opened up, allowing her cherub to get behind her as cover. The mother then brought her hands together. Between her palms, an orb of shadow energy took shape. The seraph collected energies from the surrounding area and formed it in a powerful ball of magic; then sent it hurtling towards the spirit with a flick of her wrists. It hit the wraith and blew it back several meters in pain.

The seraph's head began pounding once again from using her powers. The sharp, pulsing pain caused her to go dizzy for several moments, yet she ignored it. She knew she must protect her daughter. The mother's eyes then began glowing brightly in a blue aura as she used her psychokinesis to grab two of the Black Sun disciples. She tightly grabbed them, lifting the humans up and dashing them head-first against the ravine wall. A wet crack could be heard as the victims' skulls were split open, and the two humans landed and didn't move again.

The mother then tore off the limbs of another disciple using her mental powers and tossed the lifeless corpse against the remaining two, knocking them to the ground. She saw the spirit recovering from her earlier attack while feeling her own powers diminishing. Her wings disappeared as quickly as they came as she quickly grabbed her daughter and began making way for the cave; floating past the disciples as they tried to get back to their feet. Her head was pounding worse than ever.

"Ugh, dammit!" screamed one of the disciples, recovering from the hit.

"Shoot her!" yelled the other, retrieving his revolver from the ground. He brought the weapon up and fired several rounds. One managed to find its target, hitting the seraph in the shoulder.

She yelled out, grabbing her shoulder. Tears formed in her eyes from the searing pain. The silver bullet had dug into her scapula and burned away at the flesh and bone around it.

"*Mom!*" screamed the cherub, terrified for her mother.

The seraph held her closer and tried teleporting again but found that she still couldn't due to her head injuries. She kept herself floating and finally managed to make it into the cave. They quickly went around the corner and further into the tunnels. She could hear the two disciples running after them, their wraith giving chase as well.

The two creatures rounded the next corner and discovered that only the barren walls of the cave were before them. They had found themselves at a dead end.

No!! What do we do?? The seraph quickly scanned the tunnel, looking for any means of escape, but found no way out. She turned around, placing her cherub behind her.

I can't let them hurt my baby. Was all that ran through her mind. Her shoulder hurt worse from the silver burning her. She could feel the warmth of her own blood running down her back.

"*You need to try to teleport us to safety. I am unable to do it, I'm too injured,*" she said to her daughter. She did not want to place the burden of saving them again on her daughter's shoulders, but they were in of a desperate need to get to safety.

The cherub held on to her mother and focused her powers as hard as she could. She tried to mentally reach out into the tangles of the fabric of space around her and make the teleportation, but her young mind was unable to find the means to concentrate past her own fears.

"*Mom, I can't do it!*" she whimpered.

The seraph grimaced in pain from her injured shoulder and head. She touched her shoulder and looked at her hand. Her fingertips were crimson with her own blood. The mother knew her daughter was trying her best, but if neither of them was unable to teleport then she feared they'd both perish. In the distance, footsteps echoed off the cavern walls. The two disciples rounded the corner slowly. The wraith floated between them with a burning look in its eyes. The two humans appeared winded, yet furious at the seraph.

"Enough! This is where you both die!" yelled one of the disciples. "Wraith, kill them!"

The wraith released an aura of darkness, which hit the seraph and sent her crumbling to the ground clutching at her head. Her brain felt as if it was getting fried and her vision began to get blurry. The seraph let out a scream of agony.

"*Momma! No!*" the cherub yelled, crying uncontrollably. She couldn't lose her mother, not after already losing her father.

The seraph weakly got back to her feet, then tried to grab the wraith with her psychokinesis. Unfortunately, though, she found that she had no strength left.

"Finish her, my spirit. Make them both suffer," growled the disciple, ordering his wraith to kill the injured creature.

The dark spirit charged forward, blazing in a bright light, but was stopped by the grasp of a powerful aura. It seemed shocked, wondering in a panic as to how the weakened seraph could do such a thing. It then looked past the hurt creature. It was not the mother, but instead the cherub. The young one's eyes were glowing bright blue as she moved to her mother's side.

"LEAVE US ALONE!" she screamed, repeatedly smashing the wraith against the floor and ceiling of the cave. She eventually threw it as hard as she could against the rocky wall. It slumped to the floor, dead on the spot. The Black Sun member glanced at his deceased monster, then looked back to the cherub with rage in his eyes.

"You little bitch!" he yelled, bringing up his rifle. He racked the lever to chamber a cartridge, then aimed for the cherub. The disciple pulled the trigger and fired a round.

The cherub froze up as if her feet were cemented to the ground. She was unable to move out of the bullet's path. The projectile never hit her though, as her mother managed to jump in the way and was hit instead. The cast bullet lodged itself deep into the seraph's chest, who collapsed once again to the ground. The mother began wheezing and gasping for air as the little cherub dropped to her knees. She held onto her mother with tears streaming from her face.

"Momma...please don't die...please..." she pleaded, trembling again with fear of losing her last parent.

The seraph looked up at her daughter, a small trickle of blood beginning to run from her mouth. She slowly reached up and caressed the cherub's face in her hand. She could feel herself getting weaker, her life leaving her. The cherub started sobbing.

"No, mom! No, don't die!" she cried out. Her sobbing echoed throughout the cave. She heard the two disciples taking a few steps closer. She looked up at them with tears streaming down her dust-covered face.

Why? She thought to herself. **Why must this happen?**

Both disciples took aim, ready to finish off the seraph and kill her child. The cherub tightly gripped her mother's arm. Gunshots then rang out in deafening blasts...but it wasn't from the guns of the disciples. Spouts of blood shot out of both Black Sun members, who dropped to the ground dead. Standing behind them, just after the turn into their tunnel, was another human. He wore the dark long coat and hat like the humans she had spotted earlier. His coat was dirty and had the dark stains of blood on it, along with several holes perforating along the bottom.

The human just stood there staring blankly at them, limply holding a smoking revolver in his right hand. The cherub felt as if she still couldn't move, being frozen in fear. She only stared back at the human, thinking they were next to die. The child squeezed her mother's arm once more. The injured seraph faintly looked at the human as well. She tried moving, tried to protect her baby, but was far too hurt to do anything. The cherub thought of trying once more to teleport but could not focus hard enough to get both her and her mother away to safety. She looked down and squeezed her eyes shut and braced for death...but it never came. She slowly opened her eyes and looked back up at the human.

The human looked at the two creatures for another silent moment, then walked forward. He holstered his weapon and knelt down next to the seraph. Using two fingers, he felt at her neck. The human then reached down and gingerly lifted the wounded creature into his arms. He then looked at the cherub, sorrow dominating his emotions.

"I need to take her to get help now. Follow me, I promise to protect you," he said, before turning around.

The gunshot they had heard earlier worried Eric. The sound still rang through his head as if it had happened next to him. The hunter knew that there was definitely something wrong here. He felt much more alert than he ever had before. His heart began to race, and he tightly pulled his rifle to his shoulder. He also felt to make sure that the small leather pouch containing his soul stones was still attached to his belt. He felt there was the possibility he would need them.

Eric, along with the other hunters, continued moving towards where they think the shot came from. It was hard to tell since the shot rang off every hill and rock, almost making it sound like it came from everywhere at once. Everyone seemed tense, even the veteran Jonathan Burke seemed to not be at ease. The old hunter wasn't worried about himself; he was never concerned with dying. Instead, it was the young men under his command that he worried about. Hearing that shot only confirmed what had been speculated; there were definitely enemies here. Now they just had to find them and eliminate the threat.

As the hunters moved quickly through a ravine, Burke looked around at his men. They were scanning their surroundings for any signs of movement, just as they had been trained. Burke stopped and let those behind him pass as he wanted to take up the rear so he could watch the entire line. Once he was in the back, he looked around for another second. As he scanned the tops of the hills around them, he caught a glimpse of something. It looked like a flash of blue over a hill about a hundred meters away, but he barely saw it. He stared at the hill for another moment before turning and continuing along with the others.

About ten minutes had passed. The heat was getting unbearable. Several of the hunters quickly took swigs from their canteens, beads of sweat running down their faces. Their clothes were damp from the sweating and a few removed their hats to wipe away the sweat. Burke thought about having them stop to try and rest again, after all, the hills had gone quiet once more. Part of him thought it was a good thing, but he couldn't help but have a feeling that the silence meant something bad. He was about to say something to the others when something big could be heard flying their way. Everyone stopped in their tracks and all eyes went to the sky. That's when Burke saw people jumping up from over the hill tops, all wearing silver and black garbs. A reaper dragon then swooped down and let out a thunderous roar before unleashing a torrent of flame.

"Everyone, get down!" Burke yelled out.

The hunters scattered in every direction to different pieces of cover. Hobbs was unlucky though; he was hit by the reaper's attack and burst into flames. He began screaming as he threw himself onto the ground, rolling around trying to put out the fire. Oliver ran out to try to help his comrade but got struck by gunfire coming from the hillside. Oliver was struck several times in the chest and arm, with one bullet hitting him in the neck. Blood spurted out like a fountain as he clutched his neck and dropped to the ground, his eyes wide in fear.

"Hunters, attack! Open fire!" Burke screamed as he took aim at some of the unknown enemies. He fired several rounds at them, and he could see others pouring over the top of the hill.

There has to be several dozen of them! He thought to himself in a quick panic.

Several of the enemies unleashed their monsters. From several flashes of light, a leviathan, wraith, and banshee appeared. The beasts roared and growled at the intruders. The reaper appeared once again over the hill and was ready for another attack run. Eric was in cover as he saw the creatures being released. He quickly reached for his own soul stones and summoned both of his.

"Vesuvius, Gyrog! Come forth!" Eric yelled as his monsters were released.

Gyrog was the name Eric had given to his other monster. It was a sea leviathan; a massive serpent. It was covered in dark brownish-gray scales and had a pair of beady yellow eyes. Its mouth was lined with a thousand razor-sharp teeth.

Vesuvius appeared in a haze of light and spread his wings, looking determined. Gyrog stretched his head up into the sky and let out an angry roar. They both stared down the hostile creatures that their enemy had deployed. The vile reaper swooped back to attack Eric's beasts, attacking again with by spraying fire at his leviathan.

Eric's sea monster moved out of the way of the fiery attack with speed that one would think not possible out of a creature its size.

"Gyrog, attack their reaper. Knock it out of the sky! Vesuvius, you go after their leviathan and then both of you target their banshee!"

His creatures leaped into action. His leviathan fired a beam of energy out of his mouth and hit the reaper. The enemy dragon fell to the ground with a hard crash, injured by the fall, yet it slowly rose to its feet. Meanwhile, Vesuvius shot off a powerful blast of his own energy from the tips of his wings, hitting and electrocuting the enemy leviathan with a bolt of lightning. Vesuvius then rushed towards the banshee, but the fearsome beast leaped out of the way and their wraith countered with a blast of dark energy. Vesuvius was hit hard. Dust and smoke exploded into the air and the dragon recoiled back from the impact.

Eric winced when he saw Vesuvius hit, but stayed determined to knock out the enemy beasts. A bullet hit next to him, tearing a small chunk out of the rocky ground. He flinched and returned fire, racking off several cast silver bullets from his Glenchester rifle. He looked back at his monsters and was relieved to see Vesuvius back up, ready to continue. The enemy reaper was back up as well though and charged his leviathan and clawed at his neck. The sea creature tried jumping out of the way but was still struck. The sharp claws of the reaper tore away at the leviathan's flesh, then a bullet fired from their enemy hit Gyrog and injured him.

"Gyrog!" Eric let out in a yell, running out of cover to help his monster. He fired his rifle up at the hillside, emptying the magazine tube in an attempt to pin the enemy down as he made his way to Gyrog. Vesuvius moved to protect his master from the hostile monsters, each one attacking.

Eric got to Gyrog and examined his wounds. He was hurt, but the wounds didn't seem life threatening. The leviathan looked at his master with shame, feeling as if he disappointed his hunter. Eric gave a smile towards the beast, reassuring him that he would be okay, and then returned him to his soul stone to heal and rest. He looked back up and drew his revolver, firing a shot at the enemy.

"Fall back, we have to fall back!" yelled Burke, before being hit in the shoulder and falling to the ground. He quickly jumped back up and started to run, pulling a wounded Ross along with him.

Eric stopped and looked at Burke as he retreated, then looked back at the chaos he just then realized was being unfolded around him. Half a dozen more enemy monsters were being summoned. Too many to handle. The enemy banshee let out a deafening scream, the sound wave aimed at Vesuvius. Meanwhile, the dragon was also being attacked by several creatures at once. Eric kept looking around, frozen and not knowing what to do. He looked over and saw Oliver and Hobbs, who both lain only a dozen meters away. Hobbs was a scorched mess and Oliver was motionless next to him. He still couldn't find himself to move until Joseph grabbed him by the shoulder.

"What the hell are you doing?? We gotta get out of here, we're badly outnumbered!" he yelled at Eric, shaking sense into him.

Eric snapped out of his trance and started to run alongside Joseph. Both fired off shots at the enemy as Eric returned Vesuvius to his soul stone before he could be seriously hurt. The two ran as fast as they could out of the open space. Plumes of dust was kicking up where bullets hit around them. A few rounds smacked holes through Eric's duster.

Occasionally they would turn and fire to keep the enemy pinned. They ran around the corner into another ravine, continuing to run until they couldn't breathe anymore. The two hunters then stopped to catch their breaths once they thought they were far enough away.

"I...I think...we're ok for now," said Joseph, breathing heavily. He looked over at Eric and began to look him up and down, looking for any signs of injury, "Are you okay?"

Eric panted for a few moments before responding, "I think so, what about you?"

Joseph shook his head, looking around, "I'm fine...don't worry about me...we gotta find out where we are."

"Yeah, and we have to find Burke," Eric said. He hoped Burke and the others were alright.

The two caught their breaths and started running again. They knew they had to get further away from the enemy. The gunfire behind them had stopped, but they knew that couldn't be good. They ran alongside a tall ravine wall, and then spotted a cave entrance ahead. Joseph and Eric got within a few dozen meters before hearing a few shots being fired and then movement heading that way. The two hunters both hunkered down behind a rock and watched as a wounded seraph holding a cherub moved quickly into the cave.

"What the hell?" Joseph questioned. They jumped up and started to run to the cave when two of the enemies came sprinting into view, followed by a wraith.

The two hostiles and their spirit came to a halt and opened fire on Eric and Joseph. The wraith attacked them with a cloud of poison gas. Eric jumped back into cover and was about to return fire when he noticed that the shooting had already stopped. He paused for a second before looking over his piece of cover. The enemy was gone. He breathed a sigh of relief before freezing up with fear. Joseph was lying face-down on the ground, blood pooling under him while the cloud of poisonous gas hovered around him.

Eric jumped up and ran to his friend in a panic.

No, no, no, no! He was screaming in his head. He dragged Joseph out of the gas, then knelt down and flipped his friend over. He was barely still conscious.

"Joseph! Joseph stay with me!" Eric yelled, choking up. Joseph began coughing uncontrollably, blood running out of his mouth. Once he controlled his coughing, he looked weakly at Eric.

"What...the hell are you doing crying?" he said, breaking into a fake smile.

Tears began building up in Eric's eyes. It hurt him to see his childhood friend like this. "You're hurt Joey...I need to get you to safety."

Eric started to lift Joseph up, but he pushed Eric away, shaking his head.

"No Eric...I'm done...I'm sorry," he reached into his shirt pocket and pulled out a blood-covered letter. "Here, give this to my girl okay?"

Eric shook his head, "No, you're giving it to her. You're going to make it."

Joseph chuckled, but then groaned in pain, "Heh...ouch...leave me here Eric, I'm only going to weigh you down...I'm done."

Eric's tears started falling from his cheeks as he held his dying friend.

"Go...now...go and kick their ass..." Joseph took his last breath before passing away in Eric's arms. Eric stared at his friend's face, sobbing quietly to himself. He slowly lowered Joseph's body to the ground. He saw that his duster now had large stains of Joseph's blood. He went to say his goodbyes when he heard a gunshot come from the cave.

The hunter jumped up, wanting to avenge his friend. He unhooked Joseph's gun belt and ran as quick as he could into the cave. Eric wrapped the leather belt with Joseph's revolver on it around his own waist. He sprinted down the tunnels into the dark and rounded a corner. In front of him, he saw the two enemies who killed Joseph cornering the two creatures he saw earlier. The seraph appeared badly injured on the ground as her cherub was crying over her body. The two enemies were aiming at the young creature.

Eric didn't give them the chance to fire. He brought up Joseph's revolver and emptied its cylinder. The disciples were each hit several times and dropped dead. He slowly started walking over to the cherub and wounded seraph, stepping over the bodies of the two enemies. The cherub looked terrified; she slowly looked up at Eric with tears streaming down her face. The seraph slowly looked at him and appeared to try to move but couldn't due to her injuries.

He holstered the revolver and got down on one knee to check the seraph's pulse. It was weak, but there.

He slowly and carefully lifted the angelic creature into his arms. She was surprisingly light, barely ninety pounds.

He may have looked disheartened, and he knew how dangerous these monsters could be, but he knew he had to help them.

"I need to take her to get help now. Follow me, I promise to protect you," he said, before turning around to walk out of the cave.

[V]

Eric held the wounded seraph in his arms as he walked. He paused to look down at her. She was looking back up at him with her eyes half-lidded. He had never seen a seraph in person before. They were just as beautiful as described by those who claimed to have seen one and lived. Her skin was white. Not a pale and sickly white, but like that of pure and clean snow. Her thin, sinuous body was cloaked in a long dress that was same white as her skin, only slightly tarnished with dust and grit from the earth. Her arms, chest and hands were covered in more of the silky fabric of her gown yet was instead colored in a bright sapphire blue. Her hair was of a light blue as well; crowning her head and still managing to keep itself in a neat, curled bobbed style that covered part of her face. A pair of elongated, pointed ears protruded from either side of her head. Her eyes, though they were half-closed, were a pair of crimson rubies. They still shone even though she was hurt.

The seraph was still breathing, but it was slow and shallow. Eric shook himself from his trance. He knew he needed to get her to help immediately. He began to walk again when the seraph glowed in a bluish aura and was slowly being lifted out of his grasp.

The lone hunter turned and saw the cherub behind him, her eyes faintly glowing. She was trying to take her mother back from him. She didn't seem to understand what he was trying to do, or maybe it was that she didn't trust him. The creature had tears streaming down her face. Eric could only imagine what these two had been through, but he refused to let go of the seraph. He knew they were known for their psychic powers, and for being mind readers. He had to make it clear he meant them no harm.

"Please," Eric began, looking at the cherub in the eyes. "I want to help, she's hurt bad. I will get her the help she needs."

The cherub paused, looking up at Eric. She was shaking. Her psychokinetic grip loosened slightly, but then tightened as she tried once more to take her mother out of Eric's arms. Eric mentally pleaded with the creature, and the cherub weakened her grip again. She was looking at the seraph; her mother looking back at her. The two seemed to be speaking telepathically.

"No, I believe this human means what he says," the seraph spoke to her daughter. The cherub shook her head.

"I don't want to lose you...I can't trust him...what if he tries to kill us?" the cherub responded, trying one last time to take back her mom.

The seraph's eyes glowed slightly, the cherub's grip being weakened by her mother's own powers, ***"Listen, please. You must trust my judgement, understand? I can sense his intents. He is different from the others. Please, my sweet child, let him help us."***

The young cherub stood still for a moment, trembling. She was so terrified to lose her mother. She did not want to be alone. Yet, after another second, she slowly nodded.

The seraph smiled faintly, *"Thank you. Now, please follow and stay close."*

Eric watched the silent exchange between the mother and daughter. After a few quiet moments, the seraph looked back at Eric and nodded at him. Her eyes then closed as her breathing got weaker. They needed to go now.

The hunter shifted the seraph's weight in his arms as he reached for a soul stone. He held it out and squeezed the crystalline rock in his palm, releasing Vesuvius. The dragon seemed wore, but otherwise ready to help his master. The cherub seemed frightened at the sight of Eric's monster. She had never seen such a beast before. The dark-blue winged creature glanced to her, then towards Eric.

"Vesuvius, I need you to escort us. Make sure we don't walk into any traps, so keep an eye out. We have to find Burke and the other hunters," Eric ordered.

Vesuvius nodded, knowing what to do. The dragon went ahead, making sure the coast outside the cave was clear. Eric followed shortly behind but stayed inside the cave while his dragon scanned the area. He looked back at Eric and gave out a short, snort-like noise, signaling all was clear for now.

Eric walked out of the cave, pausing to look down at the seraph and further assess her injuries. Her wounds were worse than he thought, now that he could see them in the sunlight. She had two wounds where bullets struck her, and they leaked blood like wine.

He needed to try to patch her up now in order to hold her over until they got to help but remembered that he had no medical supplies. He needed to think quickly. When trying to run from the enemy, he remembered the two militiamen that were killed in the ambush. It hurt to think of the fallen soldiers, but he knew that one of them, Private Oliver, had a knapsack full of various medical aids.

The group began to make their way to the battle site. As they passed Joseph's corpse, Eric refused to look at him. The sight made his heart sink once more. The cherub, on the other hand, stared at the lifeless body as they walked by. She then looked curiously back at the human carrying her mother, taking note of his emotions.

The group neared the site of the battle between the hunters and their new enemy. Eric knelt down and shifted the seraph's weight again in his arms. He looked to Vesuvius, who nodded and slowly went ahead. After a few moments, the beast returned. Vesuvius nodded again, telling Eric it was good to go. The hunter slowly laid the seraph onto the ground.

"Vesuvius, stay here. I'm going to get the medical supplies," he said, patting Vesuvius on the head.

He quickly ran around the corner. The young hunter scanned the hills around him, it was still clear it seemed. He then looked ahead into the open and saw Oliver still laying near Sergeant Hobbs's body. Moving as low and as fast as he could, he went over to his dead comrade. When Eric reached him, he saw that Oliver was looking up at the sky, his eyes still wide open. His mouth was gaping as if still in shock, with both hands were clenched to his neck. He was covered and laying in his own blood.

Eric suppressed the sick feeling in his stomach at the sight. He quickly removed Oliver's medical bag.

"Thank you, brother, please rest easy..." he said, his voice trailing off. He reached out and gently closed Oliver's eyes. Eric then ran back across the open, looking around for any signs of movement.

He made it back to the others. Vesuvius was keeping lookout behind them. The cherub was kneeling on the ground next to her mother; looking at each other. Eric dropped to his knees next to the seraph and opened the medical bag. He retrieved bandages and a vial of antiseptic from the bag. He began using the alcohol, pouring it over the creature's wounds. The wounded mother winced in pain at the liquid's sting. The cherub seemed alarmed at first at her mother's pain but stayed calm when she saw the seraph continued to lay still. Eric knew it must have hurt, but she needed it. He quickly prepared the bandages and grabbed gauze out of the bag.

He began to stuff the wounds with gauze to stop the bleeding, but quickly realized he didn't have enough. He did the best he could before beginning to wrap the wounds with the bandages. Eric found that it was hard wrapping the wounds on her chest. There was a large, blade-like fin protruding from her chest through a slit in her dress; and it was in the way of a tight bandage. He was trying the best he could, but no matter how tight the gauze or bandages were; the bleeding wouldn't stop. The young man began to panic. He was trying, but he couldn't help but feel helpless trying to save the seraph. The hunter knew they didn't have time to get somewhere for her to get proper attention; they were too far away for such a thing.

He just thought if he could patch her up, that she'd have a chance. He felt that hope quickly fading away.

Eric began to choke up again as he tried to make the bandages tighter. He searched the bag for more gauze, but there wasn't any more. The panicked feeling got worse, he didn't want to fail another soul. He clenched his eyes shut, fighting back tears. Then he felt a hand gently grab his arm. Eric opened his eyes and saw a three-fingered blue hand gripping him; it was the seraph. He looked at her face and into her large red eyes. They sparkled, tears of pain collected in the corners. She smiled though, as if to try to comfort him.

The seraph fought through the pain. She looked into the hunter's eyes. She knew he was trying to save her. That he wanted to save her. Yet she also knew that she couldn't be saved. She was dying. The mother then looked over at her daughter. The cherub was trembling.

"My sweet daughter," the seraph said weakly, smiling through the pain. *"May you have many years ahead of you."*

"Mom?" questioned the cherub. She reached out and held her mother's hand. The seraph squeezed it, then let go.

"My time in this life is done, my loving child," the seraph said, reaching up and stroking her daughter's cheek. *"You must go now, please. Go and live your life."*

The cherub shook her head, she didn't want to believe her mom was dying, *"No... I don't want to lose you..."*

The seraph smiled a little more, wiping the cherub's tears away.

"I will never leave you. I promise to always be there for you. I will always watch over you from Aedurus," the seraph could feel herself slipping away. The bright red of her eyes began to fade. *"Now please...go...me and your father will always be with you...I love you, Celestial."*

The cherub stared at her mother as her life left her. The seraph's eyes faded in color and closed. Her breathing stopped. The young creature just kept staring at her, she didn't want to believe she was dead. She felt alone. She broke down crying.

Eric looked down at the seraph's body, having failed. He felt himself break apart on the inside. A lump formed tightly in his throat.

Dammit! He yelled in his head.

Vesuvius slowly came over and rubbed his head against Eric's shoulder. He patted Vesuvius on the head; he knew that the dragon was trying to comfort him. He looked at the cherub, who was sobbing over her mother. The hunter could only imagine the pain she felt. After a few moments, the cherub paused her sobbing and looked up at Eric. The two locked eyes for a split second. She then teleported in a flash of light.

Eric jumped up, shocked at what the creature did. He needed to find her; there was still bound to be enemies all over the island. He knew they wanted to hurt her, and he was bound to keep his promise to protect her.

"Vesuvius! Help me find her! I can't let her get hurt!" Eric said. The dragon nodded in agreement and began to use his hammerhead-like horns to sense for the cherub. The two began to make their way towards where Vesuvius sensed the cherub went.

Eric unslung his rifle and shouldered it. He let his beast lead the way. His heart was pounding. He could feel sweat run down his face and neck. He ignored the heat of the rocks beneath him and continued, almost in a run. The two crossed up and over several hills and through multiple ravines following Vesuvius's senses. Eric took a quick swig from his canteen and noticed it was almost empty. He put it back and continued to run when a lapguis burst from the ground.

"Dammit! We don't have time for this!" Eric yelled out, rifle at the ready. He racked the lever on the weapon, making sure a fresh cartridge chambered.

Vesuvius let out a roar and waved his arm for Eric to go on and let him deal with the lapguis. Eric stood still for a moment, not wanting to leave Vesuvius. He knew that the dragon could hold his ground against the giant stone-like serpent, but he didn't want to risk having his monster become injured.

"No way in hell am I leaving you!" the hunter called out, refusing to leave his monster. The hunter took aim and fired at the serpent, causing it to flinch in pain.

Vesuvius looked back at Eric and let out another roar, then shoved him towards where the cherub went. The dragon then charged forward at the lapguis. The serpent charged a ball of magic to attack but was tackled by the dragon. Vesuvius smashed the lapguis against the ravine wall, sending dust everywhere and obscuring Eric's view.

Eric wanted to stay and help his beast, but then heard another battle happening just over in the next ravine. He wished his dragon luck and turned to run towards the sounds of the fighting in the distance. Upon coming up to the edge of the top of the steep ravine wall, he looked down into it and saw the cherub. She was surrounded by several monsters being used by the enemy. Their disciples also surrounded her, ordering their creatures to attack her. The cherub dodged several attacks and grabbed the nearest enemy wraith with her telekinetic powers and slammed it into several other monsters. She then grabbed a stunned camazotz from the air and slammed it like a toy against the ravine wall.

The angered enemy disciples yelled more orders to their beasts as the cherub somehow managed to slowly fight them off. Then, over the next ridge a reaper dragon, the one Eric thought was part of the earlier battle, swooped in and lunged at the small creature. It caught the cherub off-guard and knocked her to the ground. Seeing the little creature get hit put a fire in the pit of Eric's stomach. It enraged him.

"Hey bastards! Up here!" he screamed, opening fire on the enemy disciples below.

Several got hit and either dropped clutching their wounds or started to run for cover. A few returned fire but missed as Eric jumped over the edge and slid down the steep wall.

He kept up the fire, keeping their heads down. He then dropped behind a large boulder and reloaded, making sure to load the silver rounds into the rifle's tube. He racked a round, then opened fire on the monsters nearest to the cherub. The lethal metal hit their marks on the beasts, who screamed in pain and jumped out of the bullets' paths. The ones who weren't killed or wounded immediately retreated a short distance towards their masters. The remainder laid on the ground as the silver cast bullets burned into their flesh and took their souls away.

The cherub was hurt by the attack she sustained from the reaper. She felt dizzy from straining her powers. Her elf-like ears then picked up the sounds of gunfire around her, causing her to look up. A short distance away she saw the human from earlier jump down behind a rock, several bullets hit around him. The human seemed to show no fear, only anger at that moment. The human removed the wide-brimmed hat from his head and tossed it to the ground before firing once again at the monsters near her.

What is he doing? She thought to herself. She wished that the human wouldn't have come looking for her. **Why did he follow me?** She pushed the thoughts to the side; she needed to get up and continue fighting.

The cherub got back to her feet. The human didn't seem to notice she was standing again. He was reloading his weapon, then fired over his cover at the Black Sun disciples. She turned and saw the reaper approaching her again. It was injured from the human's bullets and had hate burning in its eyes. It bellowed fire from its mouth, but the cherub managed to teleport out of the way. She then lifted a large chunk of stone from the ground with her mental energy, launching it towards the beast. The attack connected, knocking the reaper back into the ravine wall. It seemed to be on the verge of unconsciousness from the attack. An enemy minotaur came out of cover to help its comrade. It lifted the rock off of the dragon and threw it back at the cherub. She dodged the attack and threw a ball of shadow energy. The attack connected, but the bull-like beast merely shrugged it off.

Eric glanced over and saw the cherub fighting again. He was fearful of her getting hurt. He grabbed his soul stone and summoned Gyrog. The large water beast was slightly injured but still roared with determination.

"Gyrog, help the cherub! I got the enemy disciples covered!" Eric yelled to his leviathan, who nodded and rushed over to give aid to the cherub.

The cherub didn't like the water serpent, but she ignored it and threw another ball of energy at the minotaur. The minotaur was hit and knocked back in pain but rushed forward in retaliation. The reaper recovered from the attack and was in the air once more. The beast's eyes burned with pure anger as it stared at the cherub. It wanted the small creature dead. He swooped down for an attack when he got hit by a beam of energy from Gyrog. The attack hit hard and knocked him out of the air.

The reaper crashed to the stone earth and tried to get back up but was then grabbed in a bloody hold in the leviathan's mouth. Gyrog ripped and tore away at the dragon's neck with his sharp teeth, killing the enemy beast. The reaper's limp body dropped and didn't move again.

The young cherub watched as the leviathan quickly turned its attention to the minotaur, attacking again by firing a beam of energy from its mouth. The bull creature was hit hard and smashed into the ground as smoke and dust obscured it. When the dust settled, the cherub saw that the entire upper half of the minotaur was vaporized.

She watched in awe at the strength of the water serpent. The two creatures moved near each other, watching the enemy as they exchanged fire with Eric. Two more soul stones were used by their enemy as a banshee and draugr were released. The banshee wasted no time and screamed in a focused attack, aimed right at Gyrog. The leviathan tried dodging the sound waves but was hit. The sound sent the leviathan to the ground in intense pain as its ears started to bleed from the overload of decibels. The cherub was shocked to see the large beast fallen and didn't see in time that the draugr had moved in to attack. The undead creature smashed dark enshadowed fist into the cherub, knocking her back and onto the ground. The hit felt as if it took it all out of her. Her strength started to fade away and she felt like blacking out when she heard her mother's voice in her head.

"Do not give up, Celestial! Ascend to your true form!" her mother's voice yelled to her.

The cherub got back to her feet and felt something within her. Her entire body began to glow. She hovered off the ground and was enveloped in a shroud of light. Both Eric and the monsters momentarily stopped fighting and could only stare at what was happening to the small creature. The light was blinding to look at; Eric found himself shielding his eyes from it. A few moments passed, and the light began to fade away. When Eric looked back at the cherub, he was stunned. She was no longer a cherub.

Standing tall and strong was a seraph. She had transformed! Eric stared at her for a moment, unable to believe his eyes. Her stunning beauty was captivating all around her. The light faded away and her long, flowing gown blew slightly in the breeze. The newly transformed seraph opened her eyes. The deep red of her irides stood out against the faint blue glowing light that the rest of her eyes gave off. Her body was outlined in the same bluish hue. A pair of huge, white feathered wings sprouted from her back and spread wide.

She held her arms out in front of her, and a pulsing orb of energy appeared between her hands as she charged a ball of concentrated shadows. She threw the powerful attack directly at the draugr, who was hit. The undead beast was blown back with a huge amount of force and disintegrated to dust with a single hit. The seraph then charged up a beam of light energy and directly hit the banshee with it, shearing it in half. Several other monsters came rushing out of cover to attack her, but she grabbed them all in a powerful display of her psychokinetic powers. She held them all in place in the air as they struggled to break free. The seraph then closed her hands, crushing the skeletons of every single one of them and killing them instantly. The fairy creature felt stronger than she ever had before.

I can do this. She thought to herself.

"End this! Kill the bitch already!" yelled one of the Black Sun members, who brought his shotgun up and fired a hail of silver pellets at the seraph. Several of the small projectiles hit her in the side. The pain was horrible. She fell to the ground holding her wound in shock as it burned into her.

"No!" yelled Eric, who quickly aimed his rifle and planted a bullet in the head of the disciple who shot her.

The seraph got back to her feet, seeing saw other rifles being aimed at her. She focused her mind and bent the barrels of the firearms, rendering them useless. The creature fought through the pain of her wounds, then felt all of her energy leave her in one sudden burst. Her head immediately began pounding; it felt as if something just sucked her powers away. She collapsed to the ground on her hands and knees, gasping for air. Her wings disappeared in a burst of feathers.

What is causing this?! She thought in a panic.

Laying on the ground near her was a strange stone. It was red and covered in cryptic writings. The stone was emitting a glow and merely looking at it made her feel even weaker. She attempted to stand, to hit the odd stone away from her, but she had no strength.

Looking up, the seraph saw other disciples drawing their revolvers and aiming at her. She closed her eyes and braced for it. Shots rang out, but none hit her. The fairy creature slowly opened her eyes again and saw the human's leviathan. He had jumped in front of her and took the hits. The water serpent roared out in pain and dropped, breathing hard.

"Gyrog! No!" Eric screamed, seeing his beast mortally injured.

He jumped up out of cover and went to go run to help him, but a stick of lit dynamite was tossed in front of him and exploded. Eric was launched back as the whole ravine shook with the blast. Dust filled the air as he slammed against the ravine wall and slid down it limply. The ground still shook from the explosion and a rock slide along the ravine walls came crumbling down, with a large boulder landing on and smashing Eric's right leg below the knee; leaving him pinned where he lain. Eric screamed in agony, he never felt a pain like this before.

He tried in vain to push the rock off of his leg but couldn't. The dust settled, and he saw Gyrog struggling to get back up, trying to fight through his wounds to save his master. More shots rang out and the leviathan was hit several more times. He fell again, exhausted.

Eric felt tears running down his face. He couldn't believe this was happening. The young man lost his childhood friend and now was losing his monster. The seraph was slowly walking towards Eric, clutching her side. Another stick of dynamite rolled out and stopped near her, exploding as well. The ground shook again as the detonation jarred Eric's head. The dust began to settle, and he saw the seraph fighting to stand up once more and move towards him.

She got about ten yards away when a few more shots rang out and another bullet hit her in the shoulder. She let out a yelp in pain and fell to the ground. Looking up at Eric, she crawled a few more feet. She reached slowly reached out for him. He reached his hand out to her, but then she collapsed and fell unconscious.

Gyrog saw this and tried again to get up, to do something. The disciples were rushing out of their cover and running towards them. As they ran by, one stopped and fired a bullet into Gyrog's head, killing him. The leviathan dropped without a further sound.

Eric could only stare in disbelief at what was happening. This was it. This was the end. He tried to move the rock once more, but it was far too heavy. He couldn't feel the part of his leg that was trapped beneath it. He felt like blacking out. The enemy disciples slowly approached him, their weapons at the ready. Eric thought to reach for his own rifle, but it was just too far away. He felt so weak. The hunter reached for his revolver and drew it from the holster, leveling it at the closest enemy. His vision blurred as he heard other gunshots ring out from somewhere above him. The disciples sprayed blood and dropped. One that survived started firing at something above but was also hit several times and fell dead.

Eric tried to stay awake, but he slowly felt himself losing more strength. He saw a few figures slide down the ravine wall to his right. He could barely tell exactly who they were, but they were wearing the hunters' signature long coats. One of the duster-wearing figures ran over to the seraph and checked on her as the others ran to him. One tried to push the rock off Eric's leg but struggled. Vesuvius then appeared, hurt but not down, and helped shove the rock off of Eric's smashed leg. The dragon then poked at Eric with his snout, trying to get a response out of him. Eric just laid there, happy to see Vesuvius was alright. His head was swirling. The other blurry figure knelt down beside him and started yelling, trying to have Eric hear him.

"Eric stay with me! You're going to be okay!" the voice yelled. It sounded like Burke, but Eric could hardly tell. He was still looking over at the seraph.

She was still unconscious and lying flat on the ground. The hunter that was kneeling beside her pulled out an unused soul stone and captured her with it. She was enveloped in a glowing light and turned to dust, being sucked into the stone. Eric slowly began to black out as he thought about the seraph. He hoped she would be okay.

"Come on Eric stay with us!... Dammit we gotta get him out of here!" the voice yelled again. Eric fell unconscious as everything faded to black.

[VI]

<u>Eight Years Ago: (Eric)</u>

A twelve-year-old Eric stood with his feet slightly spread apart. His hands were balled into fists as he clutched his soul stone tightly in one hand. In front of him in a clearing was his young dragon, Vesuvius. Across from the beast was a large, demonic dog. Its eyes were dark red, and it had no ears. Skin was missing from random parts of its body, and it was ignited in hellfire. It was weakened but still bared its teeth. Behind the hell-sent canine was its owner, a large burly man. A man who could feel the sweat of imminent defeat.

"Vesuvius, finish off the hellhound!" the young Eric excitedly yelled, throwing his fist in the air.

The dazed hellhound tried to stay on its feet, then got hit by Vesuvius in a heavy tackle. The malformed canine stumbled backwards before collapsing to the floor, unconscious.

The bystanders watching the fight let out a loud cheer and stomped their feet in excitement. The roars of their voices echoed off the mountain tops of Usora. A human acting as a referee walked out onto the field and confirmed that the beast was out cold.

"The hellhound is unable to fight; the victory goes to the challenger and his dragon!"

Eric jumped up and down with joy, then ran to his monster. He embraced him in a tight hug.

"You did it Vesuvius! You won!" he joyfully cried.

Vesuvius gave out a loud roar in celebration; feeling pride for himself and for winning the fight for his master.

The two separated; Eric could barely contain his excitement. He looked up and watched as the man he challenged argue with the referee for a moment. Finally, the man gave up and handed the referee a small bag of gold coins.

The referee then approached him, smiling. As the man passed the hellhound, its owner returned it to its soul stone. The large man angrily eye-balled the young Eric, who stood in confidence at his victory.

"Congratulations, young one. You and your dragon have fought very well. I can sense a strong bond between you and him," the referee said, reaching his hand out and awarding the betted money to Eric. The boy received the coins with a huge grin. Eric looked the bag over with sparkling eyes before putting it away in his pocket. He then held out his hand.

"Thank you, sir," Eric said, shaking the man's hand with a tight grip.

"I do have to say though," the referee stated, now looking at the young dragon. "I don't think I've ever seen a young trainer tame such a beast like an azure dragon before. You must have some courage."

He could see loyalty for his master sparkling in the dragon's eyes. Eric looked at his monster as well, swelling with pride at the statement.

"I've had him since he was an egg. I always made sure to take care of him and treat him like he was my best friend," Eric said, chuckling slightly to himself. "Though Vesuvius was a bit ornery at first. I just never gave up on him, that's all."

The referee smiled at the boy, "It's good to see such strong people such as yourself. Take that money with pride. Keep doing what you do, and who knows where you'll end up."

"Thank you, sir, I will," Eric replied, shaking the man's hand once more before turning to leave.

As he walked off the battlefield, his best friend Joseph ran to catch up. The two high-fived and Joseph was grinning from ear-to-ear. They turned and starting walking side-by-side.

"Congrats Eric! You did it and got some more money!" Joseph said, clapping his friend on the back.

Eric paused to return Vesuvius to his soul stone, proud of his monster and how he fought hard. The dragon deserved a rest. He then turned back to his friend and continued walking.

"It was nothing, just hard work and trust between my dragon and me. That's all it takes to win," Eric stated, reaching back into his knapsack for a canteen. He took a quick drink and put it back.

Joseph laughed, then said, "Well, whatever it is, if you keep this up then maybe you can beat the Champion one day!"

"Thanks, I appreciate it!" Eric said excitedly.

He hoped that one day he could challenge the famous Champion. Monster fighting was the province sport of choice for those who knew the arcane arts of the soul stones. Most anyone in Usora who had control of a beast would train it to fight in pitted matches against other people's monsters.

Simple fights like the one he was in was just for the fun and money, but when one enters what is called the 'Arena', it's an entirely different fight. Combatants would have their creatures fight to the bloody death. Only the surviving beast would be allowed to move on. If one's monster was strong and beat the rest, then you would get a shot at the Champion and his creature, and a shot at taking the title of Champion.

"Well," Joseph said with a sigh. He rubbed his stomach. "Wanna go get a bite to eat? I'm starving."

"Yeah sure, I'm hungry as well," Eric said. His gut began to rumble. With his soul stone and money in hand, Eric and Joseph quickly made their way to the local restaurant.

Once they made it, Joseph quickly claimed an outdoor table by tossing his bag down into one of the chairs. Eric looked up and around at the wooden restaurant. The building seemed relatively new compared to the older establishments around it. It was located just on the edge of the small town of Beaksturm, next to a field and pond. The young boy walked out into the field and clutched his soul stone, releasing Vesuvius once more in a haze of smoke.

The dragon let out a deep purring-like sound and nuzzled his head against Eric for a short moment, then turned and laid out in the sun to relax. Joseph chuckled at the dragon and then thought of something.

"That guy was not happy you defeated his hellhound," he stated with a grin.

Eric laughed and was about to take his seat when he noticed a crowd of people nearby at a news stand.

"He'll get over it. It's not like Vesuvius killed his dumb dog," he replied, now more interested in the group of strangers.

"I guess so," Joseph replied, looking over at the crowd as well. "What's going on there?"

The boys went over and weaved between the moving bodies. Most of the people shown signs of worry or anger. Others showed shock or sobbed quietly. They made their way to the front of the crowd and up to the newsstand. The lone paperboy was frantically trying to hand out the papers as fast as he could. On the small wooden cart he was pulling along was a stack of more of the papers. Eric grabbed one and tossed a coin down to pay for it.

Him and Joseph bobbed and weaved their way back through the pedestrians back to their chairs. Once there, Eric planted the paper onto the table's smooth wooden surface. On the face of the news, the headline read:

'The Village of Rozzerdrift burned! No Survivors!'

The article went on to talk about how the small village up in the mountains of Usora was completely destroyed by monsters. It also talked about how the monsters were being led by a powerful cult. The news wasn't a first case of something like this, and it shocked Eric. It seemed to bother Joseph more than anything.

"That right there is why I plan on becoming a hunter as soon as I'm old enough. The militia hasn't been able to stop these attacks, and it's only a matter of time until a cult attacks Beaksturm," Joseph said, referring to their town and poking the table's surface for effect. "...If they aren't already here that is."

A server came by their table and took their orders. Eric made sure to order a large raw steak for Vesuvius as well. Once the server acknowledged their orders, she walked away.

Eric thought in silence for a moment, then said, "Do you think the Order actually does any good? There aren't very many hunters, and these cults seem strong. What makes you think the Order does any good over the militia?... They're also kind of controlling over people's lives."

Joseph looked at Eric in the eye. Eric saw determination as Joseph said, "It has to be better than what we have now. The militia can only do so much. The Order has saved humanity a hundred years ago, that's why they reign supreme! One day they'll change and be better though...Why don't you join up with me?"

Eric never had thought about it. He had always been too twisted up with wanting to beat the Arena and becoming Champion of Usora to consider another option.

"I don't know...I feel like I should definitely do something though. I hate seeing innocence being hurt by evil like that," he replied.

"Listen, I'm becoming a hunter as soon as I'm of age. Give it some thought okay? I'll have been a hunter for a while by the time you're old enough," Joseph took a drink from his canteen, then continued. "I'm sure I'll have you talked into it by then."

They both chuckled, then grew silent once more. Finally, Eric nodded.

"Yea, I'll give it some thought," he said.

Months ago, from present day: (Celestial)

The forest was absolutely serene that night. The small cherub craned her neck and looked up at the stars. The sky was clear and not a sign of a cloud was to be seen. She closed her eyes and focused her hearing; concentrating on the chirping of the small birds that lived around her. It was completely tranquil. The corners of her mouth curled into a small smile.

"Celestial?" she heard her name being called. *"Your father has returned, please come home."*

The cherub reopened her eyes and turned. She faced the direction of her home and began to make the short distance back to her parents. As she moved, she lowered her body to the ground and walked instead of floating. Her feet made small imprints on the forest floor as she stepped carefully around tree roots and anthills. As her home came within view, her mother was patiently waiting for her. The seraph smiled at her daughter, sending warm feelings telepathically to her.

"The forest is most peaceful, isn't it?" Her mother asked her as she got closer.

The cherub smiled back at her mom and replied, *"Yes, momma. It is."*

The seraph placed her hand on her daughter's shoulder and gently led her into their home. It was a small half-spherical hut made from tree branches and leaves. The walls were finely woven from the branches and the leaves were sewn in to act as a means to keep any rain from leaking inside. Within the walls of the small hut, her father was looking out the space between two of the branches. He sighed to himself.

"I felt...something...out there," her father said. *"But I couldn't tell what it was."*

He stepped away from the tiny opening, turning towards his daughter and mate. The father then spoke once more.

"That sense though. It felt like humans...though their kind haven't been spotted in this area for years."

The female seraph floated over to her mate, then kissed him on his cheek.

"I know you felt something, but I do not, my love. Try to relax. Everything is okay," she said, rubbing his arm gently.

He nodded, then kissed her back. The small cherub grinned at her two parents. She knew the two seraphs loved each other very much. She had hopes to one day find a mate that would love her as much as her father did to her mother.

Everything seemed to be perfect, but then her parents stood straight, as if lightning shot through both of them suddenly. Pupils appeared within their red eyes, unfolding from the centers of their irides.

"Grace, you felt it as well?" the male asked.

The female shook slightly, "*Yes...I did. You were right, there are humans out there.*"

The cherub started shaking. **Humans? What do they want?** She asked herself.

"*Momma?*" she questioned.

Her mother grabbed her gingerly using her mental powers. She was pulled into her mom's arms. They then both moved towards the wall furthest from the hut. Then, noises. Footsteps. Crunching on the forest floor outside the hut. It was slow at first, but then it picked up as more steps could be heard. It sounded like several humans hiding in the brush outside.

The cherub's father sprouted his wings but kept them folded behind him in the small confines of the house. He looked to his mate and child.

"*I'm heading outside to face them. Take our daughter and run, Grace. Do not look back,*" he said, stepping outside.

The father left the hut, and immediately could see them. More than a dozen humans armed to the teeth. They all aimed rifles at him. At the front, one of them spoke up.

"Seraph!" he yelled out. "We know there are more of you in there! Come on out and surrender yourselves!"

The male seraph spread his wings wide, floating a few more centimeters from the ground. His eyes and body glowed in a powerful aura.

"Leave this forest at once, humans!" he answered him. His voice rung through their head in a powerful voice, *"This will be your only chance!"*

Though most of the humans may have appeared somewhat frightened, none moved from their spots. The man who spoke up earlier stood, waving to the others.

"Take him down!" he screamed. "Do not kill! We need them alive!"

Gunfire erupted. The sounds were deafening to the family's ears. The father shot forward, getting hit once. The bullet burned him, but he ignored it as he tore the head from the first human's shoulders. He then followed the attack by grabbing another human from the bushes and crushing their chest cavity with his mind.

The mother, with her daughter in her arms, sprinted out of the hut behind her mate and went as quickly as she could into the forest. She could hear gunfire behind her, followed by the screams of men.

The male seraph tore apart several other humans, then turned towards another. The small person was cowering up against a tree. They made eye contact, and the human dropped their rifle. The seraph, believing them to no longer be a threat, turned away. He then felt all of his energy drain at once. A small, red rock with cryptic writings landed on the ground next to him. His wings disappeared in a flash and he fell to the ground, coughing and gagging.

That stone...it's draining me... He thought in a panic.

Several humans then surrounded him, beating him with the butt of their rifles. They then tied him up with rope, placing the red stone deep within the knots to keep it near him.

The mother sensed her mate had fallen and was defeated, but she refused to try to go back. She loved him dearly, but she needed to get her cherub to safety. As she ran, a single shot rang out. The bullet implanted itself deep in her thigh, causing her to fall and drop her daughter. The cherub got to her feet and turned to her mother, who was on all fours. Behind them, several humans were giving chase. The mother looked at the humans, then spun her head back to her child.

"*Celestial, run!*" Her mother screamed out. Tears of both fear and pain ran down her mother's cheeks.

The small cherub panicked and spun, floating away as fast as she could. As she passed a tree, the butt of a rifle came out from behind it and smashed directly into her skull. The cherub then laid on her back, fading in and out between fainting and staying awake. She was losing the fight to stay conscious. As she blacked out, she could hear a voice.

"You all gave us a bit of trouble...but don't worry, you seraphs and the like bring a pretty coin."

Present Day: (Mariah)

Mariah stood at the top of one the mountain peaks of Krehaul Island. She crossed her arms as she watched the smoke of battle in the distance. The cult leader had a bad feeling about this deep down in her gut. Demothesis was not going to be happy about this intervention by the Order. As long they get what they need for their plans, she didn't think it would matter if the hunters got involved. Everyone would parish before they'd be stopped.

A Black Sun disciple came running up the hill. He stopped about two meters behind her, panting and trying to catch his breath.

"Well? What is it?" Mariah commanded. She glared over her shoulder at the disciple with a look of scorn. He quickly straightened his stance and made sure not to make eye contact with her.

"Ma'am...we failed to recapture the cherub or stop the human helping it. We had nearly killed them both when they received reinforcements. We think it was the surviving hunters from earlier," he said, still breathing heavily.

Mariah curled her lip in anger, then spun around and smacked the scout across the face hard.

"You idiot!" she screamed, "Demothesis wanted that cherub alive! Where are they now!?"

The scout flinched in pain from the sting. He rubbed his face, but refused to otherwise move from his position, "They've managed to escape to the other side of the island. Our other members show another ship preparing to arrive to get them. Shall we pursue?"

Mariah furiously stared at the scout for another second, then waved him off with a huff. She turned back to where the smoke was coming from.

"No, we can't risk any more damage and exposure. We'll have to evacuate the island for now. The Order is sure to come back with more hunters now that they know our presence here is bigger than they thought. Tell everyone to pack up and make sure that the remaining monsters are secured," she ordered.

The disciple balled his fist and brought it to his chest in a salute, then spun on his heels and ran off to spread the word to the others. Mariah continued to watch the smoke for another moment. Further in the distance near the shore she saw the ship the scout mentioned. Seeing the paddle ship only served to infuriate her more. After another moment of watching, another member came running up to her in a panic.

"Zealot Mariah, ma'am!" the man yelled.

"What is it this time?" she said through gritted teeth. Her words dripped with venom.

"Ma'am...the other hunters...the monsters have escaped!" the disciple replied.

Earlier: (Jonathan Burke)

Jonathan Burke looked at his shoulder again. It only seemed like the bullet grazed him, but it still hurt like crazy. He pushed the pain to the side and checked on David McGowan.

"How are you doing David?" he asked.

The large man ignored his injured leg and side. He clearly walked with a limp, but Burke was proud of his hunter for sticking it out.

"I'll be fine, Jon. I'm holding up." David replied. He was wearing bandages fashioned out of his torn shirt.

"That's good," Burke nodded. He then turned to Ross Lancaster, "How about you?"

Ross wasn't wounded, but clearly seemed shaken up. "I'm fine too, Jon"

Burke nodded once more as they continued walking, "Alright let's continue on then. We have to see if we can find Joseph and Eric."

A short time passed when the group came upon a mine opening. There didn't seem to be any enemies around, and it seemed like a place that the two other hunters would fall back to. Burke waved his hunters in quietly, rifles at the ready. They went into the mine tunnel, following it down deep into the island. It seemed like the old tunnels that were used for mining ore. There were still old mining carts, pickaxes and shovels scattered about. After a while they came across a freshly dug tunnel going down deeper. The hunters took point around the opening.

"Look alive hunters, we may run into something," Burke said quietly. He took point and continued down deeper into the mine.

After a few hundred yards, the tunnel opened into a cavernous room. There were crates and various supplies spread around the large chamber. Tents and altars for worship were arranged neatly along one area. They found the Black Sun's base on the island. Lined along one of the walls were a number of steel cages holding several different kinds of creatures in them. In the center of the room was an ornately carved pedestal, and on it was a stone tablet. Several guards patrolled the area.

The hunters took cover behind a large crate. Jonathan Burke knew there was something religiously important about that tablet. He decided he needed to take it.

"Alright boys. I want you to stay here and don't make any sudden moves or sounds. I'm going to sneak over to that pedestal and take that stone; it looks important to them," he said.

The two hunters nodded, David gave him a thumbs up. The old hunter then nodded as well.

"I'll be right back," he said.

Jonathan quickly and quietly made his way from crate to crate, ducking behind them so as to not be seen. Once he got close, he noticed there was a guard that made his patrol around the tablet. He needed to take him out. Burke got closer and hid. He waited for the guard to pass while the others weren't looking before quickly reaching out and grabbing the passing guard. He put him in a choke hold while covering his mouth with his hand, so the guard couldn't scream for help. He pulled the guard behind cover and choked him out until he was unconscious. Once he was out cold, Burke dropped him and sprinted for the tablet, grabbing it.

With the ancient stone object in hand, he turned and ran back to where the others were. Once he got back behind the first crate, he saw they weren't there. He panicked a little and spun his head around looking for them when he spotted them over by the cages holding the monsters. He was about to go get them when the cages opened, and their arcane barriers dropped. His hunters were trying to release them. With the cages without their magic, the vengeful beasts regained their strength and rushed out and attacked the disciples.

Burke felt a little anger for potentially giving their position away but was happy for his hunters for helping free the creatures that were captive. The hunters quickly came back to their Burke without being detected in the chaos that was unleashed.

Jonathan nodded back to the tunnel they came through. "Let's get the hell out of here and keep looking for the others."

As they left, Burke looked behind him in time to see the guards being killed by the monsters that were getting their revenge. One disciple was torn apart by a troll as a giant woodfall spider jumped another and impaled him with its massive fangs. He grinned to himself.

Those bastards deserve this. He thought.

Once out of the tunnels and back outside, they retraced their steps back to the battleground. They figured the enemy wouldn't be there anymore, and it may prove useful in finding Eric and Joseph. On the way back, they spotted a body lying on the ground. The hunters ran over.

"Oh gods no..." David said quietly to himself.

It was Joseph's body. There was blood pooled under him.

Jonathan shook his head. If Eric was still alive, he needed to find him fast. He pushed his hunters onward. As they came up onto the site of the battle, they passed the body of a seraph. He felt a pang of sadness at the sight but continued on. The hunters kept moving until they heard a roar in the distance, followed by another.

"That sounded like Eric's dragon. Move!" Burke barked. The hunters began running towards the sound.

When they rounded the next corner, they saw a lapguis and Vesuvius battling. Eric was nowhere to be seen, and the dragon looked hurt.

"Quick, take the serpent down!" Burke ordered.

The hunters quickly brought up their rifles and opened fire on the lapguis. They pelted the serpent with the bullets, who didn't seem heavily affected but did flinch from the impacts. The dragon seemed relieved to get help and quickly attacked by bellowing blue flames from his mouth. The attack coated the serpent in hellfire and burned it alive. It then dropped to the dirt ground with a heavy thump, dead.

With that threat dealt with, the dragon ran over to Burke.

"Where's your master, Vesuvius? Lead us to him!" He said.

Vesuvius spun around and beckoned for them to follow. Just then an explosion rang out ahead of them in the next ravine. Then another explosion.

Burke knew they didn't have time. He started running.

"Let's go hunters!"

[VII]

Falling... Falling... Was Eric underwater? His sight was too blurry to tell. Noises were opaque and distant. His body was floating in a suffocating air. He tried to move his left hand, then his right leg. Then his head, his eyes. Nothing. He could not. Shortly enough, he gave up. He was so tired...

Falling... Falling...

He was at the bottom depths of a dark jail, whose bars were made of stone. The entire ground shook with an intense noise, as if the place had a thousand banshees screaming at their full capacity. Eric covered his aching ears. Every ounce of his skin was crying; his heart burst and his brain exploded. He strived to get free. He tried to look for help, so he forced himself to scream. But there was no freedom, no help. No voice.

Then, the vision stopped in complete emptiness and silence, leaving him...

Falling... Falling...

He was inside a candle-colored room, void in all directions infinitely. It was empty, but restful to the eye and calming to the mind. It was not too bright, nor too crushing. The floor was a texture of snow; the ceiling was clouds. The light air had the slightest scent of incense, of that which a small dose was pleasant. The only sound was that of a soothingly deep tone; what remained of a single, delicate note of piano after playing it. Such a peaceful place, only the mind of a pure being could possibly make it. Eric felt like he could stay there forever. Any worries, any problems, any fears were so, so far away; as distant as the stars in the night sky. No, not even that. It was as distant as a place of happiness could be from Plataea.

Out of curiosity, Eric took a single, bashful step forward. The scenery dimmed to waver in shades of cerulean, black, and midnight blue. The room became much smaller as several slow, pale shapes moved along the spherical ceiling. They crossed over one another, drawing arches and waves in the sky. It was as if someone was casting them there for the sole purpose of entertainment. It resembled the bottom of an ocean, if not a lonely one. It was a profound, submerged reality, hidden to anyone else.

It was such a fantastic place. Was this what heaven looked like? Was this the Elysian Fields?

Then, he noticed her. A feminine figure kneeling on the ground and looking at the distant nothingness. She had her back to Eric, hidden by a soft garment too large for her slender body. The curves of her form were still visible, though. She seemed to be the only focus Eric could manage after seeing her. He was left thoughtless at the sight and, even though he couldn't see her face, he remembered that she was most graceful and beautiful. There was no doubt about it; she was the seraph from Krehaul. With the same confidence, he felt he was most familiar with her. He felt he knew her exact thoughts, even. So close he was to that ethereal soul, he thought his mind had to have been tricking him. She was so far, yet he could feel her soft, thin breaths as if he was mere centimeters from her. Was she aware that she was sharing this room with someone else?

Eric awkwardly stepped back. He was not willing to disrupt the harmony of such a delicate and angelic presence. As soon as his left foot retouched the floor, she moved. She did not turn to him, but rather she slowly raised one gentle hand from the ground. She moved it up along her upper body in one, single, sinuous move. She reached forward and lightly tapped, with just the very tip of her index finger, against an invisible surface in front of her. It bent to her touch like a mirror of water and resonated across the entire room. It sent the crisp, new, lighter tone of a piano note. The entirety of the room wobbled gently.

An immense joy rushed through the young hunter. Yet, he noticed it was becoming harder to continue looking at the enchanting world. His sight became muffled, the colors smeared. He rubbed his eyes several times, not wanting the beautiful vision to be over. His touch even became numb. She was going to play another note soon, he was sure! It was not soon enough though. He fainted once more.

Eric saw a blurry light at the end of the void. The world came swirling back as he regained consciousness. His head hurt, his sides hurt. It felt like everything hurt. His right leg especially, but something else seemed off about it. He then heard faint voices around him. He tried to focus on what they were saying as he began to stir.

"He's waking up, oh thank the gods!" one of the voices said. It sounded like his mother. He hadn't seen her since he left Usora.

"Take it easy son, you took a beating," another voice said. That one sounded like his father.

Eric placed his elbows beneath him and struggled to sit up. The pain all over his body got worse. He slowly opened his eyes but could only see a swirling blurry light for a few moments. His vision started to clear up. Colorful blobs began to take shape as his vision came into focus. He tried to push himself up fully into the seated position, but then he felt several hands gently stop him. The hands slowly lowered him back down onto his back.

"Not too fast, Eric. No need to strain yourself," a voice called out. It was Burke.

Eric laid back down; his vision cleared up the rest of the way. He looked around as best he could. He was in a hospital room. Sitting to his right was his parents. His mother looked like she had been crying. They both smiled seeing their son was still alive. His mom reached out and rubbed his arm lightly.

"Thank the gods! My baby is alive!" she happily called out.

Eric reached up and clasped her hand and squeezed it. He smiled back at his parents. He was very happy to see them. He couldn't imagine how worried they must have been.

"We were worried you wouldn't ever wake up, son. I couldn't be happier to see that the doctor was wrong," his father said. Tears welled up in his eyes as he continued, "He told us it was very unlikely you would ever recover, or even simply regain consciousness."

Eric silently nodded at his dad. He felt another hand squeeze his shoulder lightly.

"It's good to have you back in the land of the living," Jonathan Burke said from Eric's left.

Eric looked over at his leader. The old hunter had his jacket off; a large bandage was wrapped around his shoulder. Eric nodded again.

"Yessir..." Eric struggled to speak, "How is everyone else in the chapter?... Did anyone else make it?"

Burke frowned, his gaze dropped to the floor. He then sighed and looked back up at the young man.

"We only lost Joseph and the two militiamen..." he began. "When we were trying to carry you out of there, we were ambushed again...David has been wounded, but he'll recover. Ross sustained minor injuries as well."

Eric was quiet. He closed his eyes and held them tightly shut. He still couldn't believe that Joseph was gone. His best friend. The young man also felt remorse for the two militiamen. They had families, friends, lovers. Why did any of them have to die? He felt himself choke up. He reopened his eyes and looked back at his leader.

"Were we able to recover the bodies?" he asked, his voice quivering.

Burke responded, "Yes. Two more groups of hunters arrived as we were boarding the ship to evacuate. They were unable to find the enemy, but they did recover the bodies of our fallen. They have all been given proper burials."

Eric nodded. He wished he could have at least been there for Joseph's funeral. He choked up again at the thought of his lost friend.

They had known each other for so long. Joseph's parents must be devastated. He remembered he still needed to deliver his friend's last letter to his girlfriend. He felt the saddened pain come back. He just then remembered something else.

"What about the seraph? Is she okay?" he asked. The weird-feeling pain came back again in his right leg.

"I don't know." Burke said, looking over his shoulder for a split second. "I was concentrated on helping you; she had disappeared by the time we got you out from under that rock."

Eric thought to himself for a moment. He had thought he saw her being captured by a soul stone. Who was the hunter that caught her? Did Eric even actually see that, or was he just seeing things? He didn't know what to think, so he just nodded and decided not to think about it.

"Thank you, sir," the young hunter said.

"No problem, Eric." Burke smiled at the young man, then stood up. "Well, I'm going to head back to my room for now. You rest here okay?"

Eric watched him as he walked away, but then stopped him, "Wait, Jonathan."

Burke turned around and look at Eric, one of his brows raised quizzically.

"What's going to happen to me with the Order?" Eric asked. "Will I still be able to serve?"

Burke glanced at Eric's parents, then replied, "We'll worry about that later. For now, you need to visit with your parents and get some rest."

Eric silently nodded. The old hunter left the room, closing the door behind him. The young man looked back over to his parents. He was glad they were here.

"We're so happy you're alright sweetheart," his mom said, forcing a smile.

"I'm fine mom, I always promised you I would be," he replied.

He tried sitting up again. The pain wasn't as bad, but the odd feeling was still there in his right leg. It hurt, but at the same time he couldn't feel anything beneath his knee. As he sat up, he looked down at his feet and saw that there wasn't anything under the covers beneath his knee on the right leg. The color drained from his skin and he felt like passing out again. He had to brace himself on his elbows to stay up.

His dad noticed that Eric realized he was missing part of this leg and jumped out of his chair to help him lay back down. He didn't want his son to go into shock at the realization.

"I know son, I know. It's okay, it's fine," his father quietly told him.

"Dad...I'm missing my leg..." Eric said in a panic; his eyes wide open. He couldn't stop staring at the empty space where his leg should have been. He was light-headed again.

His mother reached out and ran her hand through his hair. She was trying to help keep him calm.

"Hun it's okay, you will be alright. We were told a large boulder crushed your leg and it couldn't be saved. The doctor said he tried his best, but that it had to be removed. We're sorry sweetheart, but it will all be okay, I promise," she said.

Eric remembered the boulder, and the pain it caused. He couldn't believe he was missing part of his leg. He didn't want this, any of it.

"Mom, I don't want to be stuck in a wheelchair. What will I do?" he asked.

His mom thought for a moment, then said. "We'll figure something out. We could get you a prosthetic."

Eric just looked up at the ceiling. **Why did all of this have to happen to me?** He thought.

About that time, the door opened, and a nurse walked in to check on the hunter. She saw that he was awake and seemed surprised.

"Oh my! You're awake, thank goodness for that!" she said, smiling warmly. "The doctor was worried whether you would ever wake up."

"He's still a bit in shock. He noticed his leg," his father quietly stated to the nurse.

The nurse shifted on her feet, trying to keep her smile.

"Yes, it's a most unfortunate thing. We tried our best, but it was far too damaged to be saved. I am sorry."

She looked down at Eric, "We could get you a prosthetic limb if you'd wish to go that route. I promise you that with some practice and exercise, you could be walking and running again in no time!"

Eric looked back at her. He nodded and replied, "Thank you nurse."

She smiled again, then turned around to leave. Eric stared back at the painted, white ceiling. He figured he would get a prosthetic. He refused to be bound to a wheelchair for the rest of his life. He laid there for another moment, then deep down he began to feel another emotion bubbling up. He felt it quickly replacing his worry. It was anger. Vengeance. He wanted to avenge his fallen brothers and his leviathan. He wanted to make the enemy feel what he felt right then. He wanted to hurt them all...then he calmed his nerves. He knew realistically that he probably wouldn't ever be able to do it. He didn't even know where they were hiding. Like many other cults, this group seemed secretive for the most part.

He still felt the anger bubbling deep within him. He glanced back at his mother at his bedside. She was looking back at him. Her eyes were still brimmed with tears. Eric took a deep breath. He fully calmed down then once more.

"What are we having for dinner? I'm starving," he said, feeling his stomach rumble.

His parents smiled again, his mom even let out a small laugh.

"We were just about to leave for now and get something to eat. Do you want us to bring back something for you?" she asked.

"Yes please, I would love that," he said, smiling for his worried mother.

Both his parents got up to leave. His dad made his way to the door before pausing and turning around. His mom leaned down and kissed Eric on the forehead.

"I love you sweetie. I'm so happy you are okay," she said, turning to leave.

She walked out the door, his father waited for her to pass him.

His dad nodded, "Try and get some rest until we get back with the food. It shouldn't take very long."

Eric replied, "Alright dad."

"Love you son," he said, closing the door behind him.

With his parents gone for now, Eric suddenly felt much more tired than he was already. He laid his head back and closed his eyes. Thoughts of the seraph entered his head. He was positive that was her in his visions, there was no doubt! He knew she still had to be out there somewhere.

He thought again about how Burke said he didn't see what had happened to her. While he trusted the words of the old hunter, he was sure that she was captured by another hunter. He wished he had gotten a better look at her captor. The young hunter worried for her safety even still. Eric was sure she was safe, but he couldn't help but having noticed the feelings of immense despair coming from her, even in such a tranquil place they shared.

He decided not to worry for now. The hunter was sure that whomever had her, was taking good care of her. As he further thought about her, sleep began to take his mind over.

It was raining outside. Such a shame.

Still, he wouldn't want to stay in the Order's building on his special day. No, there was no way that such a silly reason like rain would stop him. After all, he finally fulfilled his dream of becoming a master; a master to one of those creatures. He would always daydream of their beauty, of their power, of how he could make them do whatever he wanted them to do. Because he was always thinking about them, he believed he deserved one. He always wanted one, he wanted an army of them, because he loved them. He would treat them well, and make sure to pleasure them. A lot. Every day, he would be ready for them.

The strange hunter walked down the streets as the raindrops patted onto his hat. He paid no mind to the occasional passerby who glared at him. He paid no attention, for something else was on his mind. He swung through a small market, coming back out with a large turkey leg in hand. He gnawed on the meat, his mouth like a hippo as he dirtied his chin and the front of his duster with a mixture of the cooked flesh and his saliva.

In a short while, he arrived at his destination. A small, somewhat run-down abode near the edge of Pratertown. The odd hunter unlocked the door and swung it open, stepping inside. He removed his soaked hat and duster, dropping them to the floor without a care. As he did this, his teeth once more hit the bone of the turkey leg. The man glared down at it to find the bone already picked clean. He sighed and tossed the bone to the side, not caring where it landed.

His stomach was suddenly no more an issue. Instead, something a bit further down moved. This was a special day indeed; for he finally had *one*.

He walked across the filthy living room floor towards the door leading to the basement. There was still signs of the creature's attempted escape from just yesterday. He really was obsessed a bit too much with the creatures, and he felt that was a bit silly for such a respectable man. Sure, maybe it was a bit excessive to have shot it in its leg- oops sorry, *her* leg, rather. Still though, he firmly believed all he had done, and all he was going to do, was necessary to capture and keep her. He would do it with force, because she would resist him.

That was absolutely shameful, but he would excuse her for such behavior. After all, she could not possibly know beforehand how much of a wonderful person he was, could she? Of course, he would teach her to stop being so silly, because he cared for her. With force, if necessary.

He was hyper that day, he could not deny it. He was practically jumping up and down as he reached the door going to the basement. He couldn't wait any more. He swung the door open and nearly sprinted down the spiraling staircase. As he made his way down, he could already hear the muffled whimpering of a soft voice from behind the next door.

"Nobody can hear you!" he shouted to her. "Don't worry, my dear. After all, I love you, don't I? I know you also love me. You are just too shy to admit it, aren't you?"

The mysterious hunter then turned the knob and opened the door to the room that the angelic seraph was chained up in.

"Why are you looking at me that way? Come on now, don't be so silly..."

[VIII]

Eric took a few steps forward, bracing himself on the doorway leading out of his bedroom. Looking down, he lightly cursed to his new metallic leg. The prosthetic had been painted black very quickly after receiving it, and though it was not visible under the pant leg of the young hunter's trousers, one could still see the ever so slight limp he had when he stepped.

Overall, Eric was well getting used to walking with it, even to the extent of running a bit, but it still somewhat bugged him. It was a constant reminder to be more careful on missions in the future. It had been nearly three months since the events of Krehaul Island, and the death of his best friend still rang like hollow bells in his mind. The seraph, on the other hand, was only a distant memory to him. While he unconsciously cared and hoped she was okay, her face was only a faded dream by this point.

The young hunter walked along the stone corridor towards the dining room of the Order's building. His steps landed with heavy thuds as his boots contacted the ancient hardwood floorboards. Entering the dining room, Eric grabbed a fresh apple from a tin bowl that was resting atop the long table and bit into it, wiping away the juices that ran down his chin.

Jonathan came into the room, having already looked for Eric elsewhere in the building. He smiled warmly at the new hunter and clasped his shoulder as he passed.

"Morning, Eric. Did you get a restful sleep?" the old hunter asked.

Eric nodded, swallowing his bite of the apple.

"Yessir, about as restful as it could be," he responded.

Burke chuckled and grabbed up an apple for himself, biting into it.

"That's good," he said with a mouthful. "I want you to meet me in the great room in an hour. You have a mission."

Eric tilted his head to the side. A mission? So soon after recovering from his injury? He didn't understand it but was happy otherwise to finally go out again. After all, he was tired of hanging around in this old structure. He yearned for the outdoor air.

"That sounds fantastic sir," Eric said. "...But who will I be going on mission with? David and Ross are paired hunters, who will be my partner?"

Jonathan took another bite of his green apple, "You will be going with David on this one. Ross has asked for some time off, and I'm sure you're itching to get back out there. David has volunteered to go with you. He will be your partner until we receive the hunter that is being transferred from another group."

Eric's gaze dropped to the floor for an instant. Burke saw this and placed a hand on his shoulder.

"Joseph was a fantastic hunter. None of us could ask for a better one...nor a better friend. Keep your head up, Eric, for his death was not in vain. He died fighting a horrible cult and helped to drive them back into the shadows. That is an honorable death," Burke said reassuringly.

"His death was honorable, that I am aware," Eric stated. His gaze was fixated on a spot on the floor, "But I wish we knew more about this cult. Who were they? Where are they now?"

Burke looked at Eric. His lips were pursed into a thin line. After a moment, he responded.

"I wish I had an answer for you. I do not know where they are. After we left, other hunters searched the island and found nothing. It was like they vanished."

The young hunter raised his head and met the older one's eyes. The trace of a tear ran down Eric's cheek.

"I promise you though," Jonathan said, pausing, "we will find them and get our revenge. They are still a threat, and we will put an end to it."

It was with those words, Eric felt a small ray of hope in his heart. He nodded to Burke, who returned it.

"Now..." Burke said, patting Eric on the shoulder. "Go get yourself ready and be in the great room soon. You may borrow my shotgun for this mission...I think you'll prefer it over your rifle for this one."

The old hunter grinned, showing his metal teeth. He then stepped away and left the room. Eric watched the doorway for another moment, then took another bite from the apple.

A shotgun? What could I possibly be hunting that will make a shotgun better than a rifle? Eric thought, leaving the dining room as well.

Again. Again, and again. The swine was at it again.

Did he not come before today already? Was he still not satisfied? Perhaps it was another day. Could that mean she was losing the track of time? Was she losing consciousness? Had she stayed awake, then surely, she would have noticed the change of date, after all. So, it was likely. That would explain why her head had felt as if a hammer had been beating against it and her vision was spinning. All of that did not matter to her anyways.

How much longer would he take? Celestial just wanted him gone. To be away from her. On this day, he was smelling worse than before. It was disgusting to her senses. As he moved her insides, she shivered at the cold and sticky layer of his sweat more than anything else.

That feeling was the worst of it all. She had already learned to not care for the crawling feeling within her violated body; she could just close her eyes and retreat to the safe space within her mind. It was only within her mind could she seem to run away.

The hunter who imprisoned her grabbed her rear and began moving with more force. His revolting smell, she was not able to endure it any more. She thought it would start to infect her; to make her smell like him, that she would emanate that same sweaty illness through bubonic skin that would cover her wholly. She would rather kill herself than live with that.

Every time the human came downstairs, it seemed like he smelt worse than before. He was more and more nauseating. If she could at least vomit, but her stomach was nothing more than bread and water. Her gut churned, and she felt as if she would finally-

He began to move faster. It caused her further pain, a lot more. Yet, to her it was a good sign. It meant he was almost done. She tightly clung her hands around the chains that bound her to the walls and endured. She felt like she was about to vomit, she was sure of it. She tried swallowing to help, her eyes answered with a tear. Then she waited.

Nothing. She would not throw up. She damned her weak, pathetic body. At least seeing her digestive acids scattered across the gray and dirty wall would have been something new. It was not ticking a second, this recurring hell she was living. Her owner would not clean it, that much was sure. At least she would have been able to smell that, instead of his disgusting stench.

As those were her thoughts, the hunter who owned her kept uttering syllables, for the good of a time he was having. He just pushed and pushed, not caring when he would be done for the simple fact that he could have her whenever he wanted. Before ending he would moan louder, from the cry of a seal to that of a whale. She did not care as she was still desperately closing to herself, deaf to any noise.

She damned her master. She damned his vile, disgusting ways. A thought then raced into her mind. The other human from back on that forsaken island. The one in the same group as the man who was raping her; his image flashed again. She damned him most of all. He played with her mother's emotions to earn her trust and got her into this! She had thought for a split moment that he was good, that maybe she had found a trustworthy human. She knew in her mind that she was now wrong!

...But yet, even she remembered the emotions she sensed in the boy...maybe he could get her out of this hell. They had already linked minds before, while the human was unconscious. She would have try to replicate that link...

Finally, her owner was done. At least for now, he was done. Even waiting for him to button his trousers and leave felt like an eternity. The way he looked at her while he cleaned himself, like he saw her as nothing more than a silly creature! For her, every time was hard. It was becoming harder every time he violated her. It became harder to endure the process. Her body was feverishly shaking, her head sweating terribly, her heart pumping violently. She damned her fragile form once more.

Chained, beaten, physically and psychologically destroyed, the creature still would not admit defeat. In fact, she still fought to preserve something. Her eyes. Her pair of vivid, most beautiful scarlet eyes were still shining amongst all that darkness. They were eyes in which no amount of genetics or magic could hope to achieve, even to the disappointment of all the wealthy human females that begged for the same.

They were gems, carefully nestled inside their white turf. Hidden treasures of Mother Gaea. She had no pupils, but instead a kaleidoscope of shapes and forms like crystals bound to one another inside those smooth spheres of hers. Rapidly spinning at any solicitation, like a dancer, widening to the smallest of beats, brightening or darkening as a reaction to the world or her body. Reacting in anger, in happiness, in joy, in depression, in fear, in passion, in love. All of these, scattering like leaves through the universe, were bound up together with love in her two eyes only.

They were like skies of infinitely blended colors. Oceans of rushing waters in crimson reds, calming or blazing. Edges of a cherry above a floor of ruby. They had magenta and violet touches here and there; merely the perfect impurities of a painter's proudest work. The colors seemed to move like a constellation of stars, and likewise would not reflect light. They would instead emanate a pale, sweet, blue light.

Those eyes were gentle. Those eyes were soothing. Those eyes were a mixture of purity and depth. Those eyes would cradle you and make you forget yourself forever. Those eyes could be alluring as well, with their long eyelashes. She would keep her face slightly tilted, her mouth barely open as if to kiss you. Leaning closer, she would faintly breathe in and out. In all this, you would already find yourself lost. Lost by just looking at those eyes.

She was protecting them from him. She would never show them to the vile human. Instead, she would hide them and only show him fake, soulless, emotionless eyes. He was not even trying to see them though, nevertheless. It was despicable, it was ugly, it was unforgivable that he would abuse her body, but not her beauty.

Those beautiful eyes, which was Celestial's entire world and her whole being, in that particular instance was crying.

Spiders. Eric hated the damned things. The thought of one of the eight-legged monsters sent a shiver up his spine.

The young man and David stepped off their horses and tied them to the post just outside the small farmhouse. Off in the distance was a large wooden barn. From the outside, it appeared as if it was no different than any other barn in the countryside. Upon further inspection though, one could see the gray and whites of webs peeking out from the windows and doors of the old dilapidated building.

"Woodfall spiders," David said in his usual deep but cheery voice. "Did you have them in Usora?"

Eric shook his head.

"No. Just the little ones. The ones that get no bigger than a button," he replied.

He couldn't pry his eyes off the barn. Though it was broad daylight, the barn seemed an area of night. There was just a dark aura about it.

"Well then, you'll be in for a shock," David said with a chuckle. "Woodfall spiders grow large enough to devour an entire horse. That's why whenever they nest outside the forests and caves, they prefer barns and other large buildings where animals were kept."

Eric shivered again at the thought of a spider being that large. He tightened his grip on the worn shotgun that Burke lent him. It was a Revere double barreled gun. The barrels had been sawed off some time ago and were only thirty-five centimeters in length. A large, toothed blade was fixated under the stock with metal straps and rivets to act as a nasty melee option. Both barrels had already been loaded with silver buckshot. A dozen and a half more shells were strapped across Eric's chest. He took a deep breath in, followed by David clapping him hard on the back and knocking the air out of him. The large man let out a laughter that seemed to rumble the ground.

"Don't worry, we got this," David said. "Hell, there's supposedly only one in there. Once, me and Ross had to run an entire grown nest out of an abandoned hospital. Damn near had to burn the whole place down."

Eric went to respond, but then the front door of the farm house opened. From the chipped wooden doorway exited the farmer and his wife who had the Order contacted. They were a middle-aged couple well in their forties. The farmer approached the two hunters and shook each of their hands.

"Oh, thank the gods you guys finally showed up!" the farmer exclaimed. He then was wildly pointing at the barn, "That thing in there damn near killed all of my livestock! Each day I'm missing more and more cattle, it's like it's taking them from my other barns!"

The man was sweating profusely. He was clearly a nervous wreck. Eric glanced around at the outside of their home. There were claw marks on the outer walls of the worn painted home. Clear signs that the beast had tried to get in before. Lucky for them, it didn't.

"Oh, please hunters! Please kill that thing before it gets us too!" the farmer's wife chimed in.

She tightly clung onto her husband's arm and stared at each of the duster-wearing men. David smiled warmly and rose his hands in a friendly manner. He smiled at the married couple.

"Now calm down. We're here to kill a spider for you, and that's what we'll do," he said, turning and tapping on Eric's arm. "Come on, let's earn our pay."

The hunters crossed the field to the barn. It towered over the two men with an enormous shadow. Details of the spider's occupation became more apparent as they got closer. Claw marks covered the outer walls from where the spider crawled all over its surface. Webs stuck out of every crack and opening in the wooden slat boards, obscuring any view into the barn's interior.

David walked up to the door and placed his gloved hand on the handle. He looked over to Eric and nodded. The young hunter nodded back and pulled the shotgun tightly to his shoulder, pointing it towards the door. David then pulled the wooden slab board door open, stretching and tearing webs that were attached to the other side of the entrance. A crawling feeling ran over Eric, but he shook it off and entered the old building.

The inside seemed to be straight out of the young man's nightmares. Everything was covered in the silky strings of the spider's webs. Barely a square inch of anything could still be seen under the white cover. Eric took several, slow steps into the barn. On either side of the giant barn was numerous stalls for horses, all of which were empty save for large web-covered balls of masses that were suspended from the ceilings above. The young hunter guessed the horses had been trapped inside those balls of webs to be suffocated and digested by the spider's acidic venom.

His eyes ventured upwards towards the opened second floor. Several more of the spider's victims were suspended from the roof high above. Beyond that, numerous stacks of hay bales were neatly stacked along the upper floor, with several stacks of the dried grass on the ground floor as well. David came up alongside Eric, looking around as well.

"It's silent," David said in a whisper. "It knows we're in here."

The two walked forward more into the center of the open ground floor, trying to get a better look around the area.

"I don't see it..." Eric said quietly. His head was swiveling back and forth looking for any signs of the beast.

David turned so the two were back-to-back.

"You can't see it...but I'm sure it can see us just fine," he replied.

The response made Eric grip the shotgun tighter. Then there, movement. It was just a flash of something. Something big. Eric tracked it as best as he could. There it was again, over the stall on his right. He spun around and leveled the shotgun in that direction, but it was gone again.

"It's in that stall," Eric said, not removing his eyes from the small enclosure.

David didn't say anything in response. He instead took a step closer to the stall. A lantern behind them fell from its hook, shattering onto the floor. The sound of broken glass made both hunters jump and spin to face the source of the noise. It was then, the spider revealed itself.

The monstrous arachnid, its body had to have been twice as large as a human! Its legs spanned nearly five meters from tip-to-tip, with fangs almost as long as a man's forearm! Its body was an oak brown, with a large black fiddle-shape on its back. It jumped onto the wall above the stall and hissed loudly behind the humans.

David and Eric both turned, and each fired a shot. The monster sped along the wall, dodging each of the hunters' shots. Its legs tapped loudly against the wall in a repetitious noise as it scurried into a new position.

"Shoot the damn thing!" David yelled, firing again.

Eric fired the second shot. A few pellets managed to hit, judging from the pained shriek the spider gave off. He broke the gun's action open, causing the fired shells to eject violently from the chambers. He fumbled for two more shells from his bandolier to reload with.

The spider quickly ran up the barn's wall and onto the ceiling. It bared its fangs and shot a string of webs from its abdomen. The strong silky material hit Eric's right arm and pinned him to a wall, making him unable to reload. The monster then hissed loudly and leapt to the side to dodge another shot from David. It then pounced, landing hard on the man.

The arachnid bared its fangs once again and tried to drive them into the large hunter. David grabbed ahold of the sharp, black fangs and pushed back with all of his might. Even with as strong as he was, it took everything to hold back the monster. The spider's two front palps pummeled David, scratching his clothing with their small claws. All six of the creature's eyes were centered directly on the man it was trying to kill.

Eric tried to pull his arm free but was unable to. He looked over and saw the spider pinning David to the ground. The large hunter wouldn't be able to survive very long. The young man looked to where his dropped shotgun laid. It was out of reach.

Eric instinctively reached for his revolver but found that it too was covered in webs and was unavailable. He panicked slightly, but then remembered. The leather pouch that hung from his left hip. It was free from the webs. The young hunter reached into it and withdrew his only remaining live soul stone. He had fears of using his monsters in battle again after losing Gyrog, but he needed his beast now.

He squeezed the stone in his palm, uttering the arcane words. Mist appeared from the stone and formed into the shape of a dragon in front of him. Vesuvius emerged from his stone.

The dragon centered a slit eye on the spider, then turned to Eric with a cock of his head.

"Vesuvius, attack the spider!" Eric ordered. "Get it off of David!"

The azure dragon roared, then sprinted at the large arachnid. He tackled the monster and smashed it into a wall, putting it into a daze.

Eric used the small amount of time he had to retrieve his knife and began cutting himself free. He then glanced at David, who was getting back to his feet. He seemed okay, but he was huffing in an attempt to catch his breath. On the other side of the barn, the dragon and the spider continued their fight.

Vesuvius bellowed blue hellfire from his gut, engulfing the spider's face in flame. It screeched and ran around the barn, rolling and tossing itself around to put the fire out. It quickly recovered and shot webs at the dragon, pinning his mouth shut with the sticky material. Vesuvius clawed at the webs, trying to remove them from his snout, but was then hit again with a larger spray and was pinned to the floor. The spider then slowly crawled its way over to the helpless dragon. Venom dripped from its fangs as it eyed its victim.

Eric saw this and was still desperately trying to cut himself free. Vesuvius fought as hard as he could but was unable to move or even make a noise. A shot then rang out. The spider was hit directly in the abdomen, sending a spray of dark blood onto the walls. The spider screeched in pain, then turned to attack the shot's source. Another shot went off, this time hitting the spider in the eyes. It sprinted forward blindly and ran into one of the stalls, collapsing.

David, the one who fired the shots, was walking towards the downed spider. He racked another shell into the chamber of his pump shotgun, then planted the muzzle against the top of its head. He pulled the trigger, finally killing the nightmare.

Eric was then finally able to free his arm and side from the web, walking away from the wall. He rotated his arm at the shoulder and stretched it. David looked over to the young hunter, short of breath.

"Well then," David said with a laugh. "There's that. You alright?"

Eric nodded, "Yeah I'm fine."

He went over to his dragon and helped to free him as well. Once Vesuvius was out of the webs and shook himself off, Eric thanked him for the help and returned him to his stone.

"Are you okay though? You're the one who had a giant spider on him," Eric then added.

David waved it off, "I'll be alright. Nothing I can't handle."

The two then looked over at the dead arachnid, letting out a simultaneous breath. Eric then glanced back at David, waving towards the door.

"Well then. Mission success. Let's go get paid," Eric said with a laugh.

[IX]

Celestial had to try again; as painful as it was. This was her only viable option for escape. After all, she had already been able to enter the human's mind, even if it had only happened once before. In the short time she was there, she discovered his name; Eric. Maybe she could do it again. Just long enough to tell his subconscious who put her in her cell and where to find her. She needed no more than only a single minute to accomplish that.

She had been trying every single day to the point of exhaustion, without any progress. The only time she had ever been successful was now further than months away in the past, when the human was still unconscious after receiving the injuries on that forsaken island. His health has improved drastically since then. She was losing him as his mind became impenetrable when compared to the weak abilities she had left.

She had to try again. She closed her eyes and focused, breathing in and out as fully as she was able to.

The practice of entering one's consciousness is, in some ways, like that of pushing a barrier. Like a sphere which is constantly closing in around you from every direction as the target's mind opposes your intrusion. If you place enough pressure with your own mind, the walls will expand and reveal to you a world in which you can either create or destroy what you please in order to influence your target's impulsive decisions. But, whenever your strength does not suffice, the walls will encircle you once more. This will cause you to feel as if you were being relentlessly crushed by an impossible force and drowned. Such an event is both mentally painful and physically dangerous to the user.

She began casting.

At first, nothing but a void. Black. She pushed more.

Still nothing but dark. Her head was slightly hurting already. More, she needed input more force.

Nothing still. She was starting to gasp for air, but she refused to give up.

Empty... She began to shiver.

Come on, please?? She begged.

Even still, there was nothing. His subconscious was putting up a stronger resistance. Her entire body was shaking wildly, and she was having trouble keeping her eyes focused.

A mass of water went up her throat. She was drowning. She knew she would pass out within seconds. It was no use, she was not winning.

More water, more weight, less air. Heavier, thinner. More, less. More, less. More, and...

...Wait!

A realization. Indeed, something was different this time. That water felt wet, like a real liquid that she could drink; like she was inside a real sea and not feeling rushes of nausea, but concrete waves crashing into her. It was not just her, but a dream. It was the boy's dream!

She was inside it, she truly made it! That night, the young man must have been drunker than ever before!

She quickly mustered all her renewed strength, resolute to leave some mark on the human's mind. The creature realized that the gates were already closing. She had no time for any of her previous plans like she had done last time. The candles, clouds. The soft lights and sounds, no time! Celestial had to say something fast! She tried to think of something essential, something that the human might recall at some later time. Something he could remember!

She whispered a single, short, miniscule word. Thereafter, the waves crashed down and crushed her fragile being. Like that, she passed out.

Eric earlier decided to go along with David and Ross to Beck's. The business was a bar, and to a small extent, a place where a man could go to find himself a 'lady for the night'. The liquor was nice, though, that night; and with the extra cash in Eric's pocket, he decided to enjoy himself.

The young hunter had already been there for several hours and managed to have more glasses of alcohol than he normally would. He decided to forget all the worries of the world and have some fun that night, though he did fall asleep for a moment at the table. He had a short and pleasant dream, though he failed to remember the details.

A few scantily-clad women hovered around Eric on and off several times throughout the night so far. Their perfumes reeked and burned his nose. They kept going on about how 'young he was' and how he was 'a nice, fresh hunter'. He ignored them and politely rejected their calls and beckonings to a private room, not out of disinterest necessarily, he just didn't want to take chances with anything he was sure they had.

Eric downed another drink, then decided to was time for him to go back to his room. Ross mentioned he was to leave as well, so the two left together. Eric didn't have enough to render himself unable to walk alone, but the other hunter on the other hand was barely able to walk a straight line. Against Ross's protests, Eric decided to help him get home.

After a few moments of complaining, Ross finally agreed. The two were now headed down the main road of Pratertown. They were going in the direction of Ross's private home. From there Eric would leave the man and head back to the comfort of this own bed.

During his time being around the guy, Eric has learned that Ross was not considered 'handsome' by the usual standards. Women generally were repelled by him, though the young hunter believed that was also due to Ross's reeking stench. It seemed to have only gotten worse since the events of Krehaul Island. 'Delicate cologne', Ross had put it, though Eric knew better.

As the two walked, Ross had been ranting about the petty observations against his persona, which lately had not been uncommon. He was bringing to surface all his previously harbored bitterness towards the opinion of others.

All of his statements were formulated without fault in the most convoluted and unbelievable ways. 'A secret plan of the Order that only I'm aware of...', or 'life on other planets', were some of the big cards he always played. Eric began asking himself if even Ross was aware of his own self-mockery. Maybe he was doing it on purpose? Maybe he wanted to convey what was an obvious lie as something so undeniably a clear, blatant fabrication so no one would hesitate to call it out as such? Maybe Ross just didn't like people and did everything he could to scare them away.

But even as much of a spoiled liar he was, to a factor which sometimes would add to be dumb, he was otherwise somewhat enjoyable. Overall, Eric thought of Ross as a rather nice guy, under the rest of his faults. It was possible that even with time, they could actually be friends.

"Haha! That one burnette had a bit too much to drink!" Ross exclaimed, now as happy as can be. "Did you see her when she smashed an empty bottle and threatened that guy for touching her ass? Haha!"

Eric grinned, the memory still in his head. He then responded.

"At least when she danced, she didn't accidentally fall off the stage!"

Ross shoved Eric, still grinning. "Right, right...I only fell off the wrong side of the stage, pfhahaha!"

Eric paused on the sidewalk for a second. Ross took a few more drunken steps before realizing that the other hunter wasn't there anymore. He stopped as well and turned around, giving Eric a confused look. Eric's grin faded into a gentle smile, as if he was thinking a somewhat nicer thought.

"That girl was kinda cute, you know?" the young hunter said.

The two continued walking. Ross shrugged his shoulders.

"Eh, I don't know. I've seen better."

"Oh yeah? Who?" questioned Eric.

Ross suddenly looked away, as if he was hiding something. He pretended to be more interested in the old buildings around them.

"Oh, come on, Ross. Is it someone you haven't presented to us? A young lady that you wish to keep to yourself?" the young man asked curiously.

"No, it's just that...it's ah...bit of a thing, a..." Ross paused, "...a *silly*...kind of thing of mine...Nothing of relevance."

A chill froze Eric's spinal column. A burst of adrenaline rushed through immediately after, burning his muscles with excessive heat. Was it the environment around them? Perhaps it was just a cold breeze. It was very brief and had already disappeared by the time he thought about it, but he couldn't figure out why he felt it. Nothing was happening around them. There was no external threat. Only the odd sense that the word '*silly*' was somehow important. The echo of a familiar and feminine voice sounded in his thoughts for just a second.

Ross didn't seem to notice the change in Eric's mood. He continued his talking.

"It's just a bit of a personal secret of mine, you know? Maybe I'll tell you one day." Ross concluded.

For Ross to state that it was a bit of a personal secret was not like any of the other lies. Eric was sure of it, and since the usually very talkative hunter was refusing to discuss it, that made the entire thing all the more questionable and shady. Eric had an irresistible urge to find out what this secret was, yet he asked himself why? Surely it was bound to be something of little concern, or even downright idiotic, yet he still felt he needed to know! So, without asking any further, the young man devised a plan to meddle his way into it.

"Anyways, it's getting a bit on the cold side out here," Eric said, gesturing slightly to the air around them. "Why don't we quickly make way to your home?"

"Well...I..." Ross hesitated.

Eric smirked to himself. **So, your secret *is* at your home? My guess was correct!**

"...I mean... my place is very messy inside. I'd rather not have you see it..." Ross said, clearly nervous. "You see it's... the maid's fault. Yeah, the maid! She resigned a week ago and my house has become filthy... haha..."

Ross was always known to laugh nervously in any form of tense situation.

Still...that is the most believable lie he's come up with yet... Eric thought.

"Anyways...so...why d-don't we go to another bar instead?" said the nervous and still drunk hunter.

"Oh, come on Ross. We just left Beck's, didn't we? Besides, I'm not going to judge you based on how clean your place is. How about when we get there, we can get some coffee put on and I'll help you clean up!" the young hunter said, trying to put on a warm and understanding smile. It was the fakest he could manage.

"Uhh... okay... that's fine I guess..."

Yes! It worked! Deep inside, Eric was very much enjoying the victory over his victim's distress. It was like when a kid defeats their friend in an innocent game.

"Great then! After you!" Eric exclaimed, waving Ross onwards.

Once they arrived at Ross's house, they stepped inside. A small, square living room. Only a minimal restroom. A single bedroom whose only luxury was an ornate writing desk with a matching electric lamp attached to its side. The small kitchen was disgusting; stacks of dirty plates and cups, along with countless gnawed-on bones and half-eaten turkey legs. Finally, there was a corridor that stretched and conjoined the rooms of the home. There was also a locked door at the end of this corridor, one that according to Ross was a door that led to an 'attic without a roof'.

That door was certainly suspicious, and the keys to it were merely hanging on a small nail imbedded into the wall next to the home's entrance. Eric took note and knew he'd have to try enter that portal.

The two hunters took seats in the pair of wooden, creaky chairs. They were arranged on either side of an old and beat up table. Many chips and gouges were taken out of its oak surface, along with cryptic writings that matched those of some arcane arts. Their meanings were unknown to the young hunter at the time.

"So, Ross. You live here by yourself?" Eric asked, deciding to break the awkward silence.

"Yep," was the short and quick reply.

Eric nodded, "What about your parents? Where are they at?"

"Don't know. Mom died when I was young, and dad never comes around. I only receive a small package once a month containing money...I guess it's his way of 'parenting'," Ross answered plainly, staring down at the table and picking at a small wooden chip.

Eric's shoulders slumped, "Oh...I'm sorry to hear that."

The other hunter shrugged his shoulders, glancing up at young man sitting across from him.

"Nah, it's past me. The only good thing is that he's rich, so I get some extra coin for myself every once in a while. Even with the pay I get from the Order, it costs a lot to have fun around here, you know?"

"My pockets are emptier than yours, I assure you," the young man stated, leaning back in his chair.

"Heh, like pretty much everyone in this town...You know, some people think that I'm well-heeled...can you believe that?" Ross said with a chuckle, breaking the chip free and tossing it to the side.

"Well, I don't think you look like one of those know-it-all braggers," Eric said.

Actually...you are... The young hunter thought.

"Sometimes I wish I was. You have all these guys out there that ruin the fun for people like us, know what I mean? All the most expensive clothes, these fancy new automobiles. They even get the most gorgeous women. They're a bunch of asses. I'd like to teach them all a lesson!" Ross slammed his fist onto the table. It wobbled at the impact, unstable as it was. A fire burned in the hunter's eyes. It then quickly puttered out, "Oh...I'm sorry...I got worked up."

Eric waved it off dismissively.

"Don't worry about it. I kind of feel what you mean."

Oh sure...I certainly feel for a man who has far more money and is in a much better financial situation than most any of us in this town. All of this money, and he still can't get a single woman for the pure fact that he doesn't care to put any real effort into anything. Oh, the poor guy...

"Do you?" Ross asked.

"Yes, I do. Don't worry about the little things, you're better than that," responded Eric, placing his hands behind his head and leaning back further. The chair he sat in was now on two legs only.

"Thanks, that really means a lot..." a pause, "you know, you're a nice person...I know we may not get along a lot...but I have learned to consider you a friend."

Eric smiled, but not for the appreciative answer. The entire time they had been talking, Ross had been drinking more alcohol. Ten empty bottles had been freshly scattered across the wooden table by this point, and not one had been consumed by Eric. Ross was starting to lag a bit, which meant this was the young hunter's time to act.

"Well," Eric bluntly said, bringing his hands to the table and standing up. "Let's get started, shall we? Surely your home cannot clean itself?"

"No Eric don't worry about it...I'll hire someone...in the morning...to do...it..." answered the drunk hunter. In his state of inebriation, Ross was already falling asleep in his chair.

"Nah, it's fine! No problem at all!" Eric called out, walking to the entrance and snatching the house keys from off the nail. "At the least, your bedroom should be clean, yes?"

Ross didn't say anything back. He was nearly out cold.

Eric walked down the corridor to the locked door. His heart was pumping faster, excited to discover the other hunter's petty secret.

"I'll just collect a broom and other cleaning supplies...this room, yes?"

He fumbled with the keys and found the correct one. He inserted the key into the door's lock.

Ross waved absent-mindedly and responded.

"Yeah…. yeah…"

And then the realization hit him. He gasped loudly.

"Wait! No, that's not!-"

He felt his heart drop at the sound of the door unlocking. He choked up and leapt out of his chair and rushed down the narrow corridor in a panic. Eric was already halfway down the spiraling staircase, descending it further. He was getting terribly close to the second, and final door that hid his secret.

Eric was laughing playfully, certain to uncover Ross's little secret and tease him further. He was cracking up and imagining the other's reaction, that rattled expression. He would finally satisfy the childish curiosity that has consumed him the last hour or so. The young hunter was so caught up with tormenting his comrade, that he did not hear the alarm and panic in Ross's voice.

Ross nearly sprinted down the steps. He was praying to stop Eric before it was too late. He could hear the dreadful and haunting clinking sounds of the keys that Eric carried with him.

The young hunter did not listen to the other's pleas. As he found the other door at the bottom at the steps, he began trying the different keys in the lock.

"This one is wrong...this one is also wrong..." Eric was singing loudly. He changed the tone of the word 'wrong' every time he said it, purely to torment Ross.

"Wrong...wrong..."

Ross's panicked steps rang out and rained down as if an earthquake hit the area.

"Still wrong.... wrong..."

Ross was almost there! He could catch Eric before-

But yet, it was too late. The door creaked open slowly.

Ross screamed, "NO!"

And then Eric saw...

That most fragile mirror, which reflected a fortress of illusions. What was once a most beautiful vision for Eric's future, cracked, split, and shattered into a thousand pieces as its image turned to dust. The young man's dream of a peaceful existence became twisted, not unlike that of a piece of delicate cloth that has been brutally torn. The battlefield came back in full force. Guns firing, bullets whistling in his ears. The fighting was once again being fought in Eric's mind, for now and ever, all before the creature's pleading, shimmering red eyes.

[X]

The basement of Ross's home was small; no more than five meters in width and seven or eight in length. The room was somewhat dark and damp; only lit by a single bulb hanging from the ceiling. The walls were dirty and gray. Broken crates were scattered about and there was cracked pipes that would occasionally leak water onto the wet floor. Amongst it all, there laid the feminine, humanoid creature in the penumbra of the cellar.

"What the hell..." Eric quietly said.

The small difference in temperature and light that opening the wooden door allowed into the room made the animal tremble. The chain in which she was bound to the wall with rattled along her body. Her long and dirtied-white dress, while a perfect highlight of her sinuous form, was nothing more than a wrinkled thin blanket that would not have sufficed for even heat conservation. She was cradling into herself; covering her torso with both of her arms and slender legs, almost as if to diminish her presence.

"Now...I know this isn't completely in line with the Hunter's Code..." Ross began, awkwardly stumbling up alongside Eric.

Eric was not even looking at Ross. He was only fixated on the void within her eyes; his own magnetized like opposite poles. The young hunter was trying his hardest to spill a word, a phrase, even a single syllable that could describe the horror that he was witnessing. Eric was oblivious to the excuses of the hunter next to him.

"I'm not doing anything necessarily wrong, right?" Ross said nervously.

Eric could only think about how long she had been kept here. All those months that had passed after he last saw her on Krehaul Island. Not only that though; her messy hair, the worn-out stance. Her unwillingness to fight back. All consequences of being forced to survive without a bed and very little food or water, along with not being able to move or see the sunlight.

"I mean, It's not like s-she's human or anything..."

There were other clear signs of abuse. Scars on her body that were newer than the ones left on her by the cult who held her captive before. On her hand, her shoulder, even on her right leg. A gunshot wound. She tried to escape from Ross before perhaps? All the signs of physical violence, and sexual as well, judging from the curled-up stance she was retreating into.

"Listen, if you're worried that we'll get in trouble, please don't! The laws don't say anything about mistreating a monster!" Ross said, laughing nervously behind his drunken and slurred speech.

Eric couldn't believe it himself at how anyone, especially a hunter, could be so nonchalantly cruel against such a poor, pure creature. A damsel she was; a beautiful girl left to be rotten in this tiny prison. He couldn't stand the sickening sight no longer. What was he to do then? Contact authorities? No. Tell Burke? That would be the worst idea.

The creature's eyes were filling up with tears, as if they were dams about to break at any moment. Oh, by the gods, those two little hearts! The brilliant rubies that were her eyes were staring so deeply, so passionately, so intensely at him!

And there it was. A single, burning tear of pity that slid down Eric's cheek.

...Free her? He thought.

It was an insane thought. The creature could still be dangerous. She could break out like a ravaged animal and kill both hunters. But-

Abruptly, as soon as the creature's abuser turned his head to her, she broke her eye contact and hid herself behind her pale form.

"The hell are you looking at?! This is all your fault, you whore!" Ross screamed out like an enraged minotaur, spitting his thick saliva at her.

She was not just searching for her freedom, the frightened creature. She was trying oh so insistently to gaze once again at Eric. She was asking with her sweet, cherry red eyes for his help. She was hoping and depending on him for rescue. He may have seen her as a simple treat, but she had never caused any undue suffering to anyone. Because she was a beast to be preyed on, but she was mistreated beyond any cause. It was because she could see the pandemonium of his morality. She knew he could be trusted to free her, to do the right thing and maybe restore her faith in humanity.

"Listen... w-we're friends... r-right? Heh, he..." Ross nervously chuckled once again, trying to get any verbal response out of Eric.

Friend? Yeah, right. Ross and Eric never had gotten along, and it was only now that the deranged hunter tried to gain the younger's friendship. Ross had been hiding under a mask of lies. He was only feeling guilty when confronted with the disgusting face he truly possessed.

"Eric?... You aren't caring about her, are you?" He asked quietly, a sinking feeling in his gut appeared.

There was still time. With a simple gesture, Eric could free her. He could shoulder upon himself the sins of the hunter next to him, the sins of the world! It could be a mutual bond, a friendship that he could forge. One that could bring together a world that has been separated for a millennium.

"Hey! You know what! You can also have her!" Ross exclaimed as the idea came to him in that instant. He immediately brightened up, not unlike that of the small electric bulbs illuminating the tiniest of writing desks. "Yeah! That's what friends are for, is it not? Friends are to share, so...just go ahead and do whatever it is that you wish to her!"

The creature glanced ever so slightly in a brief instance to Eric's right. It was an almost imperceptible movement that nobody but him could have noticed. It was her sign to him. They had become accomplices already. Something between them moved Eric's own eyes to follow her gaze. There, on a small wooden table just out of reach of the creature was her soul stone. The small crystalline rock that bound her and left her without any free will to fight back against Ross's disgusting actions. Eric saw the stone and knew immediately what she needed him to do.

"Just don't go around telling anyone okay?... It'll be our little secret...heh, he...." Ross said, before going silent at the lack of response from Eric.

Who was it that was the true beast? Her? On what basis? Just because she was 'one of them'? What else was there? What other reason could there be that would justify everything she had been through; to make her deserve any of this?

No. It was something else. It was a true evil. There was no need to attempt to reason around it. The final decision was clear in Eric's mind.

"Ross...I'm sorry about this," he said.

He drew his revolver. Before the other hunter could react in the slightest, Eric cocked the hammer and rose the muzzle to align it with the stone. With a pull of the trigger, the handgun fired. A thunderous report sounded off; the cast bullet left the gun and successfully hit the stone. It shattered on impact and broke altogether. The dim light that the stone gave off faded away as the seraph's soul was released. Eric had done it!

Yet as Ross had realized what Eric had done, he turned and looked to him with a bleached-white face. His mouth was pulled into a death-like frown. His eyes were hollow and expressed true horror.

"...What have you done?" he said, expiring.

The next image was one that would be infernally burned into Eric's mind for the rest of his existence of the last time he would ever see Ross. The hunter was impaled by several crystals of emblazed light. They impaled and stuck through his chest, arms, legs, neck, everywhere! Another brilliant crystal, the largest of those, was sent through Ross's skull. The grey matter of the hunter's brain was leaking out of the orifice that had been created. The grotesque image only took a single instant to be executed, only a single one, but it was caused by an immense hatred and a will to cause as much agony in the victim as possible.

The small basement room had suddenly become much, much colder. Eric was trembling uncontrollably as he turned to see the creature he so foolishly released. His heart was beating at an uncontrollable rate. He could taste copper in his mouth. Not only that, he was scared. Truly and fully terrified.

It was standing, floating several centimeters from the stone floor. Its body was bursting in a powerful aura of deadly energy. A set of white wings sprouted from its back and spread as far as the walls would allow them. The creature was not looking at Eric, not anymore. It no longer needed him. It was all a deception, a mask. The insensitive, psychic creature knew well how to toy with emotions and use her angelic beauty to convey empathy. She was undoubtedly an angel; and angel of death which was only looking to kill.

What had Eric done indeed?

The monster tore a heavy iron pipe from the stone walls and sent it flying at incredible speeds with a simple snap of its wrist. The pipe smashed into Eric's midsection with enormous force before he could even see it coming. The young and naive hunter quickly lost consciousness.

Some time had passed. The sound of dripping water was steady, if not slow. Eric tried to focus as much of his will as he could to hear around him. It became clearer after a few moments, and he soon regained his senses.

It did not take long for him to realize he was still in the basement of Ross's house. Where he had so foolishly freed a terrible creature simply due to his crazed thoughts. He was laying on his back. A terrible feeling in his torso shot through him as he attempted to move. He wasn't dead, that much was clear. His breathing was painful, but his body was intact. It took the hunter a good several minutes to get to his feet; his legs shakily holding him.

The attack probably would have ended his life, had it not been for his muscles instinctively tightening and constricting to cover the area that was hit. Had the blow been to the head, the most logical choice, it would have proven fatal with no chance of surviving. Why did the creature target that spot then? Was it so cunning that it expected Eric to duck into the pipe and get hit in the skull?

Why that approach then? Would it had not been easier to tear me apart, just like it did to Ross?... The thought made Eric shudder. He forced himself not to glance to his right, to where the disemboweled remains of the hunter were strewn.

The answer though was simpler than that. It was clearly exhausted already. It had planned to kill both humans as quickly as possible with what feeble powers it had left before blacking out. It first went after its rapist, then Eric. But it was most likely left dry of powers after its first move against Ross. It must have panicked then and resorted to a more indirect assault, one that failed before it fainted.

Indeed, there the creature was. Flat on the ground with its chains broken free from its neck and wrists.

That was it then. It had explained everything. There was nothing more to be said. No more words to add. No justification, no excuse, no apology, no regret. Not a 'thank you'. The creature tricked him for its survival and not a single other reason. It was from this point like they had never met each other. As if Eric had not helped her on Krehaul Island in the past. It would have killed him, if given another chance, and the hunter was now to consider it an enemy. If such a thing were true, then Eric would have to murder the monster as quickly as possible. Any other time from then on would prove to be an impossible chance.

Eric dragged himself to Ross's remains and dropped to his knees. The sight was hard to bear. A carcass that was barely recognizable as the human being it was only a short time ago. It had already reeked of death and decay.

Eric leaned forward and supported himself onto his hands and cried harshly. It was indeed his fault that the man died. It was him who sentenced Ross to death. He failed to even listen to what the fellow hunter had tried to say in his defense. Eric didn't even try to listen. He was simply being stubborn with his little idiotic views; views that somehow, he could earn the trust of a monster like that.

His revolver was laying on the floor nearby. He quickly snatched it. Then, he laboriously lifted himself back to his feet and began walking towards the defenseless beast. Sweat was spilling over Eric's body, and he was wheezing and panting in both a fever and in anger. After all, it was the creature who was a hypocrite. It was the one who killed a fellow human. It was the beast who laughed at his worthy ideals. That *thing* was the demon who had shattered Eric's hopes and dreams of living in a blissful existence beyond the missions of being a hunter. It was the one who brought back the chaos and despair into his life!

Eric was approaching the quiescent, sleeping creature. He tightly grasped the revolver's grip. Were it not for this monster, he would be living a quiet and happy life. He would be content and without trouble. Yet now, the rest of the Order would surely execute him for what has been done!

He looked on at the creature in a blind rage. The simple act of breathing inwards and outwards pained him, and that caused him to feel more enraged. At least he would bring this beast down with him. Yet, he could fake the scene; yes! He could tell everyone about how he heroically managed to injure it and avenge his comrade who had sacrificed himself to shield him from the monster's wrath after it...after it freed itself! He could tell that to the other hunters, there was no doubt!

The hunter arrived very close to its body. He could feel her soft breath, which only fabricated its innocence. She was without a doubt gorgeous and remembering those eyes of hers...those eyes.

They were so unbelievably beautiful, so ethereal that they could...no, it was a trap! Nothing more! All a fake!

His thumb moved to the gun's hammer, pulling it back to the point to where it clicked into place. The hunter then eyed down the notched sights and planted his point of aim on the creature's temple. He would kill this monstrosity. He would enjoy its death. He would...for now on...enjoy killing every other creature...after this.

He placed his finger on the trigger; ready to fire. His entire arm was trembling.

He thought to himself. **I can even learn to enjoy the death of the mother...of this creature...yes...even that was-**

A shock. Images flooded into his head. He was forced to relive the fear he felt, the anguish after having lost Joseph. He felt again the dread of losing the mother seraph after he had tried in vain to save her. He saw the twisted and deranged members of the cult they fought. It all terrorized him! He didn't want to become that. The idea was evil and against every one of his morals.

What am I thinking?! A small voice screamed in his head, trying to make him come back to his senses. He was losing control of himself, being pulled by an evil and seductive force.

He gulped. A different kind of sweat had begun running down his temples.

E... ev-even...her...mother...

A loud metallic clang sounded through the room. The revolver was dropped to the ground. Eric started to cry uncontrollably. He had let evil take him over for a split moment and it almost betrayed him forever. He just wanted this nightmare to be over. He hated it and couldn't stand it anymore. Eric only wanted to be kind-hearted and protect those around him, and instead he was almost driven to madness. It made him terrified.

I can't kill her...I just can't... He thought as he broke down, sobbing.

[XI]

What Eric was to do next, even he had no clue. He was defeated, both mentally and physically, yet he still tried to push away the deepest angst and the void that was growing inside his gut. He kept only a single, logical reasoning around what was his situation and what he could do next to save himself.

He was somewhat satisfied with himself that he managed to carry the unconscious creature to the Order's building and into his private room. The fact he also managed to complete the task without rousing suspicion made him even more slightly confident. Even if the town was bursting with life on that night, finding unlit alleyways to sneak through was not the hardest of tasks. He also knew that the other two hunters would be out for the night, and Eric hoped that they would be having a great time so as to not come back anytime soon.

He wondered about his fingerprints that stained the inside of Ross's home. He didn't care if they were found as long as they were not on anything suspicious such as Ross's clothing. Finding an alibi as to why he was there a few hours before the incident would not prove to be an impossible task. After all, it was clear that a monster was responsible for the hunter's death while Eric himself had no clear part in it. He figured he should not fear any repercussions or consequences.

Eric then asked himself; what about the creature herself then? He had very clashing feelings about her. While he did very well believe she deserved freedom, he could not forgive her for her actions even if they had been in self-defense. The young man had to admit, though, that she was such a fascinating creature. It was that thought that opened his imagination to an even wider extent. It widened to an even more wild world of forces and wonders. She was without a doubt dangerous, though her feminine pose as she slept betrayed a veiled softness of hers. There was both a grace and blood in her, and she was just a beautiful as she was fearsome.

In the end, Eric failed to reconcile his fears and morals with his attraction, and he would continue to waver in between them. Even so, there was some hidden, unknown part of himself that was slowly budding within his mind. It was a part of him that wished for powers like hers. He enjoyed the thought of superhuman strength, of psychokinetic powers, and he wanted it as his own. It was that part of him that was enticed by her mixture of light and dark, and that caused him to like her as a whole.

It took him a single second to reject the idea afterwards. He convinced himself that it must have been another trick of that demon that he was protecting. Eric damned his weak mind and his weak morals. The nausea and goosebumps he felt hit his stomach and crawl across his skin only strengthened the idea. It was like even his own body was rejecting it.

Regardless, he was still too worried about what was to come to care about such things. What if the seraph was found? In his private room, of all places?

He was far too afraid to pick her up again and carry her out of the town and into the forest. What if she woke up? Regardless, it was an impossible task for him at the moment; as weakened as he was. His spinning headache quickly bothered him enough to stop trying to catch his breath and lumber into the kitchen to find some food and water. His entire body was still shivering even as he took a small glass and sipped the water from it. He didn't dare try to consume anything solid, but he did take some fruits and placed them at his bedside. Maybe if he offered them to the creature, she would not kill him the moment she awakened.

Just as Eric stepped into the hallway and closed the bedroom door behind him, a sudden wave of pain hit his head. He leaned back against the door and slid down it to the floor, passing out from exhaustion.

The next morning, he awoke. He quickly stood up and turned; opening the door and peering into his room. The creature was already gone, along with the fruits he left for her. While his memory of the previous night was clouded, he was sure he had not eaten it.

Nevertheless, his search was cut short by the sudden ringing of the large bell atop the old bell tower in the center of Pratertown. Following the hollow ringing, there was a soft knock on the doorframe behind the young man. He turned around and saw Burke, who was leaning in the doorway and grinning.

"Good morning hunter," the older man said. "You look like hell. I saw you sleeping in the hallway last night but decided not to wake ya."

Eric rubbed his head, trying to rid himself of the small headache he had left. Fears that Burke may know about the events of last night were ringing in his head.

"I feel like hell," he said with a light chuckle.

"I bet. You seemed to have a good time at Beck's last night," Burke stated. "Now hurry up and get cleaned up; all hunters are to report to the Order's headquarters outside the city of Iodevis. The Holy Leader of the Order wants to give a speech."

Eric shook his head again.

"The Holy Leader? Isn't this kind of sudden?" Eric asked.

Burke shrugged, "Yep, but orders are orders. Now get ready, we leave immediately."

The city of Iodevis was drunk of music and lights that night. It was a nest of elusive joys and thrills. Music was pumping throughout the streets and avenues as a heart does with blood within one's veins. It was surging life to its citizens and their glittery clothing, to the brightly illuminated dance floors and ceilings, to the expensive plays of fountains and dozens of fireworks, and to the tall buildings' shimmering beacons, whose reach extended far beyond the skies and horizon.

As seen from the outside and as a whole, the city was like that of a burning sun, shining in its own light. Just like the brightest stars in the universe, it seemed destined to burn out of fuel and die sooner or later.

Among the others, the city was casting its glow onto its polar opposite. Not too far off to the south, a building stood surrounded by woods. It was as tall as a mountain and as terrible as the deepest abyss. Only a tiny amount of the flickering lights seemed to reach it, leaving the towering structure in an engulfing penumbra that would scare even the bravest viewer and leave them wondering of its true size. Such would be a peculiar way to describe any building of the sort, but an ill-fated omen were it to be said about none other than the Cathedral of the Order of the Arcane Hunt. It was the largest and highest between any church ever conceived by man. It was the main capital of the Order and home to the Holy, the One, the Only Leader of the Order Himself.

Any attempt of describing or otherwise depicting the colossal structure; with its Gothic pinnacles, the arches spanning dozens of meters in length, its enormous facade made of only the most refined white marble and filled to the top with golden statues decorated with rubies, emeralds, sapphires, amethysts and all kinds of other precious gems, its complex and geometrical decorations of ivory and delicate glass, and its spherical domes, all of them stacked again and again while spiraling to the top in a miracle of architecture and a bending of the laws of physics, would seem at the same time redundant for anyone who had not seen it with their own eyes.

Even if one could fill in the gaps within their own imagination of such a superb place, they would still be missing everything that made the Cathedral an impenetrable fortress to almost anything. Several layers of defenses would protect the palace, disfiguring its ornate beauty. Hundreds of meters of ground surrounding the building hid a thousand landmines, buried beneath the most unsuspecting patches of grass. Beyond that, under the watchful eyes of snipers perched atop the tall pinnacles was the barracks of the Hunter Elite. Veteran hunters adorned in pitch black leather trench coats and their faces covered by steel masks and armed with the most advanced automatic weapons of the time patrolled the grounds both outside and within the Cathedral. It was made up so as not a single soul could sneak by.

On the Cathedral's highest zenith and far away from the earthly looks of commoners and taking the form of a spear piercing the skies, it is said that the Holy Leader Himself resides there. It was from this room and through a mystical crystal serving as a projector that all could see in any city, that He gave all His orders to his Order and all of His speeches to the people of the land.

This was perfect. That was His only thought.

Such a triumph of His mind was the plan that He devised for the future of His Order! From such a small event such as the death of a person could He potentially gain so much power! This was the perfect chance in which He had been waiting for.

They had reported the hour prior that His son had been killed. His brain was holed by a force much more powerful than that of a gun. It was no doubt the work of a monster. There were also the fingerprints of a human found there as well. Among anyone that they could have belonged to, it was the human Eric Hahn, the new hunter who had only within the last few months been accepted into the Order. Voices had already been spreading about Hahn being a spy conspiring against the Order, and only few dared to say that he was under the control of one of those beasts. That was a neat idea, and a risky one, for it could easily been used as an excuse for his actions. No. It had to be Hahn's fault, and no others'. It had to be his fault only for the death of an innocent and hardworking hunter to the hands of one of those monsters. In reality, the Holy Leader had no idea if Hahn even had anything to do with his son's death, but he was to serve as a goat for His cause. Such a small sacrifice was nothing but crumbs.

Now all He had to do was write the perfect speech. Such a task was already happening by itself as words were escaping His mind. They were powerful. He had just begun to scribble the rough draft, and He was already liking it.

He read over his notes, grinning larger as he thought about it.

Show grief and anger of a father losing his son, one or two tears shed. Speak in a tone as low as a voice at a funeral. As a shock, describe the horrifying sight of my son's body to the crowd to underline how savage monsters are. People will react with shock and dismay. At this point, I praise them for all of their hard work. Reassure them and make myself look humble in their eyes. Underline the idea that I care about them.

"The only reason I will not give up after this terrible loss is because of all of your efforts!..." The Holy Leader read aloud, dramatizing the speech in his head.

Then reaffirm that monsters are evil, with more emphasis; also say that they are cowards. They have killed an innocent to attack Me. Stress to the people that there cannot be dialogue with the monsters, only enslavement or death of them. Then, add the surprise: there was a rebel, an enemy who sided with the beasts!

"His betrayal of Humanity and the Order murdered My son..." he continued.

Inject fear into the masses by reiterating the terrible event of My son's death.

"...even if he fought his best, he was still killed without effort by the monster!"

Claim that the creatures want Man to fear them, that they want us to believe that we're weak! Then, back to Eric Hahn, I shall point to him among the hunters with a fell swoop of My hand. Shout with anger at this point. Reveal to everyone that the traitor had been hiding within our very own ranks. To the shock of everyone in the crowd, the terror they will feel will allow Me a bigger climate of horror! And then, sentence the boy to death right then and there. Finally...then a declaration of war against anyone who dares stand against the Order, no exceptions! The wakeup call and mobilization of the Order.

"...for our future, for our children, we will wage war and win. We shall gain the dominion of the entire world and enslave or destroy all monsters!"

Afterwards, the hunters will be lining up with their shining weapons. The crowds will be exploding in a maddening cheer. The largest of festivities will commence as the provinces will be united once again and prepare for war. The militias will bow down or be destroyed, and the Order will grow ever stronger as the ground itself trembles at its march!

It would be a mesmerizing speech; simply repeating it in his mind almost convinced him of the truth that wasn't in it. It was time to begin a war, His war, and anything that was not the Order, be it human or monster, would finally be under His control or slaughtered without mercy.

The next day would begin His absolute reign. Satisfied with the speech He prepared, he glanced over at the photo of his dead son, Ross. That was why there was a large grin spreading across His face.

[XII]

It was sudden. The Holy Leader struck his lightning of truth down from the spiraling Cathedral! His index finger, seen by the crowds through the ghostly image that was being casted and showing the Holy Leader Himself, was larger than a giant's. That finger was pointing at, among all of the hunters gathered at the Cathedral's courtyard and the common peasants around them, a single lonely man. Eric Hahn, a person who was hidden amongst the identical dusters and hats was separated. He was isolated from the others and shown to the world.

The masses of people gathered there were shocked and horrified at the realization. The many hunters there were enraged, for a traitor had been amongst their ranks the entire time! Eric seemed like a well taken care of, civilized young man. How could such an innocent-looking person commit such a horrible act!

Burke and David were horrified at the news, but had troubles believing Eric was involved. Though, as soon as they moved to vocally defend Eric, the other hunters there blocked them off as the young man was dragged out into the open.

The mass of people in the crowds knew it wasn't any different. Their minds and their voices were already screaming at the revelation that was told to them that day! Only an outsider, one who was accepted into the Order with kindness; only he would do such a thing. He was only a sickened bastard, one who would dare to side with a monster! There were no excuses allowed. There would be no forgiveness! As Eric ached and shook in fear, he trembled for his fate. A few words grew into shouts at the top of the crowds' lungs. Their reddened faces had lost any control over their stretched, horrible expressions.

"Kill the traitor! Kill the traitor!" they screamed.

Above all of this, within his throne room, the Holy Leader merely stood there silently. There was nothing left to be said.

What was left for Eric to do? He was shaking violently as the only thing surrounding him was hatred. The already immense courtyard became immeasurable as hundreds, no, thousands and millions of people were now looking down with hatred at him. It was only a matter of a second that he went from being a nobody, to be the center of all of the pent-up anger of the human race.

Everyone is so angry! Everyone is so loud!... Eric thought in a panic.

Tears were running down his cheeks as he sweated profusely. His adrenaline was rushing at full capacity throughout his nerves. He was unable to look away from the crowd or the finger of the Holy Leader pointing at him. His heart was pounding like a hammer against the inside of his chest. His throat was scratched and dry. His stomach was churning with nausea.

It hurts so much...please...

Alone. He felt completely alone. He failed to even hear his own voice as he tried to give his excuses. He could not hear himself over the roar of those around him. Nobody there would listen to his plea. Burke and David were unable to try to even help, being held back by the other hunters. Eric began to find that the more the people screamed at him, the more he believed that they were actually correct. It was clear to him then. He was indeed a killer, a traitor. He was an enemy of the Order. He betrayed all of humanity and now he would be sentenced to death, as he deserved.

Still though. Eric did not want to die. He was deeply and truly sorry for what had been done. He had thought that freeing the creature was the right thing to do, that maybe he could have changed the future for the better. He didn't think it would result in Ross's death. He just didn't want to die, not like this. He...

...He was just making up excuses, wasn't he? Yet again, Eric found he was just trying to justify himself, even when everyone knew of his crimes. He was merely a coward. He formed a resentment for himself, an ego that talked to his stupid and deprived self through the voice of a harsh judge.

...**I deserve to die...**

Eric deserved to be executed for his sins. It was without a bit of doubt. Just like the seraph, the angelic creature who brutally murdered his fellow hunter. Eric asked himself again and again why he didn't kill her in the first place? Why did he let her live? What had stopped him from implanting a fix to his wrongdoings? What made him pause from killing a beast, that which was his job in the first place if not to enslave it? How could he let himself become hypnotized by her beauty and let her go after just having seen her slay another human? A savage, a siren she was! It was because he didn't kill her, he was no longer worthy of even breathing the same air as other humans.

Still...

He couldn't help but add another word, then another. The words kept on stacking up and soon fear replaced his anger towards himself. Why was he so hateful and resentful of his being in the first place? He was not only scared of the hunters around him, not only of the Holy Leader, but of his own morality. He was terrified of the internal judge he was just fueling seconds prior. He was giving up on himself, and doing such a thing wouldn't result in anything good, would it?

Quite not. Within his mind was a small voice. It told him to run away. It told him to try to escape his punishment. That voice was bringing back the sadness Eric felt as he remembered that poor seraph. How she was chained up and violated and beaten for months. He remembered her mother. An immense sadness rang through him. Yet if he was to die today, then it would be for a good cause, right?

Then why does it still feel wrong?...

Was Eric just being a coward? Was he just afraid to face death? Was it just his instincts just telling him to try to survive a just morality that was condemning his actions? Was his mind just simply picking the easy side, the side of trying to find good qualities in these creatures only because he was just as bad as them?

I hate it...

He hated it. He hated his weak mind for trying to come up with an excuse for his sins. He didn't deserve any mercy. He had to suffer!

...Or not?...

In the end, he was stuck trying to make a decision. It wasn't even in these final moments that he could come up with a yes or no answer. He couldn't say guilty or not-guilty. Even if he did make one decision, he knew he would fail to follow it. He would instead fall at the smallest of obstacles, as he always seemed to.

That was why he gave up on it all. He tried to forget everything and blocked out all of the sights and noises around him. His body became dull and numb. He slowly peered to his right and spotted a familiar sight.

Mom?...

There she was, standing amongst the crowd. Her hands were to her face, covering her mouth in shock as tears ran from her eyes. While those around her screamed vile things and pointed viciously at her son, she stood in disbelief. She knew better than anyone else about her child. She knew he would not harm another human, nor betray the Order as the Holy Leader had said Himself. But yet, she was unable to stop it. She felt powerless. She was being forced to watch her son go through something so terrible, and she was hopeless to fix it.

Eric still stared at her. His mind wandered off to the distant past. A cozy home. Nothing more than a small house within a sea of identical abodes in the province of Usora. A busy woman, giving her back to a young Eric as she cooked their dinner. The young boy would sit impatiently at the dining table, eagerly awaiting his food. All of this would come after a day of being outside and exploring the area with Joseph and a baby Vesuvius as their small protector.

It broke his heart to remember the small, quiet moments such as those. They seemed so lost, so far away from the gloom that his life had become shortly after becoming a hunter and losing his friend. Now, after the first war between humans and monsters that was waged almost a hundred years ago, the humans of Plataea was yearning for another. They screamed and demanded a bloodier one, bound to destroy anything left of themselves. Oh, how humanity was the true monsters, hidden behind fake promises for peace that they only wanted to achieve through hate. They hid behind their desires, the lust of petty belongings, drugs, sex, and other temporary pleasures. They tried to fill the void within their souls when all they ever needed was less tyrants and stupid rules. It was all wrong. Very, very wrong.

Ultimately though, there was nothing that Eric could do to change anything. He was tired. He was weak. He was just ready for it all to end.

It wouldn't last much longer anyways. An Elite Hunter grabbed Eric and tossed him to the ground with force. Without a proper ceremony, the Elite Hunter yelled orders to his comrades. He had them form a line in front of Eric and ready their weapons. Each of the black-clad hunters drew their silver-encrusted revolvers and took aim at the young man.

Eric snapped back to reality. He stared up at the covered faces of the Elite Hunters. He was once again facing death, but this would be the first time he would not resist it. He would not oppose his execution. Eric had accepted his fate. He was finally ready to die, to leave this world and all the pains it caused. He would go into the afterlife to be reunited with Joseph and Gyrog. The three would then move onto the Elysian Fields, able to be children once again for all of eternity.

The hunters cocked the hammers of their guns, ready to fire. Eric didn't care, not anymore. He gave up his faith and was going to allow himself to fall into the abyss of death. The Holy Leader Himself was going to give the order to fire. It was only a matter of seconds.

It was at that time, she appeared.

The seraph materialized in the air above the courtyard from nothing but a faint glow. Eric thought that she did really look like an angel. Her arms were wide open. Her thin, blue and white gown bent and flowed with the wind as she slowly descended from the sky. A set of beautiful feathered wings sprouted from her back and spread wide for all to see.

As she slowly dropped from the sky in that pose, it was as if gravity didn't truly have an effect on her, but rather her merely allowing it to bring her down. Time itself seemed to slow as everyone watched in awe at her theatrical entrance into the courtyard. Her appearance would not allow a single movement or thought that would differ from pure amazement.

It was just like that. All the noise. All the screaming. It was gone. All eyes were on her. Eric could once more hear the rustling of trees in the distance. The chirping of birds. He could hear her soft breath, and his own heartbeat.

"Kill it!" The Holy Leader screamed from his throne room, snapping the hunters out of their trance.

Only Eric stood motionless and in awe as she opened her brilliant red eyes. They glowed in a soft, blue light as she began a most beautiful and deadly play in front of the largest audience. She opened the show with a powerful blast of her psychic power. The blast knocked everyone off of their feet and instantly fried the brains of the hunters nearest to Eric. When the others began shooting at her, she would merely circle around and impale the hunters in the backs with crystals of light. She hopped and skipped, twirling like a dancer as she easily dodged the bullets and returned them back to their owners with her mind. With the grace of a ballet dancer, she would remove one's head with a flick of her wrist and send the removed part flying through the air.

She was moving in a deadly and gorgeous blur. By the time that the terrified hunters would process where she was going, she would simply disappear from sight and reappear elsewhere on her stage, taking another life. Even when they would almost hit her with a bullet, she would merely levitate another body in front of her to act as a shield and then flash away again. All of this was performed with the grace and elegance of a girl picking flowers from her garden.

Throughout the screams of agony, the blood that fell upon the stage in a thin, red rain, the shivering of the hunters she preyed on, the seraph would reveal the smallest and faintest of grins. Not a single soul could escape her enchanting gaze, and no survivor would ever forget the show and performance that she put on this day.

She truly enjoyed that feeling. Control, possession. Something that only a being with powers like herself could possibly achieve. Besides this, she was enjoying the revenge she felt she was getting. Revenge for being violated and beaten by such pathetic creatures. Pathetic, humans were truly that. They were so weak and powerless, one would think they'd be the humblest of beings on this planet! They deserved absolutely no pity.

Even as she hoped she could stay to kill all those present here, she knew her element of surprise was falling away. The curtains were closing on her devastating dance, and she made one last carnage. She grabbed a dozen hunters in her mental grasp, lifting them into the air and shredding them apart in dark red ribbons while she spiraled on a single leg. Her arms gracefully arched above her while her dress spun in a white disc. She then slid into a final split with her head tilted back. It was in this pose that she grabbed Eric Hahn's hand and then the two disappeared from her stage, just as she had come.

In the midst of her massacre, Eric failed to realize how scared he was. He didn't even realize that he had been teleported away and into the woods outside of the Cathedral. It was only when he saw this, that he looked down at himself. He saw how badly sweating he was. His legs were shaking, barely able to hold him up. He was safe...

...But was he? Eric looked around in a panic; looking around for any signs of danger in the patch of woods he was in. Nothing. Only the quiet and tranquil greens and browns of the trees were around him. There were no people, nor creatures in sight.

...**I've been saved...** He thought to himself.

"*Saved?*" the seraph said.

A beautiful, feminine voice was heard in his head. It sounded like a choir of angels. Sublime, it truly was, yet it spooked Eric and made him jump and turn around. There she was, sitting on a fallen tree trunk. The same, delicate creature that he had saved and been saved by. Her blue hair was in a bobbed cut, usual for her kind, with a single lock trailing down and in front of her face. Her blue and white dress, too large for her slim body, gently blew in the breeze. Her wings were gone, leaving her looking very similar to that of a female human. Someone who was colorblind would not find anything out of the ordinary about her, with the exception of a single, bony blade-like horn that stuck out from the center of her chest.

"*You appear more pale than me...that certainly is something I suppose,*" the seraph added, referring to her own, snowy-white skin.

Her words sounded in his head. Her mouth did not move with any of the sounds. As he heard her speak, her breathed voice was monotone; void of emotion.

"*You believed yourself to be safe a second ago before I spoke. Does it differ now? Do you still believe yourself to be safe?*"

Eric stood still, confused by her statements. It was not only for the way she flawlessly spoke his language; instead it was also because she sat there, completely motionless. Her face showed no emotions, utterly stoic. Her eyes were fixated on him, those killer eyes. They never seemed to close. Was she hostile? He could not tell, for the body language in which humans used as part of their communication was completely absent with her. At the very least, she was trying to talk with him. It was with that; the obvious question came to his mind.

"Why did you save me?" he slowly asked. His body betrayed his attempt to remain calm.

"*Saved?*" She asked again, adding a slight inflection to that word, as if she pretended to be shocked by the question. "*You have an... odd definition of that word, it seems.*"

Eric began to fear the worst...was she merely playing with him?

She spoke up once more. Her voice filling his head.

"*I did not 'save' you...gratitude for your actions yesterday is not something I consider. And have you forgotten already about me trying to kill you before?*"

The seraph was correct. She had tried to kill him. Then, why did she...

"*Why, you may ask?*" She cut off his thoughts, reading his mind. "*To put it simply; it was curiosity. How can one live knowing the entire world hates him? I want an answer to that.*"

Eric failed to understand what she meant that her words. She then clarified it, and it struck him like a bat.

"*You see...soon, the news of your escape will spread to every human city and village. Soon, there will be papers with your face on it, with the word, 'wanted' written at the bottom. Soon, every hunter, every soldier, every human will be going for your blood. Every soul on this planet will know that you're a traitor to your own species, and you will be hated by everyone.*"

Indeed, it was true. The words she spoke was a simple truth that he didn't realize until right then. Eric had already accepted his death, so he never had thought about a 'what if?'.

What after that then? What was Eric to do after this? He could not return to any human settlements, and the Order would be hunting for him on every inch of the continent. He feared that he could never come into contact with another human for the rest of his life...but, maybe he could...?

Reading the human's thoughts, she suddenly interrupted him once more.

"It would be foolish of you to think that any of my kind would put aside our hatred of humanity to accept you, would it not? You may have freed me twice, and even attempted to save my mother, but that does not mean that monsters will be any kinder to you. I will not be kinder to you."

Her voice, as fresh as a spring breeze, as beautiful as her appearance, was only sentencing his future to be something worse than death. As she spoke, the winds seemed to pick up. Birds flew in circles around the two beings. The surrounding trees seemed to grow and reach heights that his weak, human hands could not reach.

"Humanity. Beasts. Every living thing on Plataea hates you. Now, you are alone. Honestly, it would have been better for you to have died in that courtyard. Indeed, I did not save you, Eric Hahn. I merely made your suffering worse."

With those final words, she went silent.

[XIII]

"You are finished, now that you are all alone," the seraph spoke once again after her moment of silence.

It was true. The creature was correct.

"There isn't a single soul out there that wants to be with a traitor like you. Don't think that I will help you either."

Although... Eric thought.

"Because if I'm speaking honestly; I do not care about you any more than any other human I had ever seen in my life."

...Why is she still talking? Why didn't she just leave?

"After all, you only rescued me from that damned basement because I made you do it subconsciously."

An odd thought just then entered Eric's mind. **What if she didn't leave because she didn't want to end the conversation?**

"Even if you did act on your own accord, I do not even care."

Was there some bit of guilt in her? Was that the true reason she took him from his death sentence? Was it why she still continued to speak to him? Eric wasn't sure of it himself, and he could not be sure because of her motionless stance and a lack of visible emotions. He wanted to know though. He had to know what she was thinking for once. He had to gather his courage and speak up, before she did decide to leave him forever. What did he have to lose anyways? A life that was already over? Right...

"So, human. You-"

"What about you then? You say everyone hates me, what about you? Do you hate me?" he suddenly asked.

He was shaking with fear. It was indeed a dumb question. It made no sense to have asked it. She already made it perfectly clear that she did not care for him in the slightest. That she had no sympathy for him. Regardless though, something deep inside made him ask. He wanted a direct and unmistakable answer from her.

The seraph showed surprise. This time, it was an honest reaction to his words. She stopped for a moment to process his sudden outburst. Eric felt oddly accomplished. What should have been an easy answer had actually been something she wasn't ready for. It was more than that though. He saw a tiny bit of a hidden side to her. It was a side not of that of a unfathomable monster, but a creature. A creature with doubts just like his.

In Eric's head, that ever so slight pause of hers meant more to him and what it may had been in reality. In those few moments, he saw that she looked at him with a different look in her eyes. He didn't need any effort to decipher her memories. The memories of her being caged and abused. He refused to believe that her actions back then as a complete lie. He refused to believe that she could fake her emotions as much as she wanted him to. She indeed was capable of human-like and pure emotions.

Had something really changed in the way she looked at the human before her? Even if it had been for just a moment? It likely did not, but to the lonely human, her temporary change of attitude may had been his only hope.

"*As I said...*" she slowly spoke once more.

"I know what you said. I just don't believe it to be the truth," he said, interrupting her again.

"*And why is that?*" she hissed. Her eyes were focused on him more than ever. She even looked somewhat upset, even if it was only because she didn't like being talked over.

"Because..." Eric said, swallowing. "Because if you truly didn't care for anything that I had done for you, then why did you risk your life to get me out of there?"

Her eyes widened. That cracked it.

She knew he was right before he even finished his words. She herself did not understand why she acted out against her instincts. The thought was tormenting her. She failed to understand a part of herself, and she couldn't come up with an excuse to convince herself otherwise. He was correct; she did it because she felt sorry for him. After saving her twice now, she felt sorry for what he was going through. Why did she feel this way, and for a human of all things? She always had empathy, but humans never counted!

She had to be collected. She had to be in control, but she needed time to do that. Time to think things through. When she rescued him, she did it out of her instincts and not through her thoughts. She acted without thinking of the pros and cons. She didn't have time to understand what she was doing, otherwise he would have died, and then he wouldn't have mattered to her! It was that part of her that she damned, that part of herself that felt sorry for him!

She was becoming angry with herself. She had been betrayed by her own sense of duty, and what did it get her? A whiny, pathetic human who should have been worshipping her as a goddess, but was instead arguing with her? How dare he speak to her like this! She thought she should…

…No, that was not like her. She didn't like to think of herself as superior to another being. The human wasn't disrespecting her after all. He was just frightened because of her exaggerations. She may have hated humanity, but that was no reason to take it all out on this lonely boy. She knew she had repaid her debt to him. Now all she had to do was to let him go, and then everything would be back in her control…if only she could stay calm.

The human was an open book to her. It was because her horn allowed her to see into his emotions and thoughts, but also because he was simply too innocent and scared to hide anything. On his side though, he failed to see any of her trails of thought.

Nevertheless, their conversation was cut short by the sounds of movements nearby. The cracking of twigs and leaves in the brush left both of their minds as silent as the forest around them. Someone was approaching. Eric reached for his revolver, yet found it was gone. He looked to his left hip for his soul stone. It too, was missing. Confiscated without him knowing when he was to be executed. He cursed to himself.

Soon enough, a hunter emerged from the bushes. He was dressed in the usual garb that all hunters wore, and he sported several scars across his face and neck. At his side and towering over him was a minotaur. The large bull-like beast had a crazed look in its eyes. Scars and burns covered nearly every inch of its skin. Obvious signs of extreme abuse by its owner. The hunter was slowly clapping his hands and he had a wide, toothy grin.

"What an excellent performance you did, beauty," the hunter said, talking to the seraph. "But you couldn't possibly think that you could escape, did you? I can track any monster in these woods, no matter how fast they are."

The minotaur added to its owner's words by letting out a loud screech. The hunter continued by talking full of himself, even if he was going up against such a powerful creature as she. Eric looked over at her. She was focusing her eyes and her wings were reappearing. She was definitely preparing for a fight. Still though...the sight of the terrible minotaur and his cocky owner intimidated Eric more than he wished to admit.

What if she los-

"*I won't lose, human,*" the seraph said in his head. Though she meant for her tone to sound prideful, it came across as softly reassuring.

"You know what, seraph?" the hunter said, playing with a soul stone in one hand. "You might just make an excellent addition to the team...sure I might have to beat you into obeying me, but I think you'll be worth it..."

The hunter grinned even more, showing more of a psychotic side to his personality than sane. It was obvious to Eric though, the time for talking was over. It was time to fight.

"My beast, electrocute the angel!" the hunter yelled, pointing viscously as the seraph.

The minotaur obeyed, charging a bolt of lightning between its horns and arching the bolt toward the seraph. Just before it reached her though, she touched the ground with her feet and held her hands out in front of her. The electricity disappeared in a haze as if she simply absorbed it.

The monster then screamed in rage, then charged with extreme speed towards her. At the very last moment, she flashed away and reappeared elsewhere. It would charge again and again, but to the same effect. The act of failing to connect its attacks enraged the beast more.

"What are you doing?? Hit her already!" the hunter yelled, annoyed at his monster's failures thus far.

The minotaur's desire to kill was becoming more and more clear. Its mouth was salivating heavily. Its eyes were heavily bloodshot with anger. It would charge the seraph with extreme speed, leaving behind a rush of air and moving so fast that Eric had a hard time keeping up with it. Yet, the seraph's red eyes were always fixated on her opponent. She gracefully dodged every one of his attacks as not to leave a single mark on her perfect figure. Unlike the minotaur, who was flailing violently and screaming, she was perfectly motionless and ready to teleport as soon as it nearly reached her.

Eric felt powerless but to watch the two monsters fight. He knew he was hopeful that his life would be lengthened by her possible victory. He was scared by those powerful beings. He had thought for an instant to run away, but he was too enthralled by her. The seraph, she was the most amazing thing! For a moment, he once again saw a beautiful creature that was far beyond his own dimension. An angel to which he should bow down to. Though...

...He began to ask himself why she was not launching an attack of her own. After a dozen attempts from the minotaur, she was left unharmed, but so was the minotaur itself. Eric then thought of a single idea; one that made him shake uncontrollably with fear. He then looked to the other hunter, and the smile that he sported was all Eric needed to confirm his theory.

The reason that she was not attacking, was because she was not winning.

She seemed faster than the minotaur, but even then, only barely. She could barely keep pace with it, and by managing to dodge it attacks at the last moment, she gave herself the exact amount of time that she needed to prepare the next teleport. This left no time to attack. If she were to try, it would leave her open to what would prove to be a fatal move. She would not be able to defend herself, and there was no way she could defeat the minotaur in a hand-to-hand brawl. The minotaur was baring its teeth, and they were not just for show. While her mind was stronger than most living things, her body was weak as a stick. One single bite or connection of its horns to her body would mean a certain death.

It was because of this, she was doing the only thing she could do; stall for time. She was hoping for an opening to appear, but she knew she couldn't keep this up forever. While her opponent didn't shed a single drop of sweat, she felt herself slowing down.

The minotaur let out a vicious roar, louder than before. The hunter who owned it let out a laugh, laughing at his own monster as it lost control of itself in the fight. It drooled excessively and showed no signs of slowing down. On the other hand, the seraph was clearly fatigued. Her head was lowered slightly, and her shoulders were drooped. Even her dress seemed to weigh much more on her frail figure. She clearly wasn't giving up soon, but she wasn't enduring like Eric had hoped.

Coming to the conclusion that she would fail, Eric didn't think twice. He waited for the minotaur to rush the seraph once again, and then he spun around and tried to run off into the woods.

"Oh no you don't, traitor!" the hunter playfully called out.

He drew his revolver and fired a shot at Eric. The cast silver bullet trailed right for Eric's head, but the seraph teleported between the two humans and took the bullet in the breast instead, all while letting Eric safely escape.

She was now all alone. The human had used her to get away, and she still had the good will to sacrifice herself for him. She figured that he guessed that she would lose soon enough, and she knew he was right.

The minotaur rushed at her again. She squeezed her mind and managed to teleport out of the way once more.

She still felt betrayed. She knew that Eric had no reason to care for her, especially after everything she had said to him.

The beast rushed her again. She focused and dodged the attack once more.

There was also nothing he could have done, even if he had wanted to. To think she had felt sorry for him in the first place. Karma had an odd sense of humor in the end. She was mocking him for the demise and loneliness the human had faced, and now she was at the center of it.

Her whole body shook as she teleported again to dodge the monster's attack, this time it was a bolt of lightning shot from a distance. It was painful for her every time she teleported. Had she not used most of her energy to save Eric's ungrateful life, she could have easily killed both the hunter and his minotaur by now. But kindness seemed to be her biggest weakness. The pain from the bullet in her chest had become unbearable. She lost the strength needed to even keep herself hovering from the dirt.

"Minotaur...stop," the hunter suddenly ordered.

He no longer smiled. The minotaur seemed angered by the command, but it obeyed and stood in place.

"You know what, seraph? You are disappointing," the hunter said. "I had thought of you better than this, with the adorable and cute way you saved that worthless boy. Now though, all I see is that you are simply boring and useless. I don't need you."

***Need* me? That was all that he cared about with me, if he *needed* me???**

A sudden burst of rage entered her otherwise stoic mind. Just how stupid that all that seemed to matter to anyone was if she was useful to them or not! What was she to them then? Nothing but a toy? Something to be played with and then discarded when they were bored with her? She refused to stand for it. She would rather kill herself than be a slave to a human ever again! First that cult, then that vile pig disguised as a human, and now this waste of life? She was not going to accept it. That hunter was not free to use her as he pleased. She gathered what strength she had left and stood her ground. She stared into the hunter's soul with her cruel, crimson eyes.

"Finish her," the hunter said quietly.

Her prideful little stance meant nothing to him. All he wanted was to fulfill his own little fantasy of proving his monster stronger than her.

The minotaur let out a screech louder than any other, kicking at the dirt as if it was charging up an immense charge. She knew she would not survive the attack, but she stood her ground. She refused to take her eyes off of the fearsome sight. If she was going to die, then she would do so with pride.

The beast then charged, and the seraph readied herself for death, but the minotaur stalled itself halfway to her. From behind the hunter, Eric reappeared. He pulled the hunter's own knife from its sheath and fought to drive the blade into his neck.

The hunter fought back, trying to draw his revolver. The seraph used the minotaur's momentary pause to grab the hunter in a weak psychic grip. It was just enough to help Eric to overpower him and drive the blade to the hilt in the hunter's neck.

The hunter's lifeless corpse then dropped to the ground. Along with the body fell the minotaur's soul stone from his hand. Eric quickly stomped down on the stone, breaking it into pieces.

The minotaur, after years of horrible torture at the hands of its now dead master, died as well after its soul and free will was released. The beast dropped dead to the ground with a soft smile on its face.

Eric had gone back to save her, once again. It was a victory over what had seemed to be an impossible battle. It was also the first of more to come.

[XIV]

The death of that hunter proved to be valuable to Eric. By taking from the dead body, he was able to get a knapsack that was full of useful items. Within it included matches, a small canister of lantern fuel, a rolled up wool blanket, smoked meats, and a small number of dried berries. Also, within its contents was a few cotton bandages and medical alcohol. From the dead hunter himself, Eric secured his revolver and both of his ammunition bandoliers, of which he wrapped around his torso and holstered the gun. There were numerous other small items that he didn't think he'd need but located in the hunter's pocket was a most curious item. An unused soul stone.

A soul stone...and a monster who was in no position to fight back. Eric held the small crystal in one hand and lightly tapped it against his chin. He did this for a good half minute or so as he thought to himself. He did, after all, know how to use the object. He knew the arcane words that was needed to be spoken to capture the will and soul of any beast to the stone and make it his forever. The idea of capturing the seraph proved to be very, very tempting to him. It was tempting to make her his property, his *thing*.

It had felt wrong though for reasons that he could not explain. Every fiber of his morals screamed at him not to do it. At the same time though, he could come up with multiple reasons that he was acting in this fashion. It was clear that he needed her for his own survival. He was, after all, being hunted by the entire world now. It was important that he found himself an ally, and one like her could make the difference. He did, as well, lose his other beast, his dragon Vesuvius. The injured seraph would prove to be a worthy replacement until he somehow got Vesuvius back. It had also been her fault that he was in this scenario in the first place! He had made the decision to save her life for the third time, and what had she done to repay him? She tried to kill him before, and he feared that she would try again if he gave her the chance.

There was no longer any arguing about it. He would make her repay her debts, against her will if he had to. His own, stupid morals couldn't argue against that. He had defended her too many times. She shouldn't be allowed to refuse paying him back, even if she had the strength to.

After all, surely she wouldn't mind too much. Eventually she could like it. Even learn to love it. He thought cruelly to himself, as uncharacteristic of himself as it was. **Wasn't this how the stories are supposed to go anyways? The hero saves the damsel, and she swears her eternal love to him, and then they live happily ever after?**

That was how it was supposed to go. Instead though, she kept herself hostile towards him even after every attempt he made to show kindness to her. She only had caused trouble for him. She betrayed him and killed a fellow hunter, destroying his entire life! What kind of hateful soul was she? If she refused to give in to him...then he would have to force her!

All he had to do now was approach her frail body while uttering the arcane words: 'Adiuro te ad meum autem'. She was immobile and weak. She could not possibly escape the arcane stone's grip. The soul stone itself seemed to call out to him, begging him to do it. It was a deep and calm voice, soothing and holding promises of lust and power.

"*Pleaassse...*" whispered the creature in a feeble and heartfelt plea. Her voice was softer than water and thinner than glass, that which cracked on the second syllable as tears filled her red eyes wholly.

She was lying on the dirt ground. Her thin legs were painfully moving towards her torso, one centimeter at a time. She held her breast where the bullet hit her. Blood flowed from it like a fine wine. Even though the bullet did not hit anything vital, it was cast silver, and it burned her insides. She was trembling with fear, that frightened, broken angel.

Bandages...I need to get the bandages! Eric snapped out of his trance.

He quickly gathered the bandages in his hands and ran over to the injured creature. Tears streamed down his face in shame and guilt. How dare he to think of such cruelties! He wanted to hurt himself, to punish himself until he was numb to the pain! He immediately threw the soul stone away. He threw it with all the force and anger he could put into it, smashing the stone into pieces against a nearby tree.

Eric seemed to cry harder than she was as he bandaged her wound, trying his best to be as delicate as he could. He then gently wrapped her in the woolen blanket. The young man also thought about starting a small fire as well, but he feared it would help potential enemies into finding them.

They then sat there for what felt like an eternity. They were both motionless and noiseless. The two only awkwardly stared at each other, occasionally looking around at the foliage of the forest around them, or the ground, or even the sky. A silence permeated the air between them as neither knew what to do or say to the other.

Celestial did not understand Eric. Since the discovery of the soul stone, a monster that was defeated would be forced to become only a docile slave to its master. A servant to a human. She had seen such a thing happen many times to her friends and family. Those who were not killed in battle were forced into slavery by the vile stones. It happened to her even.

Though, this human was different. He seemed to be refusing to follow that ancient rule of his own Order. He did not make her, an enemy, his prisoner. That logic did not make sense to her! This had also not been the first time he had strayed away from the usual human logic, either. It seemed as if everything he did was much to the opposite of what she thought he would do. He even did things that went against his own self-preservation! That fact frightened her. It made her unnerved. She was unable to understand him, to predict his goals and outcomes, and she could not accept it! Why did he continue to treat her with such kindness? Was he simply stupid? Was he so entranced by her, that he forgot how deadly she was?

Still though, a small part of her wished that she would just accept that it was not impossible that such behavior could be seen out of a human. Maybe those signs of kindness and gentleness were nothing more than exactly that, with no further aim or goal beyond their apparent nature. She had been truly frightened when he took the soul stone in hand and contemplated enslaving her. If only her experiences had not taught her better, then she would have been glad that he did not bind her to it. She would have been thankful, instead of being untrusting and skeptical like she was now. Maybe he was just playing with her? Maybe there was another soul stone in the bag, and he was only trying to get her to drop her guard. But something else told her that wasn't it. She didn't know his goals, because she always failed to predict him.

It was then that a fresh feeling began to appear within her. It come from an unknown tangle within her heart. For the very first time in what felt like a decade, she finally felt as if she could relax. She felt like she could release her worries, relax her muscles and feel weak. She felt it was okay for her to be this way in that moment. That he would not judge her to be pathetic, that he would not exploit her.

She was able to relish in that feeling of weakness. She enjoyed it even if only seconds before she did not know that she wanted to even feel this way! She thought it odd for such a powerful creature such as herself to want to feel so powerless. Even if the human's compassionate actions were not at all what they seemed, she did not care. He was allowing her to rest, and that was all she cared about.

There was a peaceful, quiet feeling in the world that was otherwise bent on killing itself.

"I don't wish to bother you," Eric spoke up suddenly, breaking her from her moment, "but other hunters and soldiers are bound to be searching these woods. If they find us now, we're both going to die."

The human surely knew that there was no way she could move on her own at the moment...but that meant...

"Let me carry you," he said.

She was unable to refuse. He was right, after all.

Eric picked up the knapsack and threw it over his shoulder. He then walked over to the seraph, lifting her gently in his arms while she was still wrapped in the blanket. It very much reminded him of how he carried her mother before she died, but he pushed the thought to the side. He remembered about how surprisingly light her species were. It was as if only the blanket had any weight to it. He held her close down at his waist. Her legs hung limply down. He somewhat regretted that he could not feel her skin to the touch, but he knew that it was not a smart idea to try it. Her scarlet, inquisitive eyes looked up at him. They seemed to not be any dimmer from her injuries. They still shimmered and sparkled full of light as if fire was fueling them. She was looking oh so intensively at him.

Eric knew he had to be quick, but careful. He began moving through the thick vegetation towards an unknown destination. So far, the forest had been merciful, not much in the way of stiff branches or rough ground had thus far been in his path. Still though, every step he took was like a needle in her breast. Every time he took a step a small bit rougher than another, she slightly gasped. He tried to hold her as carefully as possible, but it still caused her pain. She endured it for what felt like hours, but she refused to take her eyes off of him. She never diverted her crimson gaze from his face.

I promise you that it'll be okay. I promised you I would protect you months ago when we first met, and I will keep that promise. I'll take care of you. Eric thought to himself.

He wished to speak those words as a means to comfort her, but he did not dare to say them. The young man had no clue as to how she would react, so he stayed silent. She heard his thoughts though. She still heard those words. Her eyes finally flickered and closed. She had fainted from her exhaustion. Her breathing remained faint, but it was still regular. That was a small reassurance about her condition.

Eric continued to carry the unconscious creature. He walked for what seemed like hours, and he had no clue to where he was going. The sun had finally dropped behind the tree line and out of view, leaving the forest in a dark shadow. He soon came across a small clearing and lowered her to the ground as gently as he could. He wanted her to be comfortable. The young man then lit a small fire and tried to relax.

When Celestial awoke, the moon was already hanging high in the clear midnight sky. An army of fireflies was already out and dancing in the air around the two. They were rejoicing in their own lunar star and answering its glow with their own. While Eric seemed happy and content with the small show that the insects were displaying, the seraph on the other hand seemed to dislike it. She did not hate the small bugs, she just merely always had an aversion to them. In short, she simply did not like them.

While she swatted at the bugs that had gotten too close to her being, it seemed hopeless. The more she flailed down, the more that came around her. She became even more annoyed when the human seemed to be enjoying the little show of hers and had gotten a laugh out of it. She shot him the gaze of a viper, and he promptly apologized.

"I'm sorry," he said, still chuckling. "It just makes me happy that you seem to be okay. I was worried about you."

"*Do not underestimate me, human,*" she shot back.

He sighed, "I know...so how are you feeling?"

"*I'm fine,*" she blankly responded.

Why does he seem to care so much about me? She thought. She felt as if she should just give up on trying to understand him.

"What about the bullet?" Eric then asked.

He was surprised of her ability to speak at the moment. The fact that she seemed to be recovering this quickly was both a relief, and a frightening realization, to him.

"*I'll remove the bullet myself once I get more rest.*" she said plainly.

Eric raised one eyebrow quizzically. He then asked, "How can you remove it? You cannot teleport something that can't be seen."

The seraph let out a light scoff.

"*So, you do know something then, human,*" she said. "*That is true, but unlike your kind, I can sense every part of my body. I have perfect control over every muscle, nerve and organ. Removing the bullet will be a simple task for me.*"

Eric was struck in awe at her abilities even more. All he could say in response was a single word.

"Amazing."

"*It was...very good of you to come back and kill that hunter. That, I will give you,*" she said, switching the subject to another. "*At first, I did not understand, but I'm guessing you only did it because had I died, then you would have too shortly afterwards?*"

Eric leaned back onto his elbows, "I suppose. Partly at least. There would be no way I would have gotten away. That hunter managed to find us there; he surely would have caught up."

"*But surely that minotaur knew about you sneaking up behind his master?*" she argued out of instinct.

The human shrugged, "I'm sure he very well knew. I don't think that minotaur was an evil creature though. Maybe he wanted his torment to end, so he hoped I would succeed in killing the hunter?"

"*I think you're very naive...*" she disagreed. Was she really this annoyed with the fact that she couldn't predict him?

"Don't underestimate me, seraph," Eric said in a playful tone.

"*Screw you,*" she uttered before rolling over and hiding herself under the blanket.

Eric was so glad. He could almost cry he was so glad. He always did believe that the monsters, no, creatures were not heartless beasts. Now, he had finally been proven right. He had talked to her. They exchanged words that were not threats. They slashed at each other with not blood, but with remarks. Sure, she was no condition to attack him, but she could have remained silent and refused to speak, or even threaten him instead! Yet because she didn't, that 'screw you' had been the least threatening thing Eric had heard in years.

He felt so refreshed, as if the entire weight of the world had been lifted off of him. He felt his heart leap with joy. Could he and the seraph become allies? Could they even become...friends? Maybe, the possibility was there. Maybe...maybe it was possible for humans and creatures to exist side by side without bloodshed after all.

Her own thoughts included very similar feelings.

She felt a rush of guilt hit her. She never thought that she would ever know that humans were capable of being kind. She never had met a human who was. All of her life she had been disconnected from them, and even when she was around humans, it had been due to her being captured and abused by them. She had been raised to be strong and combative always towards outsiders, especially if those outsiders were human. She truly hated her own kind. She had hated the way she had been raised to do things, but only now did she realize just how brainwashed she really was.

Even now, when it was so obvious, she didn't want to believe it. She had always shown no mercy to others, because she was taught that it was the right thing to do. It was because others were trying to do the same to her, and that she was just acting in self-defense. But then she asked herself; was it the moral thing to do just because everyone else did it? Who became the bad guy, and who was the victim anymore? Who was the cause, and who was the effect? She had always thought of herself as an effect of the corrupted world around her, because of her bloodthirsty enemies. Now though, here came along a single soul that defied that reasoning.

Could I hurt him...and still call myself the victim? She thought as she trembled into sleep.

[XV]

The air in the forest became covered in a thick and heavy layer of fog. Wolves and other beasts of the night let out howls, daring any potential intruder to enter their territory. Even the moon itself seemed to willingly hide behind the cover of the clouds, as if to shield Eric and the seraph from anyone and reveal their presence to not a single soul.

Eric had no idea why the forest and nature seemed to act as if to help him, but he was thankful, nonetheless. He had heard myths of a magical beast that served as the guardian of the forest, almost something like a god of sorts. Maybe it was this deity that was approving of his actions, for few humans ever could survive even a single night in the vegetation of the woods after sunset.

Maybe he was deemed an exception? As soon as the thought crossed his mind, a strong gust of hot winds blew and extinguished the small fire. Eric quickly relit it and realized better. He was merely tolerated in these woods. He knew that at the crack of dawn that he would have to leave the forest.

But what then would he do? Eric knew that at the edge of the forest was nothing but the flat plains of Avrush in every direction for kilometers. It would be far too easy there for the Order to find him.

He seemed almost bound to die, for the forest surely only cared for the life of the sleeping creature near him.

Then another thought crossed him. What was she going to do? He considered the fast pace of her recovery and knew that by dawn she would be able to stand and move on her own. By then, she surely would be able to defend herself. Maybe she would simply leave him there, or even kill him!

The chat they shared only minutes ago instantly seemed meaningless. Sure, they did talk awhile. They fought together as allies. He had even seen her kinder side, but did any of that matter though? Her kind and his were still enemies after all. Eric still did not know why she had saved him yesterday morning. The truth was, he knew almost nothing about her. He had no way to know what she was thinking. It was because of this, and because he wanted to believe that everything had good will, that he could have gave her a humanity that she did not possess.

The truth was screaming in his head. The fact that she was indeed very powerful and very dangerous. Most of all, the fact that she was hostile. He very well remembered how so easily she slaughtered dozens upon dozens of well-trained hunters back at the Cathedral courtyard. About how the blood and heads and body parts were flying. The screams of agony that filled the air. And all the while, she laughed at them. She played with her prey and enjoyed their deaths and pain of the hunters just like him. What about Ross? The image of his lifeless and holed corpse still haunted his memories. It was that dark side of hers, the one that instilled a sort of fascination in him, that was also the image of monsters that the Order had taught every human.

The fact that they shared words and her somewhat nice attitude was the only comfort for him. Though, what had seemed like a warm idea for a possible, loving friendship had crumbled into dust with a single infectious thought.

What if she had been toying with me?

She had pretended friendliness before, and that had only been when she needed his help. She had been weak, helpless, even open and loving to him! Who was to say that she wasn't acting this way once more?

Mind control. Her kind was known for it. Eric was sure of it. She was exploiting him once again for her benefit. She cried and pleaded for him not to bind her to a stone, and then she used him as a litter to get through the forest. She then talked with him, to make him feel safer. She pretended to have human-like emotions to toy with his brain. She wanted to sound reasonable to him. He was sure the creature did it so she would be safe, because she knew that if she made him think that she was good, then he would not kill her.

In short, Eric was sure that she did not care for him. All she needed was rest and then she would leave him for good.

Oh, how quickly many emotions can swirl and overcome each other within the tangles of one's mind! The seraph, her mother, Joseph, that cult, Ross, the Holy Leader. Every fear and memory of his life came back in full force. They mixed together in a blender of terror, anger and other confusing feelings. The thoughts had no clear order or even made any sense anymore. It was then that he kept thinking of her terrible, monstrous side. He firmly persuaded himself that she had tricked him once more. Though he knew he could not run away. He had been without rest, and finally his exhaustion had gotten the better of him. He fell asleep as there were still a few hours until dawn.

The next morning, the two did not talk much as they awoke. All the fears that Eric felt the previous night came back to him as he saw her stand. She closed her eyes and got into a pose much like that of meditation, but with her legs straightened vertically under her. She seemed to be channeling the energies around her, but after a moment she lost her composure and reopened her eyes. Then, she slowly turned and began hovering in the same direction they had gone the previous day.

Eric followed behind her as best as he could. The vegetation, while strongly in his way, seemed to bend and bow away from her as she moved through. It was like the brush was not worthy of touching such a perfect creature. He was unsure of what to say, but because she was silent, he felt the need to say something. The idea sounded idiotic to him, but he still opened his mouth.

"So... are you feeling better today?" he asked her timidly.

"*Yes,*" she replied in a single, cold word without looking at him.

"Oh..." he muttered. The young man pondered his next words, "That's... good then... So why... why don't you just teleport away from here?"

The more he spoke, the less his voice carried. The last few words had been nothing more than a few hushed sounds.

"*I can't,*" she replied. She seemed irritated at him, but explained simply, "*I can only teleport for short distances, and even then, only to places that I've been to.*"

"I... I didn't know that," he said. "So, does that mean you've been to the Cathedral before? And you know of that spot where we fought the minotaur?"

"*I do,*" she stated, without elaborating.

"Why is tha-" he went to say but was suddenly cut off.

Her eyes blazed in a blue aura as she lifted Eric off the ground and sent him against a tree at high speeds. The impact knocked the air out of him, but he otherwise was not hurt. She pinned him against the tree, facing her. He felt he could not move a single part of his body. Her mouth was pulled into a tight frown and her eyes glared daggers at him.

"*I don't get it!*" her voice screamed in his head.

The voice was a shocking change in her otherwise melodious and crystalline tone. She even made a verbal sound from her lungs that was like the ringing of a bell. The seraph was then left breathing heavily, a result of her shout.

Eric was frozen and terrified beyond reason at her sudden outburst.

"*I don't get it...*" she said again, her words trembling.

She was clearly upset, but her body language and face lacked any signs of hostility. Instead, they only showed uncertainty.

"What are you doing?" she asked. "*Why are you doing this? Are you playing with me, or are you simply dumb?*"

She paused, then continued with a renewed anger in her voice, *"I'm tired of trying to guess. Tell me now, why you tried to save my mother. Why did you treat my wounds? Why did you carry me to a safer spot? Why didn't you make me your slave back there!?"*

She was expressing so much rage with her words, it was not like the collected and rational being she usually was. The seraph was not willing to bargain, that much Eric could tell. Yet, he saw something else though. In her eyes, it was fear. Her eyes were trembling. Even if she tried to hide it, she was surely on the verge of tears. This human, in their short time of knowing each other, had countered the entire theory she had that humans were undeniably evil. Even after her months of rape and the years of her own personal experience, this one human made her question her entire upbringing.

Though, was this man before her truly a kind soul? Or rather, was he just that crafty? Had she truly found a trustworthy human, or a devilish liar? She could not come up with a straightforward answer. With everything she had seen with him, it made her exhausted. It made her so stressed that she could not even meditate in the slightest!

She had tried time after time to attempt to understand him. She had indeed sensed his emotions and tried to put them together. Yet when she connected the dots, all she got was a huge jumble of lines and conflicting goals. She absolutely hated the idea that she could have been wrong her entire life. She hated the idea that the human in front of her may have been just as scared, just as lonely as she was! That had been the only excuse for his behavior. So, it was at that time that she did the only thing she could do. Ask him directly, as he had done.

Eric on the other hand, felt his vision become slightly blurry and his limbs numb from her mental grasp. He saw death once again knocking at his door, so he decided to not think any further and release all his frustration at her with the most truthful answer he could give. He no longer cared about her possible reactions.

"Why? That doesn't make any sense!" he yelled out, "I didn't try to rescue you on that island or from that damned basement just to pull you down with me!"

His honesty made her flinch. He had answered her question with the same desperation as she had asked it.

"...Listen, Celestial..." he said, calming slightly.

The seraph froze in shock that he knew her name. Had he learned it in their short time sharing that room in his dreams? She did not know, but the revelation shook her to her core.

"I have been serving a regime that I didn't trust...I've been ignoring injustice only because it was the simple thing to do...I joined the Order thinking I would protect people, but now I see that it's only a fascist order."

Sadness. Regret. Those feelings emanated from the young man and she could feel it with her horn.

"It wasn't that bad at first. Growing up, I saw the hunters as heroes to almost be worshipped. I wanted to be them. They gave us security from the outside world. I didn't have to fear for my life every day because of them, so it became easy for me to accept them."

Fear and loneliness. She knew it was hard to oppose the will of the masses. She knew that all too well.

"What kind of life is that though? The Order ultimately forces you to comply with the regime's stupid rules. You aren't allowed to speak up, otherwise the militia just pulls you into the dark and beats you!"

Anger, grief and hopelessness. They were all pouring from Eric's voice and mind. So powerful were the emotions that the seraph's horn was hurting. It was glowing in a hot red, overheating. Rarely had she ever felt such strong rushes of feelings hit her! She began trembling, all the while she was experiencing the same fears, the same weaknesses as his. The worst part of it all was how those feelings, that anguish, were oh so very similar to hers! She wanted him to shut up! She didn't want him to speak anymore!

"And of course, you have to worship the Holy Leader like the megalomaniac god he thinks he is! You have to cheer for the deaths and enslavement of monsters and be willing to go fight a worthless war that they think will make humanity happy again!"

He was moving as much as his constraints would allow. He was spitting the words with anger. She knew she could not force him to contain these words. He had to get them out, and she had no right to stop him, for it was she who asked for it.

"That's what we've always been taught... but I never believed it. So... when I saw you on that island, and later in that basement... I... I..."

Eric's speech suddenly became slurred and he stuttered. His eyes watered slightly and shimmered.

"...I felt guilty... Never had I felt that guilty in my entire life. I was... I felt myself actually enjoying being in the regime, before... before I saw *you*..."

Sorrow. Unbelievable sorrow. She failed to hold back a tear as she heard the pure kindness that was mouthed in that choked pronoun. It was at that time, and it was the first time, that she noticed in his deep blue eyes there were black holes that could not reflect light but wished to.

"I was finally living in the luxuries of the Order. I had been enchanted by their power."

Guilt. He felt regret for his choices.

"Back in my home province, things were simpler. The conflict between humanity and beasts didn't seem as bad as a kid. My friend wanted to join the Order to fight evil, and I went with him. I did it to help people. To think I allowed myself to fall into the Order's cage!"

Spite. Regret was present once more.

"My friend and I joined the Order to defend humanity. The other hunters in my group. Burke. David. They were good people. I'm sure they also believed in the idea that the Order was to help mankind. But, after seeing how that hunter had treated his minotaur, I can see the truth now. I still want to believe that the Order isn't evil, but I am now afraid I have to face that truth."

Doubt and a spike of fear. His voice went quiet for a moment and his mouth hung open. His eyes seemed lost, then he found his words again. Eric then looked back into her eyes.

"...When I saw you in that basement, defenseless and crying...beaten, abused and violated beyond all beliefs...I no longer cared about anything. I didn't care that you were supposed to be my enemy. I didn't care that you could have killed me afterwards...I freed you, because I couldn't bear to stand how a human's lust, how all the hypocrisy and sins of the Order was destroying something so beautiful...so beautiful as *you* are..."

His voice cracked with emotion, but it was heartfelt and pure. She felt hope and sweetness come from him. So heavy was his emotions that it made her heart heavier as well. She was drowning in her own self-contempt, so much so that she had to hold her horn with both of her hands.

How could I have been so insensitive? She asked herself.

"...I know you tricked me into freeing you...I know that you didn't care about me on that island, or in that basement. I know you probably don't care even now...But...I'd like to think that I still would have freed you regardless..."

How horrified and scared he must have been!

What have I done?? How could I have hurt such a lonely, powerless boy?!

"I know now that a war will ensue from what has happened...that is what the Holy Leader wanted...hell, it's what humanity wanted. There is no way we can win, that much is for sure. Only more brutality and bloodshed will be the result of this... I don't blame any of this on you, though... This is what we always wanted anyways. People prayed and begged for this war, even if we didn't think we did. We prayed for a golden age of the future, instead of trying to live in the present... I wish I had powers like yours. Maybe then I could have done something. I could have tried to repent for my kind's sins...but I'm just a powerless, puny human..."

It was true. He was just a puny human after all. He was a puny human whose only defect was being too hard on himself. She wished she could tell him that, to console him in some form. She didn't think she could though, not after all she had done to him. Could she possibly make it up to him? She crushed his dreams and hopes, and now she feared that she destroyed his frail being beyond repair.

"The Order is now hunting me...had I bound your soul to that stone, you would be in just as much danger as me. I've decided to sacrifice myself for you...for if I can trade my life for yours...then I feel that's an even trade. Maybe then I can die in peace. There isn't a place left for me in this world, unlike you...I'm sure your kind has a much better life than we do..."

If only the young man knew. A better life? Yeah, right. And her, worth his life? How was a creature, one who was such an ungrateful bitch like her, worth anything at all?

"Please...do me a favor...You, and all other creatures...get together and win this war... Exterminate humanity, like we deserve... Maybe then, the world can be a more peaceful place...at least for you..."

It was with those final words, he was done. He closed his teary eyes and lowered his head.

Celestial found that she was furious at herself. Furious at that stone heart of hers. She felt an intense hatred for that horrible, stuck up part of her that saw everything like math. Goals and predictions, it all angered her now! Even though her stubborn reasoning was telling her to keep her guard up, that she would regret later of what she was about to do, she didn't listen to it. There was still time to make up for what she had done. She had to try, for he deserved it. He deserved it after everything she inflicted on him!

And so, she released him from her psychic grasp and slowly lowered him down. As he dropped gently to his knees, she hovered over to him and dropped down as well. She then reached out and held his hands.

His palms were sweaty, and terribly hot, but she did not care. She only cared about getting a secure grip. She slowly intertwined her fingers, one at a time, with his own. She did this forgetting about the worries of the world around them to get a firm grasp. She did so, looking at each of their hands, and then looking back at him with tears in her crimson eyes.

Then, with the gentleness and love of a mother, she whispered to him, "**Thank you...Eric...**"

It was all he wanted. It was all he had ever wanted in his life. Those few, small words meant the entire world to him. It was all he ever wanted to hear!

Both of their cheeks were bright red. They could barely keep their eyes open and they were both still shaking slightly. The hunter and creature felt a rush of confusing feelings and warm emotions towards one another. Among all of that, they also managed to give each other open and warm smiles. It was all they needed to forge a promise of friendship and goodwill for each of their futures.

[XVI]

Sometimes, Celestial just wish that she knew when to shut up. A few days had now passed that she had been talking with this human, and she was getting all kinds of emotional. The feelings made her dizzy and gave her an annoying headache, causing her to levitate around stumps and rocks like a drunk.

Still though, she was confident that she made the correct choice. She didn't want to miss out on the possibility of getting to know the human male before her. It was refreshing to discover that humans were capable of countless emotions, even ones that were positive! What she had experienced from him, though, had not been enough. She wanted to understand him more, so she could come to a complete decision about the human race, and if they were still worth anything. Had she simply decided to run away from him, she knew that she would regret that decision for the remainder of her life.

At first the seraph thought it would be an impossible challenge to face, the idea of cooperating with the human. Though as time went on, her fears were overcome by thoughts of the countless possibilities. There were so many things she could learn from Eric, and his behaviors and actions only raised more questions! Where did he get his good will from, in a world driven by so much hate? What had been his life before, and why did he reject the regime that so many of his similar were so fond of? What were his ideals? What about his education, his family? His thoughts? Dreams? The other humans, what were his thoughts on them? What did he think was truly evil within everything? At the bottom of her heart, Celestial hoped that maybe humans were not inherently evil, but yet just very sad creatures.

In order for the human to give his answers for her countless questions, she knew that she would have to forget all of her previous prejudices. She had to be willing and cooperative. She had to be objective with her opinions about him, no more than a scientist would. Besides, she had been the one at fault up to this point, so losing her previous attitude was the least she could do for him. There was one thing that she could say for sure so far though; he astounded her with his enduring of her company. He had not turned his back to her once, ever. Instead, he continually helped her, and even somewhat believed in her!

It was this consideration that made her feel even worse for her behavior before. In fact, guilt had almost compelled her to even apologize for it, but her own pride had stopped her. After the initial hurricane of emotions had settled, she felt that an apology was now too far away and unrealistic to consider it again. This caused her to have mixed feelings. Surely Eric had been deserving of a thousand apologies, but her pride wouldn't allow it.

A silence had permeated the air between them for the first few hours of their travels that morning. While they both promised to stay together and get to know each other as much as possible, the task was proving far more difficult than anticipated. The forest around them was not helping either. As quiet and as peaceful as everything around them was: with the tall, thin pine trees to the shorter and fatter oaks; everything was utterly the same as everything else regardless of the direction the duo looked.

"So, where are we going?" Eric asked, attempting to end the silence.

"To the end of the forest," Celestial answered, her voice sounding in the human's head like the sound of beautiful bells. *"Mother Gaea does not like your presence here."*

"I figured as much," the hunter said. "I have heard of Mother Gaea, but who is she?"

The seraph glanced to the duo's left quickly, but then returned to her usual posture.

"Legends have it that Gaea can share her immortality with any other living creature, if she wishes," Celestial explained. Her garnet eyes shimmered as she telepathically spoke. It was as if she was lost in marvel, *"She gives her thriving breath to all plants and creatures alike and oversees all the flora of Plataea. She has the appearance of both a beautiful equine and a blossoming tree and is the sister of Astreus and enemy of their third sibling, Oionos. The three are superior beings with unbound power beyond anything we can comprehend. Gaea protects all her creations but despises humans because of their blind abuses of other living things."*

The birds overhead started chirping. The song sounded as if they were singing of Gaea's holy love.

"Luckily for you though," the seraph then added, "she is among the kindest of the gods. She is the harbinger of life, not death. She even still allows humans to gather the necessary resources needed to live from her forests."

"She must be a beautiful sight! It must also be an honor for you to be able to speak to her then?" Eric commented.

"Quite the honor, yes," Celestial answered.

She took a more posed and mannered posture, as if Gaea herself had suddenly appeared in front of the seraph. The hunter and creature were now coming up on a clearing in the distance; the vast fields of Avrush laid ahead.

Celestial stopped, placing her arm out in front of Eric to stop him as well. He paused, surprised at the sudden halt.

"Up ahead, there," the seraph stated. "I'm sure an ambush awaits us. Let us move slow and silently."

Sure enough, once the two were at the edge of the forest they could see what awaited them. Well over two dozen armed humans. Some appeared to be militia with their gray uniforms and outdated rifles. A few others were definitely hunters. The dusters were unmistakable from any distance. The humans all patrolled the field ahead of them, no doubt looking for Eric and the seraph.

Eric and Celestial were still hidden by the dense foliage around them, but the human very well knew that a single step further would prove to be deadly for them both. He thought about how they would get past the group of soldiers; did Celestial plan on battling them? The hunter didn't think it was worth the risk, and she didn't seem like that one to brute force something. She was more cunning and smart than that.

The seraph was not preparing for a fight, so that helped to ease Eric's thoughts somewhat. He wondered if they were to wait until dark...no, the enemy hunters surely brought torches with them. They would be spotted for sure.

"See that cave over there?" the seraph said, interrupting Eric's thoughts. *"I'm going to teleport the two of us into it. I have chosen this exact point because it's the closest to there in a straight line."*

"Understood," Eric replied.

"By the way, human," Celestial said, still looking out at the militia and hunters patrolling the field, *"How did teleportation feel the last time?"*

Eric thought for a moment, "Well...it kinda feels like jumping, I suppose. It's like you're moving really fast while you are in mid-air."

"That is correct. It happens at near lightspeed. It's not instant," she clarified.

"Then you simply land, and feel extremely nauseous," Eric finished. "What about you?"

"More or less the same. Except for the nausea," she said. *"I can sense in my mind the location where I want to go, as if they are portals in which I can simply jump through."*

The seraph then took a deep breath, then turned to face Eric. She took his hands in hers.

"*Are you ready, human?*" she then asked, looking directly at him. "*There may be threats inside the cave. If so, then we fight our way through.*"

Eric nodded, but he lowered his gaze so as not to look into her eyes. It could have been insecurity on his part. How could one look into such beautiful irides without a focal point, and not get lost within them?

"*Look at me, Eric,*" she said, lifting his chin up. "*I promise that what you'll see will be worth it.*"

Her words did not sound like a command, but instead a favor that she asked of him. She began focusing her powers while still looking at him. Her eyes were fully open, and her crimson irises began to emit a pale, blue light as they very slightly vibrated in place. Then, two slit pupils began to unfold from the center of her eyes, colored as black as the void of the universe.

Instead of seeing the world around him, Eric could only focus on the pupils that appeared. He could see objects, stars almost, being created in her pupils while they expanded and grew larger. Soon, her pupils cover her whole irides, then her entire eyes. They still seemed to expand, past her own eyes and body, enveloping him wholly! Everything went black as he experienced what the inside of a black hole was like.

The moment lasted for only an instant. All the black vanished and the two were now inside the cave. Eric looked around and up at the rocky, wet ceiling of the cave. It took a water droplet hitting his cheek to wake him from the dumbfounded expression that was on his face.

To him, he had not just seen teleportation, it was much more than that. It seemed like something that was far more powerful and deadly than he ever imagined. What did he see? How did they work? Was she calling on an enormous amount of powers? Or, instead, did she merely create it in that instance? Was that how powerful she was? He failed to realize he was shaking slightly.

"*Well, it seems to be clear in here,*" Celestial said.

She began rummaging through Eric's knapsack while he still stood in amazement.

There are no soul stones in here. She thought to herself. After checking twice, she finally managed to relax herself and realize again that Eric meant what he said about caring for her.

"*Well?*" She then asked, actually curious as to what he thought.

"I...I don't even know where to begin..." he said, still amazed by her abilities. "There are so many questions that I want to ask."

"*Then how about you start with the simple ones?*" she said, seating herself on a rock ledge that jutted from the cave's wall. The seraph tried to be as friendly as she could, almost smiling to the human even! "*It looks like we'll be safe here for a bit, so we can relax and talk for the meantime.*"

Her voice was soft and calming. It helped to make Eric feel a little less uncomfortable. He noticed that once again, she switched back to her side that he could empathize with.

"Ok..." the young hunter pondered in his thoughts for a moment. "So, how old are you exactly? On Krehaul, you were just a cherub, but then you changed. How does aging work with your kind?"

"*My age? I have lived for just over eighty changes of the seasons. Or, rather, I think you humans would say, 'twenty years'?*" Celestial answered.

Twenty years? She's as old as I am. Eric thought, surprised by her answer.

"*Individuals of my kind do not 'age' in the traditional sense like humans or other living things. Only a few other species go through a life cycle like seraphs do. We start life as a cherub, which is our 'child' stage. One can be at such a stage for as long as thirty human years. After that point, a cherub will transform into a seraph, which is our adult stage. We can live for another century, assuming that individual lives a normal life.*"

Her gaze dropped slightly, almost as if the last part of her explanation saddened her. She then looked back up at Eric, as if her mood didn't change.

"*Sometimes, a cherub may ascend to be a seraph early. I am such an example of this, as the great distress I was in on Krehaul allowed me to transform,*" she finished her answer.

Eric nodded, "I see."

The two kept their eyes locked on each other. A silent moment passed, followed by the seraph smiling and letting out a small giggle. The sound was like that of the chime of a small bell. It was absolutely gorgeous to Eric's ears. The noise, nonetheless, snapped the human from his stare as his cheeks blushed.

"Sorry...I don't mean to stare," he said, looking away quickly.

"It's alright...another question though, perhaps?" She inquired.

"Oh, yes," Eric stated. He then asked, "How do you know the human language?"

"How else would I be able to communicate with you?" she asked back.

"So, what you are using now is not your people's language?" Eric added.

"Of course not," Celestial said plainly.

Eric had his eyes fixated on her, yet she kept perfectly still. A few seconds passed. Seconds that he refused to move even a single muscle of his body, not even blinking. Did she enjoy teasing the hunter? Was this why she kept silent? Finally, she surrendered to his gaze.

"Fine, if you so wish to know what my language is like..."

The seraph stood and took a stoic pose. She then slightly bent her torso forward, while keeping her head tilted back at a small angle. The upper part of her dress tightened around her belly and waist, leaving what looked more like a bell-shaped gown to hide her legs. She slowly opened her arms to Eric as she spoke ample, feathery words out loud. They sounded as if they could not have been inspired by anything less than a god but was incomprehensible to his brain and caused his mind a great ache. The young man brought a single hand to his temple, then the pain stopped immediately as she silenced the words.

"Was...that your real voice?" he then asked, amazed by the sounds he heard in his ears.

"Yes, but I understand that the human mind has difficulty bearing our language. While I can channel my thoughts to you in your own language, ours are much more pronounced. The human mind is much weaker in comparison to a seraph's. What a whisper is for me, would be like a command for you. It is the basis of the mind-control that our kind is known so much for, especially when we speak to you in our tongue telepathically."

"Incredible..." Eric managed to say in response.

Eric thought to himself if the creature had become more and more talkative over the short time they had been together. Regardless, he was happy she had opened up more to him, and he was truly interested in what she had to say.

Celestial thought to herself as well. She thought about the human before her once more. The seraph had been wrong about him this entire time. He truly meant his words about caring for her and the promise he made about wanting to protect her. While she knew his abilities to guard her life was not on par with hers, she was truly honored by his kindness. Feelings of happiness rose up in her again. Happiness that she went against her dumb upbringing and decided against leaving him.

The feelings she felt earlier when she held his hands came back as well. They were feelings she had never experienced before, and that confused her somewhat. She felt her eyes change when she looked at him as well. As they continued to chat, her eyes began to turn from their usual crimson to a more rose-like pink. The seraph quickly shook it off, unable to understand what it was she was feeling.

Regardless, the two would continue happily talking for quite some time and easily into the late evening and night.

Eric and Celestial had found themselves bonding more than they had thought they would. They knew that sometimes it would had been difficult. Sometimes it would be simply boring. Over time, they knew it would prove to be extremely dangerous.

At one point a few days after staying in the cave, the two even had a small moment in regard to their rations.

"Smoked meat again?" complained the seraph. *"Does that bag of yours contain nothing else?"*

Neither her eyes, nor her crystalline breathed voice in his head betrayed her emotions, though it was in stark contrast to her complaint. She had shown bursts of emotions since the two had been together, though her face expressions never matched it. Even when she was being very expressive, her face would keep to the same, stoic look. This would cause some great confusion at times for Eric. Was she joking, or being serious? Was she happy and content, or irritated and angered? It was extremely difficult to decipher at times.

"Only that, I'm afraid," he eventually replied to the creature.

"I will get sick if I consume anymore," she said. *"You take it."*

She snapped her fingers, and several strips of the pieces of smoked meat appeared in front of Eric's face, hovering in place. He took the meat and sighed, then bit into it. The hunter looked over at her. She was now chipping away at dried fruits, with another handful hovering within her reach. He realized that it was his ration of the fruits that she was eating, and figured that even with her complaints, her sense of humor had not been affected. He was about to voice his disapproval of her eating his rations when she yelled in his head.

"*Get down!*" she commanded.

The words themselves meant nothing, as Eric felt as if gravity had been multiplied a dozen times and he was forced to the dirty floor of the cave. A mere second later, countless bats flown overhead as they spewed from deeper within the dark cave. It was getting late in the evening, and they had just recently woken up.

The small bats repeatedly crashed into one another and into the stalactites that hung from the rocky ceiling. They seemed too confused by their own ultrasounds and poor sight to know where to go without bumping into things. Eventually the horde of flying rodent-like animals found the exit, forming a heavy stream of bodies and wings that lasted for several moments before they were gone.

Eric was mesmerized by the large number of them. Never before had he seen so many! He wanted to capture the moment on paper. The hunter reached into his knapsack and retrieved a small notebook and pencil. On the book's cover was the name of the dead hunter that Eric took the bag from. He quickly scribbled out the name and flipped to the first blank page.

Meanwhile, Celestial had found something of interest herself. One of the bats, a smaller one, had been left behind by the others. It was hitting a stalactite repeatedly in an endless loop that stuck straight down in its path. It would charge forward as fast as it could, but then smack against the rock. The hit would put it into a daze, but its determination went unfazed. It seemed certain that it would pass through the stone on the next attempt; or more likely, it simply forgot about the stalactite's existence as soon as it impacted. The bat would back up, furiously flap its wings and then charge forward, only to smack against the mineral once more.

Celestial found herself attracted to the bat's pattern, and its ignorant determination. After some hesitation, she floated over to the small creature. The bat quickly noticed her and stopped dashing itself against the stone. It turned to face the seraph, its mouth wide as if in greeting. It tried to fly in place, but the irregularity of its flapping wings made it somewhat hover in a figure eight pattern. The seraph smiled at the small bat, then cupped her hands closely around it. She grabbed the bat in a loose psychic grip and gently helped it around the stalactite. With nothing in its way now, the bat shrieked in joy and flew off, - in a curved line. It smacked into another stalactite and began to repeat the previous pattern.

The seraph sighed in disappointment. To her, needing help and being completely dumb were two different things. She had empathy for the first, but no feelings for the latter. It was because of the plain stupidity of the bat, that it was likely to die; either from starvation or splitting its own head open. Knowing she was not going to babysit the animal, she quickly lost interest.

"You do know that bats eat bugs, right?" Eric stated, trying to use her dislike of insects to refuel her interest in the bat.

The hunter was also drawn in by its nature and was attempting to sketch it on paper. His hand was scribbling a few wobbly lines, trying to copy its silhouette. The young man was biting on his tongue as he ever so often glanced up at the bat.

His comment struck her light lightning! Insects, bugs! The tiny, disgusting little vermin! Their segmented parts and many legs, along with the compound eyes and slimy bodies! The simple thought made her skin crawl as if the little monsters were feasting on her.

Eric was right, however. Her opinion of the bat was completely changed in that instant. It may have been dumb, but it was a most courageous beast to battle against those little demons. She elected to help it get out, but how?

"Why don't you just use your powers and carry it outside?" suggested the hunter, seeing her hesitate.

"*And when do you know how to read thoughts, human?*" Celestial responded, slightly annoyed.

"It's just a suggestion, Celest," Eric replied with a grin.

He had been using that shortened version of her name since the two began talking. At first it annoyed her, but she learned to actually kind of prefer it. She felt herself calm once more, then she turned to the bat and approached it again.

The seraph lightly grabbed the bat once more in a telekinetic grip, then carried it to the cave entrance. Once there, she released it into the open, where the bat cheerfully chirped as it flew high into the night sky.

As Celestial was performing this task, Eric thought to himself about her. He surely had met a most curious creature. He found it odd that while she hated insects, she seemed to like a creature that was equally ugly and gross. She was one who seemed to really like him so far yet hate his species. She had powers and abilities beyond that which words could describe, but she would easily overthink the smallest of issues and lose herself as if she was completely blind to the obvious choice. She seemed to be both confident and lonely, and while she tried to appear threatening and intimidating to others, to him she only seemed a bit blunt. It has been to his own surprise that her company has not been terrifying, but instead extremely enjoyable. He then thought about her eyes again. He's noticed that the way she looked at him was changing as well. It used to be when she looked at him, she would give him the usual crimson stare. Yet, now when their eyes met, they would shimmer. Her irides would dance and change to a more pinkish color.

Though he had in the past teased her about this revelation of her eye color, he was coming to a conclusion about his artistic abilities. Quite frankly, he was terrible. He was having difficulties trying to capture life on the sheet of paper. So far, he had the rough outline of the bat's wings and body, but it was all terribly out of proportion. There were two small black dots for eyes, and they were lopsided at best. He hadn't even attempted shading the picture, for that was far from his own abilities.

Celestial, now back from releasing the bat to the outside world, turned her attention back to the young hunter. She stared for an indeterminable amount of time at his ridiculous sketch. Her lack of expression created a feeling of embarrassment in Eric, who suddenly felt the urge to rip the paper from the notebook and crumple it into a ball. Before he could though, she stole the notebook and pencil from his hands and floated them in between the two.

She touched the tip of the pencil to empty space on the paper, moving it with a furious speed but with absolute precision. She quickly drew an image, not through the normal lines and layers as an artist would, but instead from right to left. She shaded the image without even touching the objects, using her powers instead. What had been the result was a perfect, realistic drawing of the bat. It was a near a level of realism that only a photo could capture.

Eric had clearly been defeated by her once more. She handed the book and pencil back to him while his mouth hung in awe. When the notebook had reached his grasp, the drawing looked even better up close.

A small smile appeared on her face, and with it, a single sad tear. Eric simply couldn't understand. It had been very difficult for her to truly express her emotions. Her kind had always taught her to hide them from anyone not her family. 'A seraph who revealed her emotions, would surely die out there', she had been horribly taught. It was because of this, the human before her was getting her all wrong though!

What was she to do then? Was she to allow her expressions to flow freely? She had been trying to be more expressive, though so far it proved to feel unnatural to her. As such, he was unable to understand her at times. He simply didn't know that she much preferred and liked his wobbly but creative sketch over her own lifeless, soulless one.

[XVII]

Several months had passed since the duo left the vast caves. The pair worked together and overcame obstacles that would make any mere mortal parish on their own.

At one point during their journey, they had to cross over a small mountain ridge. As the two made their way around a jumble of boulders, one came crashing down next to them. A large, hairy troll appeared and glared at the couple with its three black eyes, then leapt down and tried to attack the hunter.

Eric managed to get a shot off, but not in time to stop the beast in its rush. The troll slammed one long, strong arm into the hunter and smashed him up against a rock wall. The beast was then grabbed by Celestial in her unbreakable mental grasp. She dashed the creature against the stones and threw its bloody body away, then quickly hovered over to Eric and helped him back up. Luckily, he suffered nothing more than a few bruises.

In the time following that event, the two came across and was forced to fight several other beasts. More trolls stood in their way. Hordes of small goblins, large ogres, and giant snakes. All got in the way of the hunter and creature, and all perished or ran as a result. A sphinx even tried to kill the human but was torn to shreds by his seraph companion.

Eventually, the two came across a vast river that split the province of Avrush in two. The Dusk River, as it was so named, was nearly a kilometer wide and stretched for what seemed like forever. Eric and Celestial pondered about how they would cross, but then noticed a small barge only a short distance away down river.

Upon reaching the small barge, they noticed that it had been long abandoned. The wooden planks making up the square floating platform were rotted in some places, and completely fallen through in others. Overall though, it still looked worthy of floating. The hunter got onboard, then offered his hand to Celestial as help. She rejected the offered hand, instead floating onto the platform without the aid. As she passed Eric though, she gave him a playful grin, earning a small grin of his in return.

Eric pushed the small barge from the shore with Celestial's help, and the two were off. They floated down the Dusk River at a moderate pace matching that of the flow of the cold, murky water. After the first mile, it was quiet, but then Eric heard something emanating from the water around them. It was music. Singing. It was the most gorgeous sound he thought he had ever heard. Celestial was at first not aware of the sound, but then heard it as she saw Eric blindly walking to the edge of the barge. She herself was unaffected; her seraph mind being stronger.

The hunter had a blank expression in his eyes, and his mouth was hanging somewhat open. He reached the very edge of the platform and knelt down. From the water's surface, appeared a woman. She was the most beautiful thing he had ever saw. She was nude, and slowly reached up out of the water with wet hands and rested her arms on either side of Eric as he leaned towards her. The mermaid was singing softly, rising up more out of the water and getting her face closer to the hunter's. The music entranced Eric more as he felt like dropping off into the water to be with her.

Celestial panicked, then used her mental powers to block off the sound from reaching Eric's ears. He immediately stopped hearing the singing and came to his senses. The beautiful mermaid in front of him instantly changed. Instead of being the gorgeous, unclothed woman he saw only a second before, the illusion was shattered by the seraph's assistance. In front of him now was a most hideous, fish-person hybrid. Large black eyes dominated the bald and gray, scaly head.

The mermaid let out a screech at the realization that Eric was broken from its trance. Its mouth opened widely, exposing several dozen long, needle-like teeth. It reached for the hunter with its slimy, webbed hands, but was shoved away by a swift kick to its face.

It recoiled from the kick, flipping backwards and diving into the river. Its long, black fish-like tail was exposed for a half-second as it dove. Eric jumped back, frantically looking around for the monster as he drew his revolver. His heart was pumping hard in his chest at the revelation that he was almost killed once again. Celestial looked around at the murky water around them, then closed her eyes. She focused her energy and sensed everything around them. There. Under the barge.

The seraph reached out with her mind, grabbing the mermaid tightly, then pulling the monster out of the water and exposing its hideous form. Eric didn't hesitate. He cocked the hammer on the revolver and took aim. Pulling the trigger, he planted a silver bullet into the mermaid's skull.

Celestial looked once more at the dead beast, then tossed its body away. She then looked at Eric, who gave her a thankful look in return. The two continued floating down the river in silence after that. As they floated, Celestial couldn't help but feel the pulling urges of jealousy at the idea that Eric thought the mermaid was stunningly beautiful; even if it was only an illusion.

The two finally came to a stopping point along the river. Eric threw a rope out and pulled the barge to the shore. The hunter and creature then stepped off the wooden deck and onto the shoreline.

They had to stop because the river was ending at a massive lake, and they didn't want to be caught out in the middle of the open water. Once on the shore, Eric stretched his legs, then they made way into the dense vegetation of the woods in front of them.

Not quite an hour passed when Celestial came to a sudden stop. Eric paused as well, not sure as to why she halted.

"Celest, what's wrong?" he asked, using the shortened form of her name.

She didn't respond. She instead brought a single finger to her lips. It was a motion that requested him to remain silent. Finally she sensed a creature again. She knew that kind of presence anywhere. It was another seraph.

Celestial's eyes glowed as she made a tree shatter into splinters, revealing the seraph hiding behind it. It was a very old creature, even in regard to the life expectancy they live. It was a male seraph, his white skin hung loosely from his limbs and wrinkled with age. His thinning, pale-blue hair was pulled back into a ponytail and he sported a long mustache and goatee that nearly reached the blade-like horn in his chest.

The seraph rose his hands in a somewhat defensive manner, but he did not cower to Celestial or the hunter.

"*Identify yourself, now!*" Celestial yelled at him.

The old seraph spoke up. His voice was a dry and dusty as his age as he voiced his words to both Eric and Celestial, "***I am Sofos, and I promise you that I am not a threat. I am far too old to fight anymore.***"

"What is it that you want?" Eric asked. His revolver was drawn, but he found himself slightly lowering the weapon.

"***I knew that you two would show up at my home,***" Sofos answered, pointing at the two with one bony finger. "***You two have surely made a mess of things, and even managed to respark the war that ended over a hundred years ago... I remember when the war ended, did you know that?***"

Celestial shook her head, "*I think you're lost, old one.*"

It was Sofos's turn to shake his head. He squinted one red eye at the young seraph.

"*I know exactly where I'm at... I'm home!*" he said with a chuckle. "*Question is... do you two know?*"

"*Of course, we do,*" Celestial shot at him.

The old seraph laughed wholeheartedly, "*Oh, I don't think you do... have you even heard of what's going on out there?*"

"*No... and why should we care?*" Celestial asked.

Eric looked from the young seraph to the old.

"*What is happening?*" he timidly asked.

Celestial gave Eric a quick glance, then sighed. Sofos looked over at Eric and grinned for a moment, but then replaced it with a grimace.

"*It's awful,*" he began. "*Your Order has declared war on all beasts and humans who dare to stay in their way...Entire villages of innocent humans are being slaughtered by the Order just to make an example out of them and get the compliance of other settlements.*"

Eric shook his head. He couldn't believe what he was hearing.

"*They are also burning much of the wilderness around them as a means to wage their petty war...I feared the return of this conflict ever since the day it ended...and now it has returned in full force, and I'm afraid it will end badly for all living things,*" Sofos finished.

"*How do you know all this?*" Eric asked.

"*Has your companion not told you?*" the old seraph chuckled, back to his cheerful demeanor. "*The older a seraph gets, the more acute our minds become to the world around us, while our offensive abilities wane. I can see far and wide without needing to be* there. I can also sense bits of the future... that's how I knew you two would show up."

"Incredible," Eric managed to say. Celestial huffed in annoyance.

Sofos then turned and waved for the two to follow him.

"Come now, young ones. I implore you to stay and rest at my home for a while. I have plenty of food to share."

Celestial crossed her arms and at first refused, but then Eric laid his hand on her arm. She felt a skip in her heartbeat and looked into Eric's eyes. Her irides changes briefly to a pinkish color, then she felt instantly better.

"Come on, Celest," Eric said with a smile. "Some good food, a nice rest. It's just what we need!"

"I don't know... can we trust this 'Sofos'?" the seraph asked.

They both turned, seeing that the old seraph was suddenly right next them. The duo both jumped with a startle, making Sofos laugh out loud. He slapped his knee and smiled widely at the two young ones before him.

He then snapped his fingers, making a pair of pendants appear in front of him. One had the appearance of a gold star with many points. In its center was embedded a small, round crystal ball with three bands of blue and red swirling together in the middle. Sofos pulled the necklace over Celestial's head, hanging the pendant around her neck. The young seraph grabbed the pendant and looked into it. She was amazed by its beauty.

"It's called a regno stone. It's a special gem that allows a seraph to ascend and transform into a monarch seraph for a very *limited time. Very powerful indeed,"* Sofos said. **"Legends say that the stone can only be activated with its matching crystal...and a powerful bond between the two creatures who wear them."**

He then approached Eric, gifting the regno stone's matching crystal. The old seraph placed it in his hand and closed his fingers around it. Sofos then looked up at the young hunter and smiled.

"Take good care of these gems," he said. *"**They could very well come in handy soon.**"*

With those words, the old seraph suddenly vanished in a flash, only to appear a distance away in the forests. He waved the two on.

Eric then took off to follow Sofos. Celestial watched him for a moment, pushing down the odd feelings she had about the hunter once more.

The regno stone... she thought. **It can only work with a bond of love...**

She then floated to catch up and be at the hunter's side.

Once at Sofos's hut, the hunter walked away to get a fire going. Eric's image never left Celestial's head, and she felt butterflies in her stomach. The seraph felt warm every time she thought about him in the last few months, but never have felt these emotions before meeting him. They still confused her.

She thought again about her eyes when she looked at him. The hunter even said it himself; they changed color when she would meet his gaze. They would always change from their usual crimson red to a light pink whenever she looked into his eyes. The only other example that she knew of this happening was when her parents would have looked at each other. Why was she experiencing this?

Why do I keep feeling this way when I think of him? She thought to herself.

"It's because you're in love with the human," Sofos said suddenly to her.

She jumped and stood up, looking around for the source of the voice. Looking over, she saw the old seraph nearby, meditating. He had his eyes closed. Celestial felt a blush rise in her cheeks.

"You're insane. I have no idea what you are talking about," she shot back.

The old seraph laughed. He opened his eyes; his stare was like knives into her soul.

"Don't lie to yourself, young one. I can sense the feelings you have for your human. That is more than just love for another living thing. That's love for a mate."

Celestial refused to meet Sofos's gaze. She crossed her arms defensively.

"I think you're delusional."

Sofos raised one eyebrow, "You're telling me you haven't sensed the feelings he has for you? I can feel it just from your body. You and that human already share a strong bond, considering the short time you've known each other. Perhaps it's the circumstances of your meeting that pushed this bond?"

"Even so, it doesn't matter," Celestial interrupted. "Human/monster relationships are immoral. Wouldn't it be wrong for us to be mates?"

Sofos hovered up beside her; he sat down and closed his eyes.

"You shouldn't let the judgement of the world stand in your path. Love is love. It will always win one way or another. You just need to not fight it. I see not a thing wrong with the deep love between two consenting beings, for it is no different than the love two humans could share. It is no different than the love your own parents shared," he responded, slightly opening one eye and looking at her. Celest just stood there.

Maybe he's right...maybe I should say something to Eric...but what if Sofos is wrong?... She thought to herself. She then felt the old seraph's presence in her head. Celestial pushed him out of her mind.

"He does feel for you the way you feel for him, I can promise you that. You just need to find the right time to tell him," he said to Celestial.

"How will I know?" the young seraph asked.

"You'll know when it's right to tell him. Maybe instead he'll tell you," Sofos stated with a chuckle. "You must figure that part out yourself. For now, though, I must head inside my home. You can always come to me if you wish to speak again."

It was with those words that the old seraph vanished in a flash of light. Celestial was left by herself to contemplate his words.

Maybe he is right... She thought. **Maybe I am in love...and Eric feels the same...**

Deep down in her heart, even if at first she didn't want to, the seraph had hoped that Sofos was right.

Later that evening, Eric and Celest decided to go on a short walk along the shores of the lake outside of Sofos's hut. The sky was without clouds and one could see every star in the night. The moon was bright and cast a glow onto everything. The seraph lowered herself to the ground and physically walked instead of levitating. She left circular footprints in the sand alongside Eric's. Celestial stared out at the ocean. It was a beautiful sight. Eric looked up at the sky and counted the stars. In one hand, he carried a large towel.

They walked and enjoyed the night, then they came to a stop on the beach. The hut was no longer in view, and only the dense vegetation of the forest was behind them. Eric laid out the towel and the two sat down on it to keep out of the sand. They continued to stare out at the water.

Celestial was enjoying the moment, but then felt that something was disturbing Eric. She looked over to him with a slight sense of worry, though she quickly pushed it down.

"Is there something bothering you?" she asked, trying to make her telepathic voice a soothing as possible.

The hunter looked over at her. He managed a small grin, then shook his head.

"It's just... I want to thank you for trusting me Celest," he said, looking at her. "You didn't have to. You could have left me there or even killed me...but you didn't. It just makes me happy that you trust me and how far we've come now."

"*Of course, and this time has been among the best I've had in a long time...even if it has been dangerous,*" Celestial responded with a giggle. "*But enough of that...I feel like swimming. Shall we?*"

She quickly stood and pulled Eric to his feet. He gave her a confused look.

"That sounds great, but...I don't want to get my clothes wet," he stated.

She took a quick glance around, then grinned slyly at him, "*We're alone out here...who said we need to wear anything?*"

A bright red flush made Eric's cheeks burn. She giggled at him.

"Oh...I-uh," he said, stammering. His cheeks still burned. He reached for his shirt, but hesitated.

The seraph giggled once more, then reached her hand out.

"*Why don't you help me?*" she asked.

Eric gently grabbed her hand and held it as it slid back out of the blue, sleeve-like part of her dress. She held out her other hand and they repeated the process with the other sleeve. Eric had no idea that the blue of her hands and arms that extended to cover part of her chest wasn't actually part of her skin, but rather was her dress. The fabric had fit so well to her limbs that it seemed like a soft, silky skin. Once her arms were free of her sleeves, she peeled the dress away and let it fall off of her. She now stood in front of him without a stitch covering her. Her slender, yet voluptuous body was snow white from her head to the tips of her legs. Only the blue of her hair, the crimson of her eyes and the red blade protruding from her bare chest contrasted the white of her skin. Celestial slightly blushed and watched Eric as he examined her body in a loving manner.

"***Well?... What do you think?***" she asked with a smile.

Eric stuttered, "Y-your beautiful. Absolutely gorgeous."

She leaned forward and got an inch from him. The seraph then said with a graceful command, "***Your turn.***"

The blush returned to his face as he reached for his clothes. He quickly removed his duster and shirt, then stepped out of his boots and trousers. The seraph watched him intently the whole time; her eyes turning a bright, shimmering pink. Eric noticed this and felt himself regain some confidence. The hunter then took her hand.

"Let's get in the water, shall we?" he said.

The two got into the water and bathed together under the warm, moonlit night. Once they were done, they left the water and went back to their towel while not bothering to get dressed. The two sat down on towel and laid back, staring out towards the water. The moon hung over the horizon in the distance, casting a bluish glow over the scene.

After a moment, Eric looked over at Celestial. He wasn't staring at her unclothed body, but at her face instead. He always thought she was most beautiful, but he knew he had been seeing her in a different light. She no longer merely captivated his eyes, but also his heart. His eyes then lowered to her chest, to the blade-shaped red fin that protruded from her sternum and between her breasts. He always wondered what that blade was. The hunter decided to gather the courage to ask.

"Celest?" he sheepishly said.

The seraph turned her head to him.

"If I may ask..." he began. "What is that coming out of your chest?"

Celestial's face reddened almost immediately. Her thin arms went to her breasts to cover herself, almost as if out of embarrassment now.

"Oh, I'm sorry!" he quickly said. "Forget that I asked...I didn't mean to offend you."

The blush in the seraph's face faded somewhat, *"No, you're fine...I just wasn't expecting that question."*

She looked down at the fin-like blade herself, *"Basically...it's my heart. It's an extension of my sternum that encases the organ. It allows me to channel my powers through it and sense the emotions of those around me."*

The hunter's eyes widened slightly. His gaze quickly went from the blade to her eyes.

"That's amazing..." he said simply.

"Quite strange, I know," the seraph responded.

"Not at all," Eric reassured.

Suddenly, Eric felt an incredibly strong feeling. There was something that kept drawing him to her heart. It was a strong sense of desire that he couldn't back against.

"...Can I touch it?"

The redness that had disappeared from Celestial's face as they talked, had come back brighter than ever. Eric looked at her with a genuine curiosity. There were strange feelings inside the seraph; like she wanted him to do it as well.

"*S-sure,*" she answered. Her usually smooth voice stuttered in the hunter's mind as she lowered her arms back down; interlacing her fingers together over her belly.

Eric at first thought to retract his request. He had never been this bold with her before, but something inside him kept pushing him. The young man knew it wasn't her doing this. In fact, it felt like it was coming from his heart. The hunter slowly reached out with one hand. She ever so slightly puffed her chest out as he gently placed a few fingers on one side of her horn.

She let out a small exhale as he made contact, her eyes fluttering with the touch.

"You ok?" Eric asked quietly.

"*Yeah, it's just...your hand is warmer than I thought. I wasn't expecting it,*" she answered.

The two looked into each other's eyes as Eric placed more of his hand on the horn. Her cheeks were flushed a bright red, but she didn't appear to be embarrassed any more. Her mouth hung open slightly. Her irides danced and spun, changing into a thousand different shades of pink.

The air became heavy. Celestial's wings appeared from her back, spreading wide and then encircling the two, covering them. She didn't realize she was doing it until Eric looked at the feathered walls around them, then smiled at her.

Celestial's heart wasn't soft to the touch, as the hunter would have thought before. It felt smooth, almost like polished granite. It was also warm. It was warmer than a person's skin. The horn didn't feel fragile in the least. Instead, it felt like it was indestructible. He now had his whole hand resting on it, and he could feel a heartbeat within it.

A heartbeat that was fluttering.

Celestial placed one of her hands on his as he felt her heart. The two stared deeply into the other's eyes. Finally, Eric opened his mouth to say something.

"Celest?" he began. "There's something I want to say..."

She didn't respond. Her eyes blinked twice quickly. The hunter felt her heart rate increase. He gathered the strength necessary to say the next few words that could change his life.

"I...I lo-" he went to say, but she cut him off with one finger pressed to his lips.

The seraph smiled at him, then placed one hand on the side of his face. She pulled his face closer to hers. Their lips nearly came in contact; their eyes closed halfway in the rush of emotions that hit the two of them.

They were about to complete their kiss when the sound of a snapping twig was heard nearby.

The seraph tightened her wings around Eric, then teleported them both to a standing position in an instant. They were now standing side by side, fully clothed again. Eric looked down at himself, then to her. Celestial's powers were truly amazing to him.

A shot rang out, catching the two off-guard. The bullet struck Eric in the chest. He grabbed at the wound and fell to the ground, too shocked to make a noise. Celestial gasped and covered her mouth with her hands. She fought back hard against the tears that quickly pooled in her eyes.

She then felt the presence of several people. They were the presence of people she hadn't felt in a long time. It was an evil feeling. Rage boiled up in the seraph, and her eyes ignited in a bright blue light.

Celestial reached out with her mind and pulled several humans from the bushes. They were all members of the Black Sun, the cult that had captured her family months ago. The disciples struggled in her psychokinetic grasp, then the seraph tore them to shreds. Other disciples rushed out, guns drawn. She yanked the weapons from their hands and crushed their brains inside their skulls without a drop of sweat.

Still more disciples poured out from the tree line. One had in his hand, a red crystal. It was covered in cryptic runes and looked much like the one that Ross had used against her on Krehaul Island. The human tossed the stone towards her as she ripped his head from his shoulders with her powers. The stone managed to land near enough to her to do its evil effect.

Celestial's wings flashed away in a burst of feathers as she immediately felt weak. That damned crystal had once again sucked her energy from her. She dropped to her hands and knees, gasping for air.

"Look at who we found," the cult leader, Mariah could then be heard. She walked out from the shadows, laughing to herself, "The two who managed to set back our plans and make my life a living hell. Do you have any idea what kind of punishments I had to endure after what you two caused? I almost thought I'd never be able to find either of you, but when my scouts spotted you two crossing the Dusk River I couldn't resist a trip."

Eric tried again to stand. He wiped the burning tears from his eyes as he rushed forward to attack Mariah. Right as he got within mere meters of her, the disciple next to her shot him again. The bullet ripped through his chest and the hunter dropped.

"I'm not after you. I'm here for the seraph. My master wants her alive...as much as I'd like to kill both of you." Mariah said.

Mariah laughed as a large, black automobile pulled out from the brush nearby. It had a large steel cage mounted on the back of it.

"There's no point in fighting, seraph. You're coming with us, and this time there won't be a hunter to save you."

The cult leader then took a step towards Eric, saying through gritted teeth, "I want your death to be long and horrible."

She kicked the hunter in the ribs. Eric let out a scream of agony as he rolled in pain.

"*Eric, no!*" Celest screamed.

Mariah looked down at Eric as she grinned evilly, "Stay here and suffer."

She waved towards the automobile, motioning her men to get on board. They loaded Celestial onto it and took off, leaving Eric to die.

Eric managed to fight through the pain and stood again. He clutched his wounds where the bullets hit him. The young man could feel blood covering his hands and drenching his clothes. He then looked and watched powerlessly as the vehicle left.

"Celestial!" Eric screamed. He felt himself getting light-headed and collapsed again. The hunter fought to keep conscious, but then passed out.

[XVIII]

Celestial sat in her cell. She had her knees pulled up to her chest; her arms wrapped around her slender legs. Her dress tightened around her as if to act as a barrier to the outside world. There were no more tears to be shed. The seraph glanced around at the cell that imprisoned her, and past it at the barren and rocky walls that made up the caves of the vast Rigpoint Mountain range. She lowered her head and closed her eyes. It felt as if there was no hope left.

It had been two weeks since being taken once again by the Black Sun. Two weeks since seeing Eric, the one she realized she loved, being left to die. His image entered her head for the thousandth time, and she felt her heart break once more. She had lost the only person left in her life. He was left there by the water to die slowly...she had hoped he passed quickly; he didn't deserve any suffering. She knew she wasn't ever going to see him again, and the thought only made her feel worse.

The creature lowered herself onto her side and down to the cold, dusty ground. She tried once more to sleep, though she knew it would only prove to be another sleepless night.

Mariah walked by the seraph's cell. She paused, looking over at the creature curled up against the back wall. The sad sight made a grin spread across the cult leader's face. She wanted nothing more than to just kill the thing and move on but seeing her suffer brought her some form of enjoyment. Demothesis wanted her alive as his own personal toy, and his wishes were best granted. It was the only thing keeping her from just ending the monster's life for her own enjoyment.

At least I finally took care of that damn hunter. She thought to herself before continuing on.

She continued walking along through the cavern's passages, heading to her personal quarters. The mountain range of Rigpoint had served as the primary base for the Black Sun for years. It was favored for its remote location and the slew of wild beasts from which to harvest subjects for their inhumane experiments.

As Mariah walked to her quarters, she passed a group of disciples huddling and chatting quietly around a few overturned crates. As soon she was noticed, the disciples jumped to attention and went about on their duties. She scoffed and shook her head, momentarily gritting her teeth.

"What are you idiots doing? You're supposed to be watching the seraph! Take her to Master Demothesis now!" she yelled at the three disciples.

"Yes ma'am! Moving ma'am!" the lead disciple yelled, bringing a closed fist to his chests in a salute.

They took off towards the creature's cell. Mariah shook her head again. Those three eagerly volunteer to guard their captive for whatever reason, but then don't...She'd have to take care of them later. She turned and continued towards her quarters.

Back at the cell, Celestial continued to lay still. All she could think about was how she felt she had failed Eric. She thought it was all her fault he was dead and that she was back in the Black Sun's clutch. The seraph sobbed silently to herself without tears and held her eyes tightly shut, not knowing if she wanted to live any longer.

She laid there motionless for several moments, then heard footsteps approaching her. The creature opened her eyes to see three disciples standing over her.

"Well hello gorgeous," one of them said, before stomping on her head and rendering her unconscious.

Eric's head pounded as he regained consciousness. He slowly sat up; his torso was sore. The hunter found himself on a bed in a small log cabin. The young man looked around the room, then down at himself. There were two large white bandages where he was shot.

How in the hell did I get here? He thought to himself.

The oak door to the room unlatched and opened. Through its threshold entered a man Eric had not seen in a while. His appearance shocked him.

"Jonathan?" Eric asked groggily. The sunlight leaked into the room through the windows, filling it with a warm yellow light.

"Look who's awake. That's twice now you owe me, you know that?" Burke responded with a grin.

Eric couldn't believe it, how was it possible?

"Wait-what? What happened?" Eric asked. "How did I end up here?"

Burke walked over to Eric's bedside and pulled up a chair. He sat down and leaned back, looking out the window.

"I couldn't believe that you betrayed the Order. There wasn't any way," he began. The old hunter's voice was low and sullen, "We may not have known each other for long, but I know you better than you think. You have a good heart, Eric. I know you didn't kill Ross, that a creature did it instead."

The light of the sun shone between the blinds covering the window, casting horizontal lines of shadow across Burke's face as he paused. He looked at Eric, who interrupted him.

"Burke, it wasn't the creature's fault. He imprisoned a seraph and raped her for several months...I just freed her, and she took her revenge."

Jonathan nodded, "So that was the seraph that saved you from your execution then?" Eric nodded back, "Well that explains a lot.... though I still don't think you betrayed us. You did what was honestly right."

"Thank you, Jonathan, it means a lot to hear that...what about the Order though? What's happening in the rest of the world?" Eric asked worriedly.

"You're still being hunted across Avrush. The Holy Leader knows that you're still in the province. You're just lucky I found you before the Order did," Burke said as he continued. "I patched you up as best I could and carried you to the nearest road. David met me there with a carriage and we brought you here to Ivoryport. Luckily for you as well, this town has rebelled against the Order and isn't looking to kill you... You had lost a large amount of blood, but luckily the surgeon who lives here was able to stabilize you."

Eric nodded again, then asked, "How long have I been out?"

Burke simply responded without a change in emotion or tone, "Two weeks."

Eric was aghast. He could only stare at his old chapter leader incredulously. **Two weeks? Has it really been that long?...** He wondered. Then he suddenly remembered something. Celestial's image appeared in his head.

"Celest!" he cried out. Burke seemed startled by the sudden outburst, "Those bastards have Celest! I have to go save her!"

Eric began to jump out of bed. His wounds were still sore and throbbed in pain. He searched for his prosthetic, but Burke laid his hands on Eric's shoulders and slowly tried to push him back onto the bed.

"Listen, I know it's a lot to take in... but I don't think your seraph is alive. That cult is known to experiment on creatures, and then killing them," he slowly said.

Eric stared at him in disbelief. He shook his head, "No, she's still alive. I know it. Their leader wanted her alive for a reason. Otherwise they would have killed her already... and... if she is dead...then I won't stop until they all are too."

Burke respected the hunter. The old man smiled to himself. He then glared at Eric's bandages. Seeing the large, white clothes wrapped around the young man's torso didn't inspire confidence in his condition.

"Even so...you're in no condition to fight right now. You need to rest," he said.

Eric shook his head. He didn't care what condition he was in. He was hellbent to find Celest. He responded, "That is not going to stop me. I'm going after her no matter what."

The room was silent for a few moments. The two hunters had their eyes locked onto each other. Burke watched as he saw a fire burning in Eric's eyes. He saw fierce determination to find and protect the creature he had sworn to defend, but he also saw something else. He knew what it was, he found the young hunter and the seraph at the same time as the cult did. He saw the kiss they nearly shared. He decided not to push the thought onto the young man, though.

Finally, the old hunter sighed and responded, "You don't give up do you? Alright then, but don't expect to just go in and win. You'll need help."

Eric gave Burke a quizzical look, "Who? The Order sure as hell isn't going to do anything. So beside you personally, who could possibly help?"

Jonathan smiled again. He patted Eric on the shoulder and then stood and walked to the other side of the room. From there, he retrieved Eric's prosthetic leg and handed it to him. Eric began attaching it to the scarred stump below his knee.

"I know a few people who could help...but we'll need time to learn more and find where the enemy hides, but we'll find them yet."

Burke reached into his pocket and retrieved a small folded sheet of paper. He gave it a quick glance before putting it away, "Get dressed and come on. It's going to be a long road ahead."

The old hunter finished his statement and began for the door. Eric only responded with a silent but determined look, followed with a nod.

Celestial's head hurt. Bad. She reached up to hold her head, but her hand hit something metal. She opened her eyes and saw what looked like black glass over her face, shading anything she saw like a cloudy overcast. The seraph was laying on a stone bed inside an ancient, rock walled room. She looked down at herself. Most of her body was covered in shiny metallic plates, whose surfaces where etched with arcane writings. The plates glowed slightly with some sort of mystic power.

"Awake already, it seems," said a voice with a chuckle.

The seraph looked over and saw a tall man with slicked blond hair. The stranger must have been in his early thirties or so and had deep, black eyes. He gave a slight grin as he approached her. He wore garments that were similar to the ones worn by the disciples, but more elaborate in design with gold inlays and thicker material.

"I am the leader of the Black Sun...and your new master," the man said with an evil tone. He then bowed slightly and gestured to himself with one hand, "I, am Demothesis."

Celestial leapt from the table, floating several centimeters off the floor. Her eyes glowed as she tried to grab the cult's leader. He laughed as her own attack turned on her and she was thrown to the ground. She slowly rose back up as he muttered a few quiet commands. In one hand, he held a crystal similar to a soul stone, but was black with more cryptic writings across its surface. It glowed with the same frequency was the armor she wore.

"Foolish creature. You have no free will anymore. You are under my control now," he said, squeezing the crystal.

The armor's glow intensified and gave of a deep tone, one that made her head pound horribly as she screamed in pain and dropped to her knees. Demothesis kept laughing at her torment until he ordered the pain to stop. She stayed on her knees, unable to fully believe what was happening. She couldn't use her powers anymore at her own will...only when forced to.

Demothesis walked up to her, kicking her to the floor and onto her side. She weakly looked up at him.

"You understand now...there's no point in trying to fight back. This armor acts like a soul stone, but the issue with the stones though...they limit a monster's potential...this arcane armor does not. It amplifies your power even beyond what you can normally do...You're mine now, and you will do as I say," Demothesis said, looking down at her with no emotion in his face.

About that time, Mariah and the three disciples from yesterday entered the room and stood at attention.

"Are we ready for the testing, Zealot?" Demothesis asked, looking over his shoulder at Mariah.

"Yes, Master Demothesis. we are ready to commence the tests," Mariah replied. She then waved towards Celestial while looking at the disciples, "You three, take her to the proving grounds."

The three disciples nodded. They moved to the armored seraph and lifted her. The group then walked out of the room and down several long corridors. Eventually they made it to a large, open cavern within the base. Celestial looked around, seeing Demothesis and Mariah off on the side watching. The disciples then tossed her to the ground. She laid there in a heap, then slowly stood up. The armor then took control of her, forcing her to stand straight.

On the other end of the arena was a lapguis. The massive stone serpent stood ready to fight her. It then attacked her by opening its mouth and firing a beam of light at her. The seraph held up her hands, but not due to her own actions. The armor took control as it made her absorb the attack. Her head then pounded as she was forced to attack back with her mental powers. She groaned in pain as she overdid the move, grabbing the lapguis and slamming it into a wall with her psychokinesis. She was then forced to close her hands, crushing the serpent's body and ending its life. On the sidelines, the Black Sun's master clapped his hands.

"Good...but too easy...another one," Demothesis ordered as Mariah looked on with a grin.

A banshee walked out onto the arena. It didn't waste time and screamed a powerful sound wave at Celestial. Her head was squeezed, then she teleported and reappeared elsewhere. The creature kept screaming its terrible directed screech, but the seraph teleported every time just before it hit her.

She didn't want to fight, but each time she tried to stop, pain hit every nerve in her body. She truly felt as if she had no control or free will. It was pure agony. She then was made to attack back. She teleported across the arena and charged a ball of shadow energy, throwing the overcharged dark orb and disintegrating the banshee. Her own attack also caused physical pain to herself. She was being forced to put more energy into the attacks than she safely could.

Demothesis chuckled, "Impressive, but I want to see more...keep them coming. I want to see the fullest extent of her powers."

Celestial felt devastated. She felt like there was no way out. Any ounce of hope she may have had was completely gone. She would be stuck in the cult's control until she died. The armor hurt her, forcing her to concentrate on the fights. Creature after creature. Fight after fight. She killed them all. Even when they made her outnumbered, she unwilfully and painfully beat every challenger into death. She was forced to use every attack she knew and used them all far beyond what she safely could. Her entire body hurt. Her body was screaming for the fighting to stop. She just wanted it all to end.

Finally, Demothesis held out his hand, motioning the fights to stop. Celestial then felt all her remaining strength drain as she fell to the ground in a heap.

"That's enough for today," he said, waving the seraph away, "Take her back to her cell. There's much planning to be done."

The three disciples ran over and began dragging her. On the way to her cell, they were talking to one another. Then one turned to her.

"Back to your new home you go...I think we should all celebrate your victories..." he said, a sick grin spreading across his face.

That disgusting stare gave her the most sickening feeling in the pit of her stomach. All she could do was cry and hope she wasn't heard.

Eric sat impatiently. He glanced at pocket watch, counting the seconds and minutes. He was tired of waiting. After a week of searching, a week of interrogating disciples they've captured during their search; they think they finally found where Celest was being kept. Now he just had to wait while Burke planned their attack.

The young hunter couldn't stand the wait. He kept tapping his foot against the floor of the patio repeatedly. Finally, he stood up from his seated position on the wooden bench and opened the front door to the home. He walked inside, paying no attention to the various decorations and trinkets that were lazily placed around the front room. A nearby radio was on, discussing the various events happening across the province.

Nobody else was in the room, and Eric huffed out of annoyance. He continued into the hallway; moving past the small, modest bathroom, the bedrooms, and then finally to the last door.

Eric placed his ear to its sanded-smooth wooden surface. He could hear a distant, muffled, conversation on the other side.

Who could Burke be talking to? Eric asked himself.

He listened more, not able to understand the muffled voices. Then, he could hear someone approaching the door from the other side.

Eric stepped back a couple meters, then leaned against the wall of the hallway. The door clicked as it unlocked, then opened quickly. Jonathan came through like he was in a hurry, almost running into Eric. The old hunter stopped in his tracks, clearly surprised at the young man's unexpected appearance.

"Oh, Eric! Ha!" the old man exclaimed, placing his hand on Eric's shoulder. "You scared the hell out of me! Haha!"

Eric didn't smile, he only simply asked, "Is everything ready to go? I'm tired of waiting while she's in danger."

Burke's face turned to a look of seriousness. The wrinkles on the old hunter's face creased as he frowned. He gripped Eric's shoulder tighter.

"We're just about ready to go. I was on my way to get you," Burke said, pulling Eric into following him down the stairs and into the house's basement.

The two hunters made their way down the stairs. At the bottom, it opened up into a small concrete room. The musty smell that accompanied most basements was not absent here. The floor lacked any covering, save for a brown rug that laid out in the center of the room. On top of the rug, a shambling table stood. Various items, such as papers and a pictograph projector covered the table as a single bulb gave a dim yellow light to the room as it hung from its thin wire.

Standing around the table were two others. One was David. Dark shadows were cast under the large hunter's eyes. Even after Eric's accusation, David elected to stay by Eric's side and give support.

Eric nodded to David, who curtly returned the nod. The other person, a woman, Eric did not know. She wore the usual hunter's duster and hat. One visible grey eye looked at Eric, the other was hidden by her long, blonde hair. She gave a small smile of friendliness towards Eric, reaching her hand out to shake his.

When they shook hands, the woman gave a slight bow of the head, her smile widening.

"I am Alice Winters, good to meet ya," she said.

"Alice here was to be our new hunter from another chapter before the whole ordeal happened with you. Because of what the Order has turned into, she left with us," Jonathan said, gesturing towards the female hunter.

"Yessir, but it seems that our worries about this cult though have materialized into something more serious," Alice stated, resting her hands on the table. "Using the seraph they took from Eric, they captured the three Guardians...for what though, we don't know yet. That seraph probably does though."

Behind the woman, a white screen came to life as the pictograph projector flickered on. Several black and white photos were then displayed. The pictures appeared to have been taken from within dense brush. In the background was a large lake, and the focal point of the photos was one of the Guardians being beaten mercilessly by a force unknown. Then, the photos showed another creature with several the Black Sun disciples on either side of her. It was Celestial. She was covered in metal plates and had a helmet covering her head and face. The metal plates were covered in arcane etchings.

The seraph was glowing in an aura as her own powers overcame the mythical creature. Celestial appeared in a state of constant pain as she clearly had no control over her movements; being forced to use her powers past what she safely could. Under the helmet's visor, her mouth was twisted in a scream of agony as she was forced to attack again.

The photos continued changing, showing the cult members rushing the Guardian. They captured it in an arcane cage not unlike the one that held Celestial. The projector then shut off.

The pictures hit Eric like a knife. He could feel his heart being wrenched at the sight.

How could I let her get captured by these monsters? I promise I will save you Celest...I just hope you can forgive me.

Eric fought to hold back tears. He then said in a low and shaken voice as it rose to a hurt and angered yell, "I have to save her, those bastards are hurting her!"

He slammed his fist on the table; it rattled with the hit. His head hung low as he couldn't begin to imagine the pain that Celestial was in. Alice placed her hand on his. Eric looked up into her eyes as a single tear ran down his cheek.

"I promise you we'll save her. We'll all be at your side the whole way," she said with a voice as soft as a mother's.

Eric looked around the room at the others. Jonathan stood with his arms crossed. He gave a slight smile to reassure his fellow hunter. David gave another curt nod to Eric, looking determined to help stop the cult. He felt better, knowing he had friends to back him up in his time of need. He would make sure to stop the cult and bring Celest home and into his arms no matter what.

"We have some final preparations to make," Burke said. "Then, we'll be ready to head out."

"When?" Eric asked. He was done waiting.

"Tonight, we leave," Alice said, pointing to a map of Avrush that was spread out on the table. She pointed to a point on the map that was circled, "That's where we now know the cowards are hiding."

The point circled on the map was at a remote location in the mountain ranges of Rigpoint Mountain.

"And that's exactly where we'll be heading as well," Burke cut in. "We know their base is underground much like what they had on Krehaul Island. With that mountain range being a part of an active volcano, the area probably isn't the most stable. So, we'll go in, rescue your seraph, then level the whole base with demo."

The old hunter pointed to the other side of the room. Piled in the corner was several demolition charges. Eric was surprised at the explosives. He looked back at Burke with one eyebrow raised.

"How in the hell did you get all that?" Eric asked in a shocked manner.

Jonathan laughed, then replied, "Sometimes, some things just simply go 'missing'. The explosives were actually stolen by the cult...I just happened to steal it back."

Eric grinned, he was gaining more confidence in what was going to happen.

"Well alright then," Eric said, straightening his stance. "Why don't we get down to business and kick some ass?"

The others smiled and looked around at each other, they all seemed ready.

"Sounds good hunter," Burke said with pride in his voice. "Oh, and Hahn?"

Eric looked at him, his eyebrow raised in question. Burke tossed a small leather pouch to him. The young hunter opened the pouch to find a glowing blue soul stone within it. He instantly knew it was Vesuvius. Eric then looked back up at Burke with a surprised face.

"It's good to hunt with you again," the old man said with a grin and a wink.

[XIX]

The black armored carriage was nearing the Rigpoint Mountains. The mountain range grouped in a massive cluster that stretched for miles, with a volcano squatting in its center. Eric stared out the window as the carriage rushed down the dirt path. His face showed no signs of emotion; he just stared out the window with a blank expression. After a moment, Alice tapped him on the arm, breaking him from his trance. He looked over at the female hunter.

"You seem worried. That seraph must mean a lot to you," she said with a look of sincerity on her face.

Eric replied, "She means the world to me. I saved her from Krehaul Island after both her parents were murdered by these same freaks. She was taken from me by Ross...who did horrible things to her before I freed her again."

He looked away, sadness crept into his voice, "I promised I would protect her from all danger...and I failed. I have to rescue her."

Alice rested her hand on his shoulder, giving him a warm smile, "She'll be okay. We'll get her out of there, I promise you that."

Eric looked back at her, managing a smile in return. After a moment, she reached forward to the front of the carriage and banged on the sliding metal plate separating them from the carriage driver.

"How close are we?" she yelled over the hollering winds when the plate slid open.

"We'll be there in 5 minutes ma'am," the driver responded, then slammed the plate back closed.

"Alright let's do this. Get ready hunters!" Burke ordered, racking a round into his rifle's chamber.

Eric and David followed suit, preparing their rifles. Alice checked her revolvers, then pulled a soul stone from her pocket. Eric looked at it for a moment, then grinned. He checked his pouch to be sure Vesuvius was still there. The carriage then made its stop at a clearing on the northern end of Rigpoint Mountain. The four humans on board leapt from the carriage's belly.

"I'll be posting a few miles down the road. I'll pick you up in an hour's time," the driver called out from his seat atop the steel carriage.

"Sounds good, you'll hear from us," Alice replied.

She then squeezed her soul stone and uttered the arcane words to summon her beast. Eric noticed and followed suit. He figured the more monsters they had ready, the better. Twin blue fogs of smoke appeared from their stones and took the shape of two monsters.

Vesuvius was released from his stone, letting out a roar. Next to Eric's dragon, a nearly identical azure dragon appeared from Alice's stone. The female dragon returned Vesuvius's roar with her own. The two beasts then looked at each other in satisfaction. Alice and Eric also gave each other a surprised look. Then they both smiled and laughed.

"You got an azure dragon too?" Eric asked with a grin.

"They're loyal and effective," the other hunter replied.

It then went quiet. The four humans glanced around at each other, all nodding in affirmation that the mission was a-go. Eric began to move towards the mountains, but Burke grabbed his arm. Eric felt a pang of aggravation for a moment. He turned to the old hunter.

"What now?" Eric asked, annoyance creeping in his voice.

Jonathan pointed to the wood line around them. From the shadows, more than a dozen duster-clad people revealed themselves. They were all hunters, but they each wore a blood-red band around their right arm. Two of the hunters approached their group.

"Earnest York, of the Driftwallow, Avrush Chapter." York said, shaking the hands of Burke and Eric.

The other did the same with a grin, "Michael Cummings of the Beaksturm, Usora Chapter. We're all ready for action."

Burke nodded, "Good, let's get moving. There's no time to waste."

Eric looked at Jonathan, confused.

York saw Eric's confusion and clarified what was happening with a wicked grin, "Do you think all hunters are just blindly following along with the Holy Leader? That man is a nutcase and a tyrant. After we destroy this cult, we're going after the Cathedral."

Burke then nudged Eric with his elbow, "Welcome to the newly formed Preservation Coalition of Usora. Not every province is going along with how the Order is leading things."

The group laughed, then got serious and moved to get things started. Michael Cummings paused and looked at Eric. The young hunter couldn't make eye contact; he felt shame at Michael's stare. He gripped Eric's shoulder and had a look of sympathy and understanding on his face.

"It's good to see you again Eric. It really is. Let's do this...let's kick some ass and avenge Joey," Michael said.

Eric looked up at Joseph's older brother. He nodded. Michael smiled again and then turned and ran to meet up with the others. York jumped up onto a rock so everyone around could hear him.

"Alright lads! The Order may have failed and became evil, but we as hunters still have a job to do, and the fire in our hearts to defend our homes still burns hotter than a lava troll's ass!" York yelled to the hunters. "They got a taste of the Pratertown Chapter on Krehaul Island and ran away like cowards when we got there! So, let's get in there and introduce ourselves to those poor bastards!"

"Let's hunt!" all the hunters hollered in unison.

The twenty hunters formed up, weapons at the ready as they made their way towards the cult's base. The three chapter leaders took point, with Eric and Alice right behind them. The female looked over at Eric, a confident grin spread across her face. He looked over at her, then grinned as well. He felt the fire in his heart burn brighter.

I'm on my way Celest...hang in there. Eric thought.

The back of her helmet hit the wall as Celestial yanked her head back in pain. She gritted her teeth, trying to kick the disciples away from her, but then a bolt of lightning ran up her body and she screamed in pain. The other disciples laughed and hit her with the cattle prod again, sending more of the agonizing jolts of energy into her. She instinctively tried to use her powers, but her head started pounding as the helmet and armor stopped her.

"Come on sweetheart, we figured you'd love this by now!" one of the disciples said with a wicked grin.

The others kept laughing. They threw a bucket of water on her, then hit her again with the cattle prod. She screamed in agony and went limp. She felt her strength just drain.

"Hurry up, we don't have time. We have to be at congregation soon. We'll deal with her later," another of the disciples then said.

The first one dismissively waved him off, balling his hands into fists. He swung hard, punching the defenseless seraph in the gut. The two disciples were silent as they watched.

The hit knocked the air out of her. She let out a yelp of pain as she wanted to double over but couldn't due to the chains holding her wrists up. She knew she was spared from the disciples' other "fun" for the time being, but that they'd be back soon. She was tired of it all, she just wished they'd kill her already.

Why must this happen? She thought as tears ran down her face.

The time passed painfully slow. She took several more hits to her abdomen, then it was over for now. The disciple stepped back, rubbing his knuckles and stretching his hands after throwing the hits.

"Next time beauty...don't fight us so much...I'll be back to get what I want later," he said with an evil laugh.

A moment of silence permeated the cell, then a series of echoes from the halls; the sounds of fighting in the distance. A bell alarm sounded outside the cell. The disciples looked at each other, then ran out of the cell as the door closed and locked.

What's happening? Celest weakly wondered.

She hung by her wrists. Her body was still limp, her abdomen throbbed in pain; the burns from the cattle prods still stung. She slowly raised her head in attempt to listen.

The fighting sounded as if to be getting closer. Gunfire rang out in the halls and the sounds of monsters clashing echoed. After what felt like an hour, it died out. Celest rested her head back against the wall and closed her eyes. Her mind was racing as she tried to listen for anything. Voices echoed, and footsteps could be heard as the alarm's bell was shot out. Then silence.

"Check this cell, we're going to move down this hallway and clear the next few rooms," the voice of an older man yelled out.

She heard a loud clang as the cell door unlocked, then the loud creak as it swung open. She felt a presence enter the cell slowly. She refused to open her eyes. Was the presence here to finally kill her? She tried reaching out with the blade-like horn protruding from her chest to sense any emotions. Even with her powers heavily limited by her armor, she still felt strong, overwhelming emotions coming from the person in her cell. Then a voice weakly called out, one that cracked with emotion. It was one that reawakened her tired mind and sent a thousand emotions running through her at once.

"...Celest?..." Eric quietly said.

Hearing that voice sent many emotions through her. She couldn't believe what she just heard, it was impossible! She thought her mind had finally broken, that she was hearing ghosts. Yet she had to know. Her eyes shot open as she looked at the source of the voice. Standing in the entrance of her cell, was the human she had fell in love with and thought was dead; and he was crying.

"*Eric...you're alive...*" she managed to say. She felt tears collecting in her eyes. She couldn't believe it.

The hunter ran across the cell and to her side. He went right for the chains bounding her to the wall. He reached into his knapsack, pulling out a set of bolt cutters. He gently clipped the chains around her wrists, releasing her. The seraph collapsed to the floor, but Eric caught her on the way down. He pulled her into a tight hug as they both were on their knees. They both began weeping into each other's shoulders.

After a few moments, Eric pulled back and looked at her helmet. He searched for a way to remove it as his tears left wet trails down his dust-covered face. His hands fumbled around on the helmet's surface, looking for any signs of latches or clamps to take it off.

"How do I remove this thing Celest, please tell me," Eric said, his voice choking up. He looked her up and down as he saw her exposed skin covered in marks of abuse.

"*You cannot...it can only be taken off with the crystal...and the ones that were just in here have it...*" Celestial slowly said.

For the moment, she didn't care. She was so happy to see Eric again. She pulled him into another hug. They sat like that for another moment, then pulled away again. They looked into each other's eyes.

"*Why did you come for me?*" the creature asked.

"I promised you I would protect you..." the hunter whispered.

"*I thought you were dead...*"

Eric gently hushed her. He then echoed a phrase from what felt like long ago, "Don't underestimate me, seraph."

The two shared a quiet laugh. Eric smiled slightly for a second, but he then became full of sorrow again.

"I'm so sorry I couldn't save you sooner...I promise you I tried!" Eric cried out. He looked again at the bruises covering her, "What did they do to you?"

Celest shook her head. She caressed Eric's face. Her touch as still as soft as he remembered.

"**Don't worry about it...I'm better now with you here,**" she said.

Eric kept looking her over at her injuries. He saw the obvious and horrifying signs of her beating at the hands of the cult. He looked horrified. The young hunter could see tears leaking from under her helmet.

His heart broke, feelings of failure hit him hard. **Why didn't I find her sooner?** He thought. Then anger replaced his anguish. He looked into the black lens that hid her eyes.

"I will kill every one of them..." he said, his voice low and with pure hatred creeping into it.

Celestial went to say something in response, but then she froze up. Her body began to glow as she stood, floating a few centimeters above the stone floor. Eric stared for a second, then realized something was wrong. He jumped up and spun around with his rifle shouldered. In the doorway, a Black Sun disciple stood. The man smiled wickedly; in his right hand, he held a black crystal. Eric was just about to pull the trigger when he felt his body being thrown against the cell wall. He dropped his rifle as he was pinned. The disciple started laughing.

Eric strained against the invisible force holding him where he was at. He slowly managed to turn his head to see it was Celestial holding him there with her powers. She groaned in pain as she was forced to do it by the disciple with the crystal.

"Oh, this is too good..." the disciple taunted. "A creature being forced to murder its old master!... You know what to do seraph, finish him..."

The disciple squeezed the crystal, and Celestial screamed in agony as she began to crush Eric with her powers against her will. Eric's face began turning red as he could feel his entire body being smashed by the force. He gritted his teeth and tried to fight it, but he couldn't escape her grasp. He let out a scream of his own as his bones felt like they could snap into pieces at any moment. The disciple laughed as the whole thing happened in front of him.

Celestial's body fought hard against the control of the armor, and for just a moment, she regained control and let go of Eric. He dropped and crumpled to the floor. The seraph screamed, grabbing at her helmet in a vain attempt to remove it as it sent waves of pain over her entire body. Eric quickly regained his composure and drew his revolver, cocking the hammer and firing a single round as the seraph was forced to grab him once again. He felt like he was going to be ripped apart by her unwilling attack.

The bullet left the muzzle just before Eric was grabbed again. It rang out in its deafening blast as the projectile screamed towards its target: the crystal. It hit, knocking the arcane item out of the disciple's hand as it blew the crystal to pieces. Eric was dropped to the floor again. The disciple stared at his empty hand, then down at the broke object. His eyes then slowly looked up at the seraph. She was staring him down like the Angel of Death itself. His skin turned a ghostly white as he realized what happened. His heart felt like it stopped in place as he could only feel pure terror.

The disciple tried to speak but was immediately grabbed by her mental power as Celestial's armor shattered into pieces and fell off of her. The disciple was slammed against the wall with a huge amount of force, shattering bones. He screamed from the pain of the bones turning to dust, then was silenced by Eric firing a single round into his head. Celestial dropped the corpse, then collapsed to her knees while holding her head.

The hunter clumsily stumbled over to her, dropping to his knees as well in front of her. He wrapped his arms around her as he pulled her into the tightest hug he could manage. Her heart shard jabbed him in the chest, but he didn't care. She was freed from her torment. They both began crying as they held each other. After a few moments, once the sobbing stopped but the tears of joy kept running; they pulled away and looked into each other's eyes. Her crimson eyes sparkled and turned to their pinkish color as she got to look at him again without that damned helmet.

She went to speak but was cut off as Eric caressed her face; pulling her in and kissing her. It was deep and full of love. It was everything she had hoped for. Her eyes closed as she melted into Eric's arms, pressing her lips back against his. It was pure bliss; happiness neither of them had felt in a long time. She didn't want the moment to end before Eric pulled away. He continued to hold her face as he broke into the happiest of smiles. She smiled as well, the first in a long time.

"Celest, I-I... uh, ha," Eric said grinning and stuttering.

"*I love you, human,*" Celestial said, cutting him off.

His eyes sparkled at the confession.

"And I love you..." he responded with a slight chuckle.

She let out the first giggle she had in weeks, her chest hurt doing it but she didn't care. She was so happy again. She reached up with one hand and gently brushed his cheek with her fingertips.

They kissed again, sitting on the floor in true bliss. The two were unaware of the large hunter and the dragon that was standing in the doorway.

David let a grin spread across his face. Burke had told him that the two had something between them, but he had never seen anything quite like it before. Though their love was a terrible taboo; he was happy for his fellow hunter.

David cleared his throat and the two newly found mates were both snapped from their moment. They both stood up and looked over at him, their faces flushed a bright red. He smiled a little more. Vesuvius let out a noise not unlike that of a laugh.

Eric went to say something in defense, "David! I-I can explain..."

The large hunter waved him off with a chuckle. He then nodded his head for them to follow.

"Come on love birds, there's plenty of time to get reacquainted later. We still have to level this place."

Eric and Celestial nodded. She floated over to the door. Eric grabbed his rifle and followed suit. David left the cell and started to walk down the corridor. Eric and Celestial paused to look at each other again in the eyes. She smiled and grabbed his hand, interlacing her blue-gloved fingers with his.

"**Let's get out of here...**" Celest said as the two left the cell. She refused to look back.

[XX]

As the two new mates left the dark cell and entered back into the corridor, Vesuvius gave his master and the seraph a curious look. He cocked his head to the side. Eric patted the dragon on the head as he moved passed. Then, satisfied with the situation, the dragon took up position behind them.

Once outside the cell, the group moved down the hallway and into a large storage room. Crates and other containers were stacked and scattered throughout the room, dimly lit by the occasional electric lamps that hung from the rocky ceiling. This room looked as if simply part of a cave system. The corridors, smaller rooms and cells were more finely finished, if not spartan in appearance, in chiseled stone bricks.

"The others should be just ahead in the next hallway," David stated, glancing around the room at the dark spots hidden from the light by the crates.

There it was; movement on their right. Then their left. The group came to a halt. David and Eric brought their rifles up and aimed to either side of the room, being sure to put Celestial in between them. Silence. The seraph closed her eyes and focused. She felt for any signs around the room. Then there it was. That evil, sick, twisted presence, hidden behind a crate. She felt hatred hit her, and her eyes shot open. They glowed a bright blue as the crate hiding the person was shattered into splinters. Now in the open, stood was a cult disciple, another of the group that beat her.

Celestial grabbed him before he could react, slamming him into the floor. Then she rose him into the air, throwing him up into one of the lights. It shattered in a spectacular flash of light and sparks, electrocuting the disciple before he was tossed to the ground again. The whole time, he screamed. While this was happening, the third disciple that abused her came from behind a crate on the other side of the room. He opened fire on the group. The seraph spun, holding her hand out in front of her. She crushed the gun in the man's hands, but not before a bullet managed to hit David. The large hunter fell with a yell, clutching his chest where the round hit. Eric ran to him to try to help, but David just simply waved him away.

"Ugh...I'm fine...it just knocked the wind out of me..." he stated, trying to brush off the injury.

Eric helped David slowly to his feet, worried for his friend. The disciple dropped the destroyed gun and drew his revolver, firing a shot. Celestial redirected the bullet back to the man, hitting him in the gut, then grabbed him with an invisible force. Dragging that disciple across the ground, she slammed him next to the other. She then held both of them down, slowly crushing them into the floor. They began to both scream in agony.

"*These...these monsters...they are the other two who beat me...*" Celestial said, her voice dark.

Eric looked at her. He only ever saw that much hate in her eyes once before. These men, these monsters as she put it, deserved everything they had coming to them. They both screamed in agony as they were further pressed into the floor. Then finally, Eric couldn't stand it anymore. He knew she wanted her revenge but didn't think it was right for her make them suffer. He walked over to the two disciples and shot them both dead; one round in each of their foreheads. They laid limp and their breathing stopped.

Celestial's eyes dimmed, seemingly confused. Eric went to her and placed his hand on her shoulder.

"Celestial...I know you felt as if you had to kill them...but they shouldn't suffer. It isn't right," Eric said sullenly.

She cocked her head, "**What do you mean?**"

Eric tried to smile, "Revenge is one thing, but to make anything, even vile people like them, suffer unnecessarily is wrong. I hope you understand and forgive me if you don't."

She stared into his eyes, then nodded.

"*I think I understand. Thank you, Eric.*"

He nodded back, then turned his attention back to David. The hunter was leaning on Vesuvius, who was helping him stand. There was a large amount of blood covering his shirt and duster. Eric threw off his knapsack, then reached into it and recovered the bandages and gauze from inside its canvas interior.

"We have to patch you up, David. Please sit," Eric said.

The man didn't protest. He dropped to the floor, dropping his duster and ripped his shirt open. The wound looked bad. Eric shoved gauze into it, causing David to wince.

"Damn, not too rough. You're supposed to be helping!" David called out.

Eric chuckled, ignoring his complaint. He wrapped the bandages around his chest, tying it taught against the skin. Once that was done, David reached into his pocket and retrieved a flask. He downed a swig of whiskey, then put his duster back on.

"Alright I'm fine. Let's keep going, shall we?" he then said. The group continued on their way.

After several minutes of walking, they caught up with Burke and the others. They had just finished securing the living quarters of the Black Sun's base. It looked like hell broke loose inside it. Shattered glass, tools and corpses were scattered about. Tables were broken and flipped to be used as cover. Bullet holes riddled the room, along with splatters of blood. The hunters were down several men, but they were holding up otherwise. Among them floated one of the Guardians. It was a small, gray, feline-like creature with two tails that each ended with a red jewel; a third red jewel was embedded into its forehead, much likened to a third magical eye. It floated a meter off the floor in a seated position near York.

Upon entering the room, the small creature saw Celestial and yelped in fear. It quickly floated to be behind York, shaking and slowly peeking from behind the hunter. The seraph felt awful. She remembered being forced to attack the legendary creature. She had hope she could make up for it somehow.

"David, Eric, it's good to see you're both alive. I see you also got your seraph back." Burke said, nodding towards Celestial.

"It is as it seems Jon. Let's get a move on. I'm sure Michael and the others are waiting," David responded.

Burke nodded, then turned to Eric.

"Eric, did you learn anything from your seraph about the enemy? What are they planning?" he asked.

Celestial spoke up for herself, *"The Black Sun used me to capture the three Guardians. Those guardians are the key to releasing Oionos, who they worship, into our world. They plan on using the Guardians to do exactly that. I suspect that their leader, Demothesis, is at the ancient ruins at the peak of Rigpoint now."*

Burke rose an eyebrow at the creature. She stood emotionless as she spoke her words in the minds of every human there. The old hunter was impressed by her ability to speak.

"Well then, I guess we can be glad we took one of the Guardians back, yes?" Burke said. "Once we blow this place, we're going up the hill to take out their leader. We must stop this 'Black Sun' from ever being a threat again. Let's go."

The group of hunters quickly left the living quarters and followed the signs on the wall to the entrance tunnel.

Once out of the room, Celestial tried to approach the Guardian, but it simply kept York between it and her. He seemed to notice, glancing at the small creature and then to her.

"The hell did you do to it? It's terrified of ya," York questioned the seraph.

Celestial felt worse and didn't respond to York's question. The small creature stared at her from over the hunter's shoulder.

"I'm sorry...I didn't want to hurt you..." Celestial said to it, letting her emotions show in the words. The creature looked at her, cocking its head to the side.

Silence was the only thing the group heard as they moved through countless corridors. Eric had a shiver go up his spine. He didn't like the gut feeling he had. Celestial felt it as well, placing her hand on his shoulder in reassurance. Then, the sounds of gunfire were heard in the distance. Several monsters could also be heard fighting as well.

"Pick up the pace hunters, let's go!" Burke yelled. The hunters and the three creatures started running. Once they got close, the sounds of combat grew louder. Soon it became deafening.

They entered the entrance tunnel. It was a cavernous room, opened on one end for vehicles and cargo to leave and enter. It was large enough to hold several small buildings at once. The rocky ceiling was more than a hundred feet high, supported by a dozen rock columns a dozen feet across. Packed around the columns was the explosives that the hunters brought with them; all ready to blow. Several empty and horseless carriages and even a few automobiles sat in the middle of the open tunnel. Large crates and concrete barriers were scattered around the room to act as cover.

Michael and the other hunters were in the middle of the room, surrounded on all sides by the Black Sun. Several the cult's monsters were deployed and helping their masters in pinning down the hunters. In front of it all though, was Alice and Mariah. The female hunter stood in the open, her azure dragon in front of her. Her beast looked worn out but stood her ground as she faced down

Mariah's harpy. Several bullets whizzed past the two human females' heads, but neither moved. They simply stared each other down. Finally, Mariah reached her hand out, yelling her command.

"My harpy, slice the dragon's throat!" Mariah yelled. Her creature flew through the air, gaining a spin as it threw its claws out.

"Korra, dodge it!" Alice ordered.

Her dragon tried to leap out of the way, but the previous fighting had already worn her out. The attack connected, sending the dragon smashing in the ground and sliding a dozen feet back towards Alice.

Alice cried out for her dragon, running to her and kneeling beside the her. The hunter returned the beast back to her soul stone, knowing her dragon couldn't go on without being hurt worse. The harpy then tried to attack Alice directly, but was engulfed in blue fire.

"What the hell?" Mariah said, shocked. She turned to see where the attack came from.

Eric's dragon, Vesuvius, stood furiously. He was unable to stand seeing another of his kind being hurt. He roared in anger towards the cult leader as he started walking towards her. Eric and Celestial followed as they both wanted vengeance. Alice went to draw her weapon but was pulled into cover by a nearby hunter who rushed out to get her.

"Ma'am, with all due respect, please stay in cover. You're going to get hurt!" yelled the hunter. The female hunter huffed in annoyance but stayed instead; firing at a few nearby disciples.

Mariah look shocked at the sight of Eric. She couldn't believe he was still alive. She then gritted her teeth, fuming in anger.

"You! You're supposed to be dead!" She yelled, clenching her fists.

She then reached for more soul stones; summoning a woodfall spider and wraith. The two monsters stood their ground, staring down the azure dragon. Several more creatures on the cult's side then turned to face them as well.

Vesuvius let out another defiant roar. Eric wasn't going to let his creature fight it alone. He shouldered his rifle when Celestial floated past him and took up a place next to the dragon.

"Celest, what are you doing?" Eric worriedly asked. "You're not in any shape to fight."

"*I don't care.*" She responded, "*I won't let your dragon do this alone.*"

Her eyes then glowed. She grabbed both of Mariah's creatures, throwing them back with tremendous force. Mariah's face turned red with rage.

"Get her!" Mariah screamed.

The half dozen monsters around her all moved to attack. Celestial rested her hand on Vesuvius, teleporting them both to dodge the attacks. She then charged an orb of energy, throwing it at a banshee and knocking it to the ground. Another wraith rushed forward, but then was hit by the dragon with a belch of hellfire. Celestial quickly moved back to the dragon's side. They watched as the other creatures slowly approached them. An orc then charged. She grabbed it with her mind, slamming the orc to the ground, shattering its bones. It was then finished off by Vesuvius; the dragon biting down on its head and crushing its skull with his jaws. He let out a roar, eyeing the other enemy beasts. Then, as if from nowhere, he was attacked by a minotaur that charged the dragon.

"Behind you!" Celestial yelled.

Vesuvius spun to see his attacker but was hit hard. The dragon was thrown back by the hit and landed on his side. He tried to get up, but the minotaur rushed him again, trying to gore the dragon with its horns. Celestial tried to help but came under attack by a wraith. Eric saw this happen, and took aim at the minotaur, firing several silver bullets into the bull-like beast from his lever-action rifle. It flinched and burned at the impacts and soon dropped dead.

Eric then ran over to Vesuvius. He dropped to his knees next to his creature, returning him to his soul stone for safety. The hunter then stood back up. He felt anger rush through him as he threw his rifle back to his shoulder, firing at the disciples that took cover nearby.

Celestial ripped the wraith into pieces, then tore a chunk of stone from the floor. The seraph smashed the stone into the giant woodfall spider, crushing its head. She then used the same stone as a shield for Eric, blocking several bullets that nearly hit her love.

A banshee kept up its attack from a distance, aiming for the seraph. Celestial teleported out of the way of the deadly sound wave, then fried the monster's brain with her own energy.

Mariah watched on, fuming in anger. She couldn't believe they were being beaten by a bunch of beings she considered weak.

Under the covering fire of her disciples, Mariah made her escape from the fight to rendezvous with her master.

Eric continued to fire at the enemy, only pausing to reload. He had no concern for his safety, not realizing he had no cover from the hostile bullets that smacked into the ground around him. Michael saw this and rushed out and pulled Eric into cover behind a concrete barrier.

"The hell are you doing?" Michael said, "You're going to get yourself killed!"

They looked at each other for a second, then Eric nodded and they both started to fire at the disciples as they shot back.

Celestial glanced around, looking for Eric. She then saw him behind cover, firing at some disciples who were returning his his shots. The seraph then started floating as quickly as she could towards Eric, failing to notice a stick of tossed dynamite stick rolling towards her. It detonated and shook the entire tunnel, filling it with dust.

Eric's teeth rattled at the blast, then he started coughing as the dust became extremely thick. He could barely make out Celestial in the distance. She was trying to stay on her feet. The exchange of gunfire continued throughout the tunnel around her, with neither side able to see the other. A bullet then struck Celest in the shoulder, causing her to scream and fall to the ground.

"Celest!" Eric yelled, leaping out of cover to run towards her.

Michael cursed to himself and shook his head, looking over at Jonathan. The old hunter spit out a lip full of tobacco, then cupped his hands around his mouth to yell.

"Hunters, pin 'em down!" Burke yelled to the other hunters, who promptly threw out more bullets towards the cult in an attempt to keep their heads down.

Eric reached Celestial as she was attempting to stand again. Bullets smacked the ground all around them. Eric grabbed Celest's hand as they started to run back for cover. As they ran, a bullet hit Eric's prosthetic leg; knocking it out from under him. He fell to the ground, unable to stand. He tried to fix it when Celest grabbed him and painfully squeezed her mind, teleporting them both back to Michael.

Joseph's older brother was still firing back over his cover, only giving a relieved glance towards Eric and Celest. The young hunter sat and leaned against the barrier they hid behind. He then reattached his prosthetic, noting its damage but otherwise saw it was still serviceable. Celestial grabbed her shoulder in pain. A trickle of blood ran from the injury. Eric stared at the wound, then hesitantly reached for his pouch. He pulled out an old soul stone; the very same stone Gyrog was bound to before he died. He held it up to the seraph, who's eyes widened at the sight. She physically winced.

"Celest please...you're hurt. Please let me put you in a soul stone. You'll be safe in it," Eric said with a worried tone.

"*No... I can't... please don't make me...*" Celest begged.

Eric knew why she didn't want to. It reminded her of all her past imprisonments. He looked into her cherry eyes as they were locked with his. They glimmered with tears.

"I promise you I will release you from it later...I know you hate the stones...but you're hurt, and I don't want to lose you," Eric said, his voice choking up.

Celestial continued to look into his eyes. She knew he was worried about her, but she couldn't do it. She slowly shook her head.

"...Please...I don't want to lose you..." Eric quietly pleaded once again.

She shook her head again, then leaned in to kiss Eric gently. Their lips parted, and they looked into each other's eyes mere inches away.

"**I promise you won't lose me,**" she said, gently brushing her hand against Eric's cheek. After a few moments, Eric slowly nodded.

She then stood up, still clutching her wound.

Eric watched her as she left the safety of their cover. He yelled for her, but she ignored him and floated out into the center of the fight. Bullets whizzed past her, but she refused to let her petty fears get the best of her. She could feel her parents watching over her; giving her strength. Her eyes glowed a bright blue light as she gathered her power. Black slit pupils unfolded from the centers of her eyes, focusing her energy. After several moments, she threw her arms out, and a wave of psychokinetic power pulsated throughout the cavernous room.

The force harmlessly passed by the hunters, who felt it as if it was simply an earthquake. The force of the attack immediately blew back the cult's automobiles and carriages, violently tossing and smashing them into the walls. The several dozen cult members and their monsters were also thrown back with great force. Their weapons were ripped out of their hands by the seraph's power. Once the attack was over, Celestial closed her eyes and collapsed to the floor, greatly weakened after expending all her energy in the attack.

Behind the hunters, at the end of the tunnel, a train of black armored carriages came into view. They rushed into the cave and roughly came to a halt, their doors already open.

"Come on, let's get out of here!" The lead driver yelled across the distance.

The remaining hunters jumped up and began running towards their ride. Only Eric stayed behind, running in the opposite direction towards his mate. Fire from one of the nearby wrecked automobiles blew out, igniting the fuel that leaked from its fuel lines and across the floor. The blaze separated Eric from Celestial. He was about to try to run through the fire when the seraph's body began to glow. She was lifted into the air and floated safely through the fire as a barrier of protective energy surrounded her.

Once she was in arm's reach of Eric, she was released by the invisible grip that held her. The young man caught her and looked around to see who was responsible for it. He turned and saw one of the Guardians floating a few meters behind him. The legendary creature stared at him curiously.

"Thank you," Eric said, emotions showing in his voice.

The Guardian smiled, then turned and started floating towards the carriage. It was then cut off. A strange-looking seraph, donned in the same kind of armor that Celestial wore, teleported in front of the Guardian. The odd seraph grabbed the creature, screaming in an unholy agony, then disappeared. Eric cursed to himself but continued to run. He had to get back to the transport, then go after the Guardian.

The surviving hunters were taking cover behind concrete barriers that separated the transports from the disciples. The members of the Black Sun were still trying to recover from Celestial's attack; only a few of them were rushing for their weapons.

Eric, carrying the wounded seraph, ran back to the group. Once there the hunters started to board the carriages as the huge horses whined and kicked at the ground, ready to take off. Eric laid Celestial on the floor of the carriage, then turned and saw David staying behind. He rushed over to the hunter's side.

"David, what are you doing? Let's get the hell out of here!" Eric yelled, grabbing the man's shoulder.

The large hunter merely shook him off. Eric looked back at him confused.

"No, I'm not going to make it...that hit did more damage than I thought," David said, pain tainting his voice.

Eric shook his head, "No... There's no way you're dying here! Let's get out of here and blow this place to hell!"

David laughed, then turned and started coughing and hacking. The violent hacking forced him to catch himself on a concrete barrier. He cleared his voice and stood back up straight.

"That's just it..." he shrugged, "There's no way to blow the demo with a timer. These bastards will have it disarmed before it goes off, so someone is going to have to stay behind to light the flash fuze manually... I'm a dead man anyways, so I'm doing it."

Laying on the ground next to them was a length of the fast-burning flash fuze. The long cord snaked across the floor and off towards the first set of demo charges. Eric shook his head again. He felt his voice choking up.

"No, there has to be another way..."

"There isn't another way. I'm not afraid of death, and I always figured I'd go out with a bang. Get out of here, I got this." David said, tightly gripping Eric's shoulder.

Eric closed his eyes to fight back tears. He then shook his head.

"That's a one-way trip," he quietly responded.

"Eric. Look, behind you, at her. At your seraph," the large hunter said as Eric glanced over his shoulder at Celestial. She was sitting up in the open carriage and was watching Eric intently. Her eyes sparkled in the light as Alice was tending to her wound. David continued, "What you two have is something very special. Some may not like or understand it, but it's special. She needs you, and I know you need her. So, go, leave me here."

Tears streamed down Eric's face. The young hunter then turned back to his friend. He nodded, pursing his lips into a thin line. David reached his hand out. Eric glanced at it, then took his hand and shook it. Their grips were tight. David's smile widened, showing blood-stained teeth.

"It's been an honor, David," Eric said. They let go. He took a few steps back.

"The honor has been mine," David replied.

Bullets then started flying past their heads as the cult members fully recovered. David dropped behind cover as Eric spun and ran as fast as he could back to the carriages.

The horses pulling the armored transports began to run as Eric reached them. He jumped and caught the edge of the open door, being dragged along. Burke and Alice then grabbed Eric's arms, pulling him inside. Once inside, other hunters slammed the doors closed as the train of armored cars turned and sprinted away. Inside it, Eric laid on the floor as Celestial pulled him up into a tight hug. She could feel the pain he was going through. He watched David wave them away as they left the tunnel entrance.

David watched as the transports left. He nodded as a tear slipped out and crawled down his face, feeling content and peaceful. His chest throbbed in pain, but he ignored it. The large hunter sat down with his back to the concrete barrier and stared out into the sky outside the massive cave exit. Then, slowly reaching into his duster pocket, he retrieved a fresh cigar he stole from Burke. He chewed on the end, struck a match, and lit the cigar.

David took a puff, then blew the smoke and watched it swirl and wisp in the air in front of him. He smiled, placing the cigar back into his mouth, tasting the tobacco and copper of his blood mixing. Memories of his past entered his head. His childhood, his family, his time as a hunter. He felt no regrets. The man then shed another tear as memories of his late daughter entered his thoughts. He then reached over; taking hold of the flash fuse and pulling it near.

The gunfire stopped. Numerous disciples came running over to the wounded hunter. They pointed their rifles at him, ready to kill.

He smiled bigger, confusing them with his defiance. Wasting no time, he pulled the cigar from his mouth and pushed the lit end to the fuse, igniting it. A pop. The fuse burned to the charges in a near-instant flash. Cracks of thunder could then be heard all around them. The disciples looked around and then, noticing the fiery blasts David unleashed, scattered and ran. Fire and smoke filled the entire mountainside as it rocked from the detonations. The ceiling of the cave system then fell in as more explosions rang out and the base collapse. The hunter bravely embraced his death.

"I'm coming home, sweetheart," David McGowan said, closing his eyes as the blast engulfed him.

On the Elysian Fields, a paradise splayed out for countless miles for all those considered worthy of a happy afterlife. At its entrance, the massive golden gates slowly swung open. Inside its threshold was a small girl who eagerly stood, awaiting a new arrival. She tightly clutched the metal bars of the gate as a large man appeared from a cloud of light.

The little girl ran to him, and the two embraced, reunited once more. The child then took his huge hand in her own tiny hand, then led her father onto the Elysian Fields. It was there that David could find his peace for all eternity.

[XXI]

Eric and Celestial fought their way through dozens of disciples on the way up the side of Mount Rigpoint. They moved on ahead of Burke and the other hunters. The mates had made it to a small flat clearing only a hundred meters from the peak. Mariah now stood in their way. Along with her was the strange seraph that recaptured the Guardian. The sight confused both Eric and Celestial.

"What's wrong, seraph?" Mariah called out with a cruel grin. "Don't recognize your own mother?"

Celestial gasped. There was no way! Yet, as she refused to believe it, the imprisoned seraph spoke out to her with a weak and ghastly voice.

"Celestial...run..."

Eric glanced over at his mate. The seraph was fighting back hard against her tears. It was her mother, Grace.

"Necromancy can do amazing things!" Mariah yelled. "It cannot only bring the dead back to life, but it makes the subject much more loyal than any soul stone can!"

Celestial and her undead mother stared each other down. She gritted her teeth and fought back her emotions. She didn't want to fight her mother, but knew she had no choice as long as Grace was under the control of that infernal armor. She stared into the black visor covering her mother's face. Mariah stood a short distance behind Grace, grinning.

"This is where the world ends and a new one begins!" Mariah yelled, holding her arms out wide. "A new world! One for the Black Sun only!"

The wind blew dust in small whirlwinds, causing everyone there to shield their eyes with the exception of Grace. Eric was behind Celestial. He glanced at his mate, then back to Mariah. He felt a sneer spread across his face. Vesuvius then took a few steps forward and got beside the seraph, letting out a low growl.

"Celest, keep yourself focused!" Eric called out to her. "We have to concentrate on stopping Demothesis!"

The seraph nodded, but she didn't take her eyes off of her mother.

"Mother...please fight it." She said to her.

Grace moved, seemingly as if she was trying to reach up to her helmet. Mariah caught this and muttered a word, causing an electrical pulse to surge through the undead seraph. She screamed, dropping to her knees momentarily as the armor quickly took over again.

Eric and Celestial both winced seeing her get hurt, but they didn't lose focus. Mariah then threw her hand out.

"My slave, attack!" She ordered.

Grace stood and brought her hands together to charge an orb of shadow energy but was stopped by a large monster slamming into her at high speeds. She flew back and smashed into a boulder protruding out of the ground. In the spot where she was standing only a second earlier, was Alice's dragon. The azure dragon hit Grace with a fast tackle, and then turned and bared her sharp teeth towards Mariah. Alice slowly walked up to be next to Eric and flashed him a smile.

"Sorry it took me so long. I got held up for a little longer than I thought," she said with a confident grin.

Eric nodded at her, then turned his attention back to Mariah. The Black Sun Zealot seemed enraged by the female hunter's interference. She muttered another control word, causing Grace to teleport off the rock. She appeared next to Mariah for a split second, then disappeared again.

The pair of dragons, Celestial, Eric and Alice glanced around to see where Grace went. Then Eric sensed it. He looked up and saw Grace several dozen meters above Alice's dragon, charging a beam of light.

"Alice! Your dragon!" he yelled to Alice, pointing up at Grace.

Alice looked up as well. She yelled for her dragon to move, yet nothing could be done in time. Grace fired the powerful blast straight down. The sword of light trailed its way to the female dragon...only for Vesuvius to shove her out of the way and take the hit instead.

Both hunters and Celestial were shocked by Vesuvius's selflessness towards her. Alice covered her mouth in shock and her eyes widened. Mariah laughed from her spot.

"Worthless. Well that takes care of one dragon," she chuckled to herself.

She then became shocked as well as the smoke cleared. There was crater where the blast hit, but in its center still stood Eric's dragon. He seemed shaken and weak from the attack, but still let out a roar and glared daggers at Mariah. Eric took his chance, he threw his hand out.

"Celest, go after your mother! Vesuvius, attack Mariah!" he yelled.

Celestial ripped stone from the ground and chucked it at her undead mother. Vesuvius opened his mouth, unleashing a blue orb of burning energy right at Mariah. Grace teleported, making the rocks harmlessly fly through where she just was. She appeared in front of Mariah, then absorbed the dragon's attack.

"I have no more time for this!" Mariah screamed.

She then mouthed another silent command, causing Grace to scream in agony as she was forced to grab both dragons with her psychokinesis. She slammed the dragons into the ground, then tossed them against the rocks.

Gunfire then filled the air as a group of Black Sun disciples came rushing down a mountain path from the top. Eric and Alice rushed into cover. Celestial quickly went to Vesuvius's side and protected herself and him by forming a barrier of her mental powers. Vesuvius still seemed slightly dazed. He shook his head to refocus himself.

"You still good?" the seraph asked.

The dragon nodded, letting out a huff.

Celestial nodded back, then turned to see Grace only a mere five meters from them. She charged another light beam, smashing straight through the protective barrier. Celestial was sent to the ground. The sudden break of her protection made her head pound. Vesuvius stood his ground, then charged forward in an attempt to crunch down on Grace and incapacitate her. Unfortunately, the undead seraph teleported again, dodging the attack.

Vesuvius was angry at the miss, but immediately had to move to avoid getting shot. The disciples kept their fire up from their cover from the side. Eric drew his revolver and began to fire at the disciples. Alice followed suit, drawing her weapon and shooting an enemy in the face as he charged towards them.

The two hunters began dropping the disciples, making Mariah curse loudly. She now knew she would have to fall back. The cult leader looked to Grace and uttered an order.

The undead seraph groaned in pain and viciously attacked Alice's dragon further with her psychic powers and threw Eric's dragon as well when he tried to attack her again. She then teleported to dodge an orb of energy from Celestial and this time appeared right in front of her. The daughter was caught off guard, then received an electrified fist into the side of her head from her mother. Grace then grabbed her by the neck with one hand. Celestial immediately felt all of her psychic energy drain. She tried to teleport from her mother's grip but couldn't. Mariah let out a laugh.

"You know how the armor works!" she yelled. "It disables any creature's power close to it and renders them useless!"

"Celest fight back! Get away from her!" Eric yelled. He started to become very worried.

The seraph pushed at her mother to try to get her to let go, but it was of no use. Grace groaned in pain but held on tight. She then teleported them both to Mariah. Then, Grace laid her free hand on the Black Sun leader. The three teleported away from the fight.

"Celest!" Eric called out.

He panicked inside. Alice placed her hand on his shoulder to try to calm him.

"They must have gone to the top of the mountain," she said. "We must hurry and catch up!"

Eric nodded, then looked over to where Vesuvius was. The dragon was now tied up battling against the enemy disciples. The beast was back on his feet and blew hellfire at a group of the enemy. The disciples burst into flames and screamed. They tried to put the blue flames out, but ultimately succumbed to the fire. Vesuvius then rushed over to Alice's dragon. She was still on the ground and was struggling to get back up. Alice left her cover, pulling her soul stone out to return her beast.

"Korra, return!" She ordered, but the soul stone's red light was disrupted by a fiery blast that hit only a few meters in front of the hunter. The blast knocked her to the ground and made her drop her soul stone.

Eric rushed from cover and grabbed Alice under her arms. He started pulling her back into cover as another groups of disciples descended towards them. They opened fire and had a mancubus unleashed. The large monster lumbered down the mountain path towards them. It appeared like a mass of molded fat with two stubby legs. Its head was small with a pair of beady black eyes. Attached to each of its arms was a set of launchers, made to fire arcane balls of explosive fire.

"Vesuvius! Attack the mancubus!" Eric ordered.

Vesuvius stood over Alice's dragon and released an orb of blue power from his mouth. It scored a direct hit, dropping the obese monster to the dirt. It laid there for a moment, then jumped back up and quickly fired its twin canons, sending fire towards the dragons. Vesuvius knew he didn't have time to pull the female away from the danger; instead getting in front of her and took the fiery hits. It blasted into an explosion, sending smoke and debris into the air. The force of the blast knocked Eric and Alice back. The hunter was dazed for a second, then recollected himself as the smoke cleared.

Eric was worried about his dragon but saw that Vesuvius still somehow managed to keep on his feet. He could tell the beast was about out of the fight, but the dragon kept a determined look on his face. Alice scrambled up, grabbing her soul stone and returning her own monster before she seriously got hurt.

Come on...where's our help? Alice worriedly thought to herself.

Eric left his cover, standing in the open in a sudden daze. He looked over at Vesuvius, who was barely standing. He then heard a disciple yell an order.

"Mancubus, kill the hunter! Fire!" the disciple yelled.

The monster rose its cannons and fired a blast of hellfire at Eric. He braced for the hit, but heard it explode in front of him. When he opened his eyes, he saw Vesuvius. Third degree burns and scars covered the dragon as he dropped to the ground, then stumbled to get back up. Eric felt dread raise in him. He had to call back Vesuvius back to his stone. He pulled out the dragon's soul stone but was stopped when a bullet hit his prosthetic and he fell down. The soul stone fell from his hand and rolled away from him. Alice rushed out and pulled Eric behind the nearest rock to use for cover.

Vesuvius looked back at his master. He was safe from the attack. That's all that he cared about...his master being protected. He stumbled again, then regained his balance. The dragon knew he was hurt but couldn't let it stop him. He looked back to the mancubus and bared his teeth. He was going to defeat one last opponent. A tear left the dragon's eye as he put the remainder of his energy into one last charge.

Vesuvius rushed forward in a blaze of light, smashing into the mancubus and sending him flying back. The monster slammed into the mountain side and collapsed. It attempted to stand again but was pinned down by the dragon. Vesuvius ripped into the monster's neck, tearing out its jugular and killing it.

The dragon then climbed off the dead mancubus, and finally fell from exhaustion. He knew he was now in the middle of a bunch of disciples, but knew it was the distraction his master needed, even if it wasn't the one he wanted. The disciples shouldered their rifles and aimed at the dragon, who stood back up and growled angrily towards them. He didn't have the energy to attack again but tried anyways. As soon as he moved, the disciples opened fire. Bullets ripped into the dragon, tearing away at him.

Eric's heart stopped seeing his dragon being gunned down. His eyes immediately began collecting tears as he felt as if he could feel those bullets as well.

"Vesuvius! No!" Eric screamed. He tried running over to him, but Alice grabbed him and pulled him back into cover with tears in her eyes as well.

"Eric, there's nothing you can do! You're just going to get yourself killed as well!" she said, her voice breaking.

Vesuvius whimpered in horrible pain, but defiantly stood his ground. He looked around at the disciples, who were all shocked at the dragon that seemingly refused to die. The dragon then looked to the sky and gave one last defiant roar. It pierced the skies and was later said to have been heard for miles. Once his lungs were emptied, the dragon dropped to the ground one final time. He closed his eyes and awaited his end.

Eric and Alice brought their guns up and fired on the disciples surrounding Vesuvius, dropping them. The hunter was fighting as hard as he could to not break down as he emptied his revolver. Every memory he had of Vesuvius flooded his mind. From the day he got him, to just then; Eric thought of every moment he had with his dragon. He felt his heart nearly break.

Gunfire was then heard behind Eric and Alice. They looked back and saw Burke, along with the other hunters charging from the mountain pass below. The disciples rushed for cover as bullets flew at them, being killed or otherwise pushed back. After a few intense moments, the gunfire stopped. The coast was clear.

Eric rose from his cover, looking over to where his dragon laid. He ran over to Vesuvius's side and dropped to his knees, lifting the creature's head into his arms. Tears ran down Eric's face as he looked over Vesuvius's wounds. He was far too gone to get any help now, and it was only a matter of time before he would pass away.

"Vesuvius..." Eric said quietly. "I'm so sorry..."

The dragon was looking into Eric's eyes. He slowly turned his head upwards and let out a pained groan. His breathing was very shallow. The hunter started sobbing. He petted him on the head slowly and gently, meeting Vesuvius's gaze. The dragon had a look of intense pain but stared directly into his master's eyes. After a moment, Eric spoke up.

"Vesuvius..." Eric quietly said, clearing his throat. "I'm so sorry... Go peacefully, ok?... Thank you for being at my side all these years..."

Eric broke down again, bringing his forehead to Vesuvius's. The dragon still smiled behind the pain he felt. The hunter held his dying monster for several moments. The dragon's breathing became raspy as he started gasping for air. Eric held tightly onto him, trying to comfort him as he passed. He trembled as he sobbed but refused to let go. Within seconds, though it felt like an hour, Vesuvius's breathing stopped. The dragon closed his eyes for the last time, and his heart pumped no more.

Eric then slumped to the ground in silence. After a few moments, Alice went over and softly spoke to him.

"Eric...I'm so sorry," She said while fighting back her own tears, "But we have to keep going...Celest and the world is in danger still."

The hunter looked up at Alice, then slowly nodded. He stood, adjusting his prosthetic to make up for its damage, then could feel the stares of the hunters around him. Looking around, he saw that the hunters were all looking at him. They all had looks of sympathy in their eyes. Michael then approached him.

"Eric...I'm sorry." He said.

Eric shook his head. He spoke in a dark tone, "It's not your fault. Those bastards did this...and they will pay for everything they had done."

Michael stood there for another moment. He then spoke to Eric.

"Eric, we don't have time. What should we do?"

Eric looked around for a moment. More gunfire was then heard as another group of disciples rushed them from the side. The hunters took defensive positions and returned fire.

"I want you guys to push them back!" Eric yelled to Michael over the gunfire. "Get rid of them...I'm heading up to the peak."

Michael gave Eric a bewildered look, "You're not going by yourself, I'm going with you!"

Eric shook his head, "No, this is my fight now! I'm ending this myself!"

He took Michael's rifle out of his hands, then spun on his heels and ran up the mountain side before any of them could protest. Eric refused to stop. He refused to look back. The young hunter couldn't bring himself to, as he knew he might not come back down that mountain.

Enough. It's time for this to end. Eric thought.

[XXII]

Eric ran up the mountain path upwards and upwards to its peak. Eventually, the path bath came to an end at a set of stairs.

This is it. He thought.

The hunter slowly made his way up the stairs, hearing the Black Sun leader chanting something. The wind had picked up greatly as the young man climbed the stairs, making hearing exactly what Demothesis was yelling difficult. After several moments of going up the ancient stone steps, Eric reached its crest.

In front of him was the ruins of an ancient temple. Its roof was gone a millennium ago. Only dusty and broken pillars remained behind. In the center of the ruins was a large square with a triangle carved into the old stone floor. Spread evenly around the giant runes were each of the three Guardians. They were all in a trance and glowing. The Black Sun's leader, Demothesis, stood in front of the old glyph, facing it and had his arms spread wide. Behind him was Mariah and several disciples, who were all kneeling and praying. Off on the side was Grace, still holding her daughter by her neck. Eric's mate still seemed weakened with her psychic powers diminished in her mother's grip. They all had their backs to Eric and didn't notice him.

Demothesis spoke again, yelling as a portal ripped open in the floor of the ruins. The portal bubbled and popped like tar, but was darker than the darkest black. It sparkled like the stars in the night sky.

"Come forth, Harbinger of Death, Oionos!" Demothesis summoned. "Take shape in our world once more!"

The portal grew larger as a black mass began to emerge. The god started to take shape as black muck fell off of it. Two glowing red eyes appeared from the darkness as it spread its wings. They were as wide as the ruins itself, tipped in blood red spikes. The black liquid continued to fall from its body, revealing itself to everyone present.

It was a large draconic beast, yet centipede-like in appearance. It had several dozen pairs of bony legs tipped with blood and its segmented body was an almost black-gray in color. Gold half-rings circled its back and it had a large golden crown perched on its head that traced down the sides of its face. Red stripes covered its black belly. A pair of massive, black crab-like arms and pincers were attached to the body section under its head. The huge pincers slammed down onto the stone floor of the ruins to help support the beast up. The newly emerged monster let out a roar, filling the air with a deafening rage that bellowed from its circular mouth, which was lined with a thousand needle-like teeth. The demon deity seemed in great pain as red chains were bound around it, placing the god under the Black Sun's control.

Eric watched in awe at the giant monster, then shook himself out of it. He needed to stop the Black Sun and stop them now. He shouldered his rifle, engaging the first disciple on his left before they saw him. Two shots rang out in quick succession, and the disciple dropped with a scream. The other jumped, then spun around while preparing his own rifle. It was too late for the disciple though, as Eric placed two more rounds in the disciple's chest and he dropped. The disciple clutched at his chest for several moments with gurgling sounds emanating from his mouth.

Demothesis and the others turned to see the hunter standing there, aiming directly at the Black Sun leader.

"You're too late!" Demothesis yelled to Eric. "With Oionos under my control, nobody can stop me!"

He gestured to the legendary monster behind him.

"God of Death, go forth! Destroy this world and create for me, a new one!" Demothesis ordered.

The god tried to fight back against the red chains, but the chains tightened and forced it to comply. It then glowed brightly and unleashed a terrible wave of energy, causing the earth to shake. The pillars that still stood after all these thousands of years cracked and buckled at the power. The floor of the ruins split and cracked as the sky turned a dark blood color. The energy caught Eric off-guard, knocking him off his feet. The wave also seemed to catch Grace off-guard, making her drop Celestial for just a split second. The seraph used that opportunity to teleport to Eric, feeling her energy come back.

"You did it Master Demothesis!" Mariah exclaimed. "The world...it is ending!"

The entire world shook slightly as it began to slowly fall apart. Eric decided he was going to take Black Sun down before they could celebrate. He brought his rifle up, firing a round at Demothesis. The bullet struck the Black Sun leader in the chest, making him fall. Mariah saw this and spun around, drawing her pistol, but had to quickly duck to avoid being shot as Eric opened fire on her as well. Celestial rushed in a blaze of energy towards her mother as Grace tried to intervene in the fight. The mother and daughter battled each other as they darted around the ruins in flashes. Eric and Mariah exchanged fire back and forth, neither being able to hit the other. Demothesis simply laid on the ground, gasping for air as his life began to leave him. Bullets flew back and forth between Eric and Mariah, with large chunks of stone being ripped from the floor and thrown between the seraph and her undead mother. The Black Sun leader grinned to himself; he did not fear death. He knew it was only a matter of time before this world was done anyways.

Eric jumped from around his cover, firing several more rounds. One finally hit its mark, smacking into Mariah's leg. She yelled in pain and fell down, then jumped up and hobbled for cover. She pulled her dying master with her when she saw that Eric was reloading.

Mariah held Demothesis in her arms behind a fallen pillar. Demothesis looked over to where the God of Death stood, then back up at Mariah.

"Mariah...we won," he quietly said.

Mariah felt a tear run down her face. She was happy that they were successful but was saddened to lose the one she considered her master. Demothesis coughed, then smiled at Mariah.

"Don't cry...today is a glorious day," he said. His voice was getting weaker.

Mariah nodded and they both turned to watch their god. The giant beast let out another roar, one that seemed to shake the entire world. The monster went to give off another wave of its power but was interrupted by a large white orb of light forming in the sky above the ruin. Another portal ripped open in the heavens above. It was beautiful. Rings of blue with waves of a rainbow of colors exploded as ribbons of every shade were spiraling outwards from the orb's edges. From it, a massive new creature appeared.

The creature was a silver, serpentine dragon. Its length seemed almost immeasurable. The body, more than a dozen meters across in thickness, twisted and swirled around itself through the air. A pair of long arms ending in razor sharp claws opened towards the mountain top. Its head was elongated; its mouth lined with a thousand teeth. A large, glowing red orb, much like that of a star, rested in the top of its head and in between its two blue eyes. The dragon let out a roar, loud enough to split the clouds and return the sky to its normal blue color with its holy sound alone. The Black Sun leader looked up at the god. He frowned at the sight.

"Astreus..." He whispered, his eyes losing their color. "So, He did come to interfere..."

Oionos and Astreus, the titanic God of the Stars, exchanged words; their language indecipherable to all mere mortals. Oionos then swung one gargantuan claw at the god's face, but the dragon simply went further into the air to dodge it. Astreus flew high into the sky, then turned to face His brother. The God of Death's eyes then glowed as He charged an orb of abyssal power inside His mouth. He fired it at Astreus. The beam of energy cut through the air, powerful enough to stain the sky with black power. Astreus bowed His head and surrounded himself with a screen of light that appeared from the orb in His skull. The dark attack hit against the shield, harmlessly being absorbed. The God of the Stars then reached out, grabbing the other and shattering the red chains bounding the monster.

Releasing His brother from their enemy's control, He opened His mouth and bellowed. From His mouth, the god blew holy fire that burned white hot, engulfing His brother and reopening the dark portal to the dead realm. The God of Death tried to fight back against His sibling, but ultimately failed and was pushed back into Aedurus. His legs and massive claws scrapped and dug into the stone floor but slid off as He fell into the dark hole, blazed in white light. The portal then shook and began to destabilize. It would soon collapse on itself and engulf and pull the entirety of the mountain top into Aedurus. The three small Guardians, also freed from the Black Sun's control, fled to the side of the Star God. Astreus then let out another deafening roar that shook the ground, returning the world to normal and reversing the damage Oionos had done.

Mariah and Demothesis watched on. They both had no words. They only knew that they had now failed.

"No..." Demothesis said. It was his last word, passing away right there in Mariah's arms. The surviving Black Sun leader started crying as she knew they lost. She then looked back up at the god.

Astreus remained hovering high in the air. He looked down at the creatures on the ruins, then turned and flew away. As He flew, the portal in which He entered the world reopened. The God of the Stars went through the portal, followed by the Guardians, leaving Plataea once more.

Celest let out a sigh of relief. The world had been spared. She looked over to Eric and smiled. He managed to get a smile out as well. She floated over to him and took his hands in hers. The two were then about to share a kiss, but the seraph was hit by a large piece of stone smashing into her and knocking her back hard. It was from her mother, who was still under control of Mariah. The sudden attack snapped Eric back to reality.

Grace was glowing in her armor. She screamed in pain as she grabbed another stone and threw it at Eric. He barely managed to dodge it.

"Grace! Stop it!" he yelled.

It was of no use though. The imprisoned seraph fired a beam of light at Celestial, who was still recovering from the earlier attack. The beam hit her and knocked her to the ground.

Mariah crawled from behind her cover. Rage had taken over her grief. She glanced over at the unstable dark portal that was ready to collapse, then back to Eric.

"I will not let you leave this mountain!" she yelled, now pointing to the portal. "I'll keep you here and take you all to hell with me!"

Eric glanced at the portal as it was growing and bubbling its dark energy. He looked back at Mariah and opened fire. Bullets struck the stone pillar she hid behind, and a ricochet managed to strike her in the arm. Mariah dropped back into cover. She reached for Grace's control crystal and squeezed it, forcing the mother to attack again.

Grace then grabbed Eric with her psychokinesis and sent him flying back into one of the ruin's pillars. He slammed into it and felt several of his ribs break. The hunter let out a scream in pain and dropped to the ground, sending more tendrils of pain shooting up through his body. He writhed on the cold stone. He knew he had to get up. He had to help Celestial in the fight to release her mother.

Celestial gasped in horror at the sight. She never saw Eric show so much pain. He had always stood so defiantly in the face of adversity, but this was too much. Seeing him scream in agony and pain sent such strong emotions through her. Her heart burned with a newly found strength. She had to protect her love. She had to save him and her mother.

The seraph pulled herself to her feet. She found the energy to float up off the ground and stared down Grace. The armored seraph grabbed Eric against her will and tossed him like a toy across the ruin's floor. He groaned as he rolled and clutched at his chest. He tried to get back up but was grabbed again and thrown high into the air.

"*No!*" Celest yelled, grabbing Eric in her own psychic grasp.

She gently lowered him to the ground, then immediately had to teleport to dodge a ball of shadows thrown by Grace. She rematerialized across the battlefield, then threw a ball of magic of her own. Grace merely teleported to the side and dodged the attack entirely. She then teleported once more, this time appearing right in front of Celestial.

Before she could react, Grace slammed an electrified fist into Celest's gut. Her insides were wrenched and shocked from the hit as she was sent to the side and landed on her back. She laid there for a moment in a daze, then was hit by a piece of torn stone thrown by her imprisoned mother. She went limp and felt herself black out.

With Celestial out of the way, Grace turned her attention back to Eric. He managed to pull himself up and was standing once more. He wiped away the blood running from his mouth as he called out to her.

"Grace! I know you can still hear me!" he yelled. "You have to fight it! Fight back!"

Grace hesitated, then clawed at her helmet in a desperate attempt to remove it. She let out a scream of agony as the armor activated its countermeasures and retook control of her.

The undead seraph then grabbed Eric once again and slammed him into another pillar. Eric felt several more bones snap and his insides get jolted. He was then held up against a pillar as he felt his entire body being crushed in Grace's grasp. He braced for what seemed like the end. His mind began to black out; his vision went blurry. Then, suddenly, the stone that hung from his neck began to glow.

Beams and tangles of light shot out of the stone and whipped their way to meet the same tangles of light coming from the pendant that Celestial wore. Once they connected, the unconscious seraph became engulfed in a white light as she began to transform. Her dress turned a dark black in color, contrasting her white skin, and bellowed out like a wedding dress. The blue sleeves of her arms turned black as well and formed into long gloves ending at her elbows. Shiny, stainless armor-like plates appeared across her body for protection. Her blue hair lengthened and curled tighter around her pointed ears, which in turn pointed more upwards and appeared to be sharper. Her heart became enlarged and split into two halves, forming twin red spikes protruding from her chest. From her back, her wings faded and then were replaced by three pairs of glorious wings, sprouting and spreading wider than they ever have before.

The blinding white light dissipated, and the newly transformed monarch opened her eyes. They glowed brightly with blue energy. She then looked over at her love.

"*Eric!*" Celest screamed. She then called to her mother, "*Mother, stop!*"

She charged a beam of light in one hand. It was blinding to any mere mortal that dared to look into it. She swung the beam like a sword, slamming it into her mother and sending her flying. Grace then reappeared in the flash of an eye, then tried grabbing Celestial with her power. It was useless, as the monarch's psychic powers were now far stronger than ever before. Celestial shrugged off the attempted attack, then reached out with her hands, grabbing Grace and holding her in place. Her imprisoned mother let out a scream of agony as she was being forced to fight back.

"*Mother! Come back to us!*" Celest yelled in her native tongue as she used her powers to rip Grace's armor off of her, now that she was strong enough.

With the armor forcefully removed, Grace fell to the floor. Celestial hovered to her mother, and gingerly lifted and held her. The older seraph opened her eyes.

"*...Celestial?*" her mother said weakly. She then smiled and reached up, caressing her daughter's face, "*Look at you, my child. You have turned into a most beautiful seraph. Your father...would be so proud...*"

Celestial felt tears run down her face. Her mother wiped them away, then went limp as her life left her once more.

"*Momma...*" Celestial said quietly.

Her mother's body glowed slightly, then turned to dust and blew away in the winds. Celestial watched the dust blow away, knowing the armor was the only thing keeping her alive, yet under an evil control. She couldn't let her mother live like that, but she still was hurt from ripping her mother's lifeline from her.

She then felt weak from the sudden burst of energy she had. The monarch seraph fell forward onto her chest, exhausted.

Mariah looked up from over her cover. She saw that Grace had been freed. Rage boiled in her veins as she could only seethe in anger at the realization that the Black Sun was done for. Master Demothesis and most of the others were now dead.

It's all because of that damned hunter and seraph... She thought as she stood up.

She reached down and picked up Eric's revolver, which had been dropped. She checked to make sure that there were rounds chambered as she walked towards where Eric limply lain. He was trying to stand back up, seeing that Mariah was nearing him.

"I'm tired of you!" She yelled, leveling the pistol at him. "You ruined everything for us!"

She cocked the revolver's hammer.

"This is where you die, hunter!"

Eric bravely faced her. He didn't say anything in return. He was ready for it. He just simply gave her a mocking grin. The smile made her even more angry. She fired the gun twice, sending two bullets through Eric's chest. The hunter fell backwards against the pillar behind him and slid down it. His breathing immediately became harder and shallower. The burning sensation seared his chest.

Mariah then re-cocked the gun's hammer and approached him. She planted the muzzle of the gun against his forehead.

"YOU. DIE. NOW!" she screamed. She went to pull the trigger but heard the metal of the gun groan.

The pistol twisted and bent in an invisible hand, rendering the handgun useless. Mariah then felt the color in her skin drain as a primal fear suddenly took over. She looked over, and a short distance away she saw a monarch Celestial hovering a few centimeters from the ground. She looked beaten and battered, but her eyes burned in an intense blue light.

The monarch seraph released all of her energy. All of her rage. All of her hatred towards the Black Sun member that was the cause of her parents' deaths. The cause of all of her misery. She impaled Mariah with a dozen crystal shards of blazing light. Mariah was bloodily impaled through every part of her body. The woman looked down at her torso, seeing the jagged shards protruding from her chest. Blood ran down her body, and she felt her soul begin to leave her. She then looked back up at Celestial with an open mouth.

"*You feel that?*" Celestial said in a low tone. Tears of pain and anger were flowing down her face. She turned her wrists over, causing the crystals to twist in Mariah's abdomen. "*That's from my parents... I want you to suffer, you bitch.*"

The monarch then held up one hand with her fingers splayed wide open. In her palm, a dark orb ripped open in the fabric of space. It expanded, pulling the mortally-injured Mariah towards it. Soon, the black hole was large enough to swallow a human, and the dying Black Sun Zealot was sucked into the hole, screaming.

"*I am banishing you to a place between dimensions. There, you will know neither death or life for all eternity,*" the monarch Celestial stated. Her voice quivered with power as the evil woman was sucked away. The rip in space then shut.

Then, having expended the last of her energy, the seraph fell to the ground as well. She collapsed onto her front, turning back into her normal form, gasping for air as she felt herself spent. Her vision was still blurry as she tried to focus her sight on Eric, who was still barely alive.

Eric and Celestial then felt the ruins shake as the portal to Aedurus continued to destabilize; ready to collapse.

[XXIII]

Every nerve and muscle in his body screamed and begged with pain for Eric to stop, but he didn't. He coughed, sending splatters of blood from his mouth to the ground. It was hard for him to breath. He could feel one of his lungs being filled with blood and the bullet wounds in his chest were searing in pain. He began to feel cold. He ignored it all and rose to his feet.

His prosthetic leg gave way from its damage and the hunter fell again. He dropped to his knees once more and fell forward, catching himself on his hands. Eric swore and reached down, ripping the prosthetic leg off and tossing the broken limb to the side. He knew deep in his heart he wouldn't need it anymore. Then, fighting against every bit of pain he felt, he pushed himself up and onto his remaining leg while bracing against the stone pillar nearby. He looked forward and saw Celestial laying on the ground only ten meters ahead. She was struggling to push herself up as she weakly looked over and met his gaze. She slowly reached up with one hand and then collapsed.

Eric hobbled forward on his one leg. The only thing running through his head was that he had to get to Celest. They didn't have time; the portal was going to destroy the mountaintop soon. All he could think about was that he had to save her. He hobbled a few more steps, then couldn't keep his balance and fell once more. He refused to give up as he started to crawl towards his love. She looked at him and began crawling towards him as well. After several agonizing moments, the two finally crawled up and laid next to one another.

He wrapped his arms around her and pulled her in tight. She looked at him through half-open eyes. Several trickles of blood ran from his mouth as Eric turned his head to cough up more blood. She could feel tears collecting heavily in her eyes at the sight of the one she loved being so hurt. They locked eyes for a moment, then Eric reached towards his belt. He retrieved the one soul stone he still had, an empty one, and held it between them.

"Celest...please...you'll be safe," Eric said. His voice was choked up and raspy from his injuries.

Tears ran down her face as she shook her head.

"...We don't have time to get away...save yourself..." Eric pleaded as tears pooled in his blue eyes.

She pulled his head towards her and kissed him. She held it for several moments, then their lips separated.

"*No...*" she said, shaking her head again, "*I won't leave you.*"

Eric's tears broke from his eyes and ran down his cheeks.

Save her. Was all he thought.

He grabbed at the stone that hung from his neck and ripped it from its cord. The hunter then placed it in Celestial's hand and closed her fingers around it. She stared at her closed hand then, with sadness, back at him.

"I love you Celest..." He said, his voice broken. He pulled her in for another kiss.

As her eyes closed from the lip-lock, she heard Eric quietly mouth arcane words behind the kiss and was enveloped in a haze of light. Her eyes opened and locked with his as she felt her heart shatter.

"*Eric?...*" her voice choked. The light was getting brighter as she began to be pulled into the soul stone.

"I'm sorry...but I have to save you...like I've always promised," Eric said.

Celest's eyes never left his as she was turned into a mist and pulled into the stone. It glowed warmly in a blue light, then faded. The hunter started sobbing and held the stone close to his chest.

"I-I am so sorry Celest...so sorry," Eric said as he sobbed.

He rolled over onto his stomach and slowly pushed himself up onto his knees. Blood almost completely filled one of his lungs, making his breathing even harder. He had to consciously think to breathe.

Save her. Breathe in.

Tears continued rolling down his face as he stared at the soul stone that contained the love of his life.

I always promised to protect her. Save her. Breathe out.

He kissed the shiny surface of the crystal, clutching it tight in his hands.

...I will save her...even if it means I have to die. Breathe in.

He knew what he had to do. What had to be done. He looked at the soul stone one last time.

"I love you...so, so much," Eric quietly spoke his last words.

Do it! Breathe out.

He cocked his arm back that was holding the soul stone. One last thought of all the memories he shared with Celestial went through his mind. One last thought of his love for her. One last tear left a trail down his face. He threw the soul stone as hard as he could. It flew through the air, spinning as it went and fell down the mountainside. He fell forward as he threw it, landing on his hands and then collapsing to his chest.

Breathe in.

All of his fears vanished. Eric suddenly felt content and peaceful. He knew she would be safe from the blast. It was all he wanted; for her to be safe. He knew the world would go on without him. He knew Celestial would eventually move on. He knew he truly loved her with all his heart. The hunter closed his eyes and smiled. He didn't feel cold anymore.

Breathe out.

The portal imploded, then rapidly expanded explosively as it devoured the ancient ruins. Eric Hahn only felt warmth as he was engulfed by the fire it sent in every direction.

The soul stone dropped sharply in its fall from the mountain top. Down below were the other hunters. Michael was sitting against a rock, being treated by another hunter for a wound he sustained. The group then looked up and saw the soul stone falling towards them. Alice gasped, feeling a sense of dread in her gut. She watched the crystal fall towards them, knowing what this had meant, and she had difficulty holding back her emotions. The soul stone hit the ground and broke with a sharp crack. It sizzled, sparked, and the light within it dimmed out. A mist then emerged from the broken remains of the stone, releasing Celestial.

The seraph appeared in a haze of light. She was standing for a moment, then toppled over. Before she hit the ground, Alice rushed over and caught her. That's when the implosion of the portal was heard. Plumes of fire and debris erupted from the mountaintop. The sound awakened Celestial's mind as she managed to collect herself. Her head turned upwards and her eyes widened at the sudden realization at what happened.

She attempted to teleport back to the mountaintop, but her pounding head prevented her from doing so. She then tried in vain to run up the path to the ruins but was held back by Alice. The female hunter had tears streaming down her face.

"Celest, he's gone! There's nothing you can do!" Alice called out, trying harder to hold her back.

"*Dammit, let go of me! I have to go get him!*" Celest demanded as she fought against her grip.

Another string of explosions rang out as it got louder. Smoke, fire and dust bellowed and mushroomed into the sky. Celest froze and stared up at the smoke. She tried to feel for his presence, for his emotions, for anything...but there was nothing. Her heart felt as if it grew cold from the lack of Eric being there. Her eyes were wide and glimmering with tears. Among the dust and small rocks that fell from the mountain, a single piece of color fell with it. It was a torn strip of fabric; tattered and burnt at its edges. The piece fluttered gingerly in the wind. Celest held her hands out, and the fabric fell into her palms. It was a piece of thick denim; a piece of Eric's duster. She stared at it, then tightly gripped the cloth and brought it to her face, sobbing into it. She fell to her knees as she couldn't contain her tears anymore. Everyone around watched as she broke down.

Alice wrapped her arms around the seraph. Celestial didn't return the hug; she just tightly held onto the the fabric as she cried. After a moment, the seraph did turn and return the embrace, crying into Alice's shoulder as she mourned.

The hunter could only hold the seraph. She had no words to say that could bring comfort to the creature. She looked over at Burke, who even had a tear as well.

Burke looked back up at the mountain top. The dust had mostly cleared, but fires and smoke still bellowed from the peak. He squeezed his eyes shut for a second, then reopened them and watched the seraph mourn.

"Rest in peace hunter..." Jonathan quietly said.

The steam ship slowly came to a stop at the docks of Beaksturm, Eric's hometown in Usora. The surviving hunters of Avrush disembarked the vessel, with Celestial behind them.

The seraph stared out at the small town that was sprawled out before her. She remembered Eric telling her about how one day he was going to show her the place where he grew up. Now, here she was, but without him. Around her neck, she still wore her monarch stone, and now Eric's matching stone was now hanging with it. The piece of Eric's duster was holed and the cord around her neck was drawn through it, having the fabric strip cradle the two stones.

The seraph grasped the stones, fighting back a tear once more at the thought of her fallen mate. She never would have thought that the life of a human, of all things, would mean so much to her. Here she was though, still hurt by his death.

Jonathan Burke and Michael Cummings both looked at the seraph, then to each other. The old hunter then turned to see a militia member approaching the group. The soldier saluted to Burke, who didn't return it.

"Welcome to Usora, sir," the militia member said.

"Indeed," Burke replied. "I was told Usora, along with its chapters of hunters, have stood up against the Holy Leader and his ways."

The soldier shifted his weight on his feet, looking at the old hunter. He then replied.

"Uh, yessir. We will not stand for a tyrant. Where do you stand?"

Burke laughed, followed by a grin from Michael.

"We don't like tyrants either. We're here to link up with the Preservation Coalition and fight for Usora."

The soldier nodded. A squad of more militiamen approached the lone man from behind. They all had looks of approval on their faces.

"That's good. That's damn good," the soldier said, now offering his hand for a shake. "I'm Colonel Otis Rodgers. I'm commander of the Usora naval defenses. We could use the extra help."

Burke took his hand, then shook it.

"We're here to do what we can. We must stop the Order," he said.

The Colonel nodded again, then looked behind the old hunter at the seraph. He met her eyes for a split moment.

"What about the seraph? Is it safe?" he asked.

"Yes, *she* is," Michael spoke up, correcting the Colonel. "Her name is Celestial. She was the partner of Eric Hahn."

The Colonel's eyes lit up, "Eric Hahn? Where is he now?"

Burke shook his head, "He's gone. He sacrificed himself to stop the return of Oionos."

"Ah...I see," Colonel Rodgers said, looking once more at Celestial. "Well then, please follow me. We have much to do in preparation for an invasion from the mainland, and we do not have time."

The soldier turned and walked away. The hunters all glanced at each other, then followed the Colonel.

As the hunters followed the militia, Celestial watched them for a moment. She then looked up into the sky and wished for Eric to be with her again. The seraph felt that his lack of presence now left a void in her heart. She decided to stay with the hunters that Eric fought alongside with. She did not fully trust them herself, and her previous instincts told her to run away. Yet, she knew though that it was these same instincts that told her to run from Eric. She was able to trust him, so she knew she had to try to help the hunters. The creature knew they would need her in the upcoming fight, and she knew it is was Eric would have wanted.

Then, catching the attention of every living being there, She appeared.

A blinding light appeared in the sky above everyone.

From it, a large creature faded into view. Everyone stared in awe at the sight. Very few had ever seen the creature that now appeared before them in the sky. The mythical beast galloped slowly through the air in circles on its way to the ground. It landed with grace in front of the group of humans and seraph.

It had the appearance of a large, white equine, with a gray underbelly and face. Its legs were tipped in golden hooves. A large cross-like golden ring wrapped around its abdomen and had the blossoming buds of flowers growing from it. Its eyes were of an emerald green, with deep red pupils glowing against the rest of its beauty. The creature's presence alone demanded a holy respect to it. Mother Gaea, the Goddess of Life, slowly looked around at the mortals in front of Her. Her gaze went to the hunters. She glared at them for a moment, then Her holy eyes moved across the militia members and finally rested on the seraph.

The militia all rose their rifles at the goddess, ready to shoot.

"Hold your fire!" Colonel Rodgers ordered.

Burke spoke up as well.

"There's no point in shooting, we can't hurt Her," the old hunter said. "We'll only succeed in pissing Her off."

The Bringer of Life slowly and gracefully took a few steps towards Celestial. She then spoke, her voice resonated with a holy power that nearly made the humanoid creature bow.

"You, seraph," Gaea said. "*Do you believe humans to be redeemable?*"

Celestial was confused by her goddess's question, but she attempted to answer it.

"*My Lord...all my life I have only seen the horrors and atrocities that humanity has done to Your creations,*" she began, feeling tiny under her Creator's gaze. "*You know this more than I do. I have, myself, been abused and violated by humans. I thought all humans were deserving of extermination...*"

Celestial glanced over at the group of humans near her. They all watched intently as the creature and goddess exchanged words that could not be understood by their minds. The seraph then looked back to Gaea.

"*...but...there is one human that changed my mind. His name was Eric,*" her eyes began to fill with tears. She never wanted her emotions to show, not in front of humans, and not in front of a deity. Yet here she was, allowing herself to openly cry.

"*He taught me that humans are capable of kindness and caring. He showed me that they ARE redeemable, Mother Gaea...and now he is gone, having sacrificed his own life for mine...*"

The seraph trailed off. She lost her voice by looking into the eyes of Gaea. The goddess stood silent for a moment, then wordlessly ripped a hole of light in the air next to her. Celestial looked to the white tear, then saw a human emerge from it.

It was Eric, donned in his duster and hat, clean and unharmed. He stepped from the portal of light and back into the world of the living, then smiled at Celestial.

"Celest, I'm home."

The seraph covered her mouth in shock. She couldn't believe the sight before her. The young man took a step towards Celestial, but the creature shot for him and grabbed him up in a tight embrace. Eric laughed and struggled against her hug, then kissed her on the cheek.

"I don't think I've ever seen you be this emotional," he said with a laugh.

The seraph pulled away, then smacked the human. He recoiled, touching his red cheek where she hit.

"What was that for?" he asked, surprised.

"That's for putting me into a soul stone," she replied, then kissing him. Once they parted their kiss, he then asked.

"And that?"

She smiled, *"That's for being selfless."*

The goddess watched the exchange between the two, then floated away into the air. When the portal to Aedurus collapsed, the Bringer of Life stepped in at the last moment and took Eric away before he could be taken to the underworld. She watched the entire event from her seat and was shocked at the human's selfless acts towards a creature. She never thought before that humans were capable of being rational beings, but the one before her had proven the goddess wrong.

Mother Gaea galloped through the air as everyone watched on. She disappeared back to her seat in a flash of blinding light. Back on the surface, Eric and Celestial released from their embrace. The hunters and militia then looked at the couple. Some of the militia gave looks of disgust at the two's display of affection, but a few others smiled. Burke chuckled at the sight.

He then waved the group away, allowing the two to have their moment alone. As they walked away, Eric and Celestial looked back into each other's eyes.

"So, what now?" Eric asked.

The seraph floated a small distance away, then turned back to her mate. She held out one blue hand.

"Take my hand, human," she said, smiling. *"Take my hand, and together we shall open everyone's hearts to a new era."*

It was with those words, the hunter took the creature's hand, interlacing their fingers tightly together. The two then began to make way to catch up with the others. They felt a storm coming. A storm of blood that threatened to plunge all living things into a terrible darkness.

And it was a storm that they vowed to help stop.

Hunter's Notes

Factions:

Order of the Arcane Hunt - Also called simply the 'Order'. An ancient order, whose members are called 'hunters'. They specialize in firearms and arcane arts; being specially trained to fight monsters.

The Black Sun - A cult of necromancers. Heavily armed and in wide possession of mystic soul stones. They worship Oionos as their deity.

The Preservation Coalition - A splinter faction, comprising of the Usora province and its chapters of hunters.

Arcane Gear:

Soul Stone - a mystic crystal-like stone. Serves as a means to capture and control any monster's will by binding its soul to it.

Disruptor Gem - a black stone, covered in cryptic runes. Can be used to disable any monster's powers. Very useful against the more dangerous species.

Mentioned Weapons:

Glenchester 1873 - a lever-action rifle, very common and popular within the Order and other factions for its reliability and ease of use.

Richmond-Taylor 1860 - a common revolver. Single-action, six round capacity. Originally a cap-and-ball gun, many have been converted to fire cartridges.

Revere Shotgun - a double-barreled scattergun. Inexpensive and simple.

Mills Shotgun - pump shotgun, among the first of its kind in the world

Springdale 1864 Trapdoor - outdated single shot rifle. It is still in common use by militia forces as of 1895.

Schmidt 1895 Autorifle - an advanced automatic rifle, very expensive and only ever seen in the hands of the Hunter Elite.

Arcane Gear continued.:

Black Sun Control Armor - metal armor plating infused with dark magic. Can be used in lieu of a soul stone to control a beast without limiting its power. Can also serve as a means to keep a monster brought back by necromancy alive. Control of the monster is done by its corresponding black crystal.

Regno Stone - a pendant created by ancient seraphs. These are worn in pairs by mates of the high-ruling class within their tribe. The stones are said to allow a seraph to transform into a mythical monarch seraph.

Humans:

Hunter - a member of the Order of the Arcane Hunt. The hunters are trained to specifically to combat monsters and potentially capture them using soul stones.

Elite Hunter - veteran hunters that have proven themselves fiercely loyal to the Holy Leader. They wear black trench coats instead of the usual gray dusters and are armed with the most advanced firearms.

Humans continued.:

Disciple - members of the Black Sun. They are necromancers and worship Oionos as their god.

Zealot - second in command of the Black Sun. The only Zealot is Mariah, after having brutally killed the other Zealots without their leader's knowing.

Holy Leader - the high commander of the Order. Only a direct descendant of the Order's founder may be the Holy Leader.

Fauna:

Mermaid - half fish, half humanoid. Their bodies are covered in black, slimy scales. They have large eyes and long, needle-like teeth. They sing beautiful songs that enchant any human hearing it, giving the illusion that they are a most beautiful woman or man. Once their prey gets close enough, the mermaid will reveal their true form and drag their victim down into the depths to devour them.

Fauna continued.:

Minotaur - a large, bull-like humanoid. They have the torso of a man, the legs and head of a bull. They can fire lightning from their horns and are very fast when charging.

Wraith - Ghost-like creatures, taking the appearance of a hooded figure without legs. They call on shadow magic and poison gases for attacks.

Draugr - frail, undead zombie-like beasts, usually resurrected from human corpses. While fairly weak on their own, in numbers they can prove to be a threat to even a hunter.

Leviathan - a massive water serpent. They can fire beams of energy from their mouths and have razor-sharp teeth. This species can survive on land and are responsible for many shipwrecks.

Ogre - seemingly related to goblins as they are visually similar but are much larger and stronger. These monsters pose a bigger threat than their goblin cousins.

Fauna continued.:

Hellhound - a canine monster. They are constantly missing chunks of skin and flesh and are ignited in hellfire. The beasts virtually feel no pain and hunt in packs, ripping to shreds anything that gets in their way.

Woodfall spider - a massive arachnid. Known to live in damp caves but have on occasion moved into abandoned buildings and even barns.

Troll - a large, ape-like beast with three eyes. They are covered in thick hides and fur that is colored depending on their environment. Fire trolls, and ice trolls are in particular more dangerous than their woodland cousins.

Camazotz - a large species of bat, known to prey on anything smaller than itself, namely humans.

Sphinx - a winged lion with a human-like head. These massive creatures are very rare, but when seen are very dangerous. It is only recommended to hunt these in two pairs of hunters in order to take one down.

Fauna continued.:

Reaper Dragon - a rare species of dragon, these pitch-black dragons are massive with fifty-foot wing spans and can bellow fire that can burn anything to a crisp in seconds.

Banshee - these monsters were once thought to appear like a woman, but recent missions by hunters have shown this species to be more frog-like in appearance, but malformed. They are the size of a human and walk upright. Their screams can be directed in a focused beam and can kill with their high decibel range.

Cherub - a young seraph. They have the appearance of a small child with light blue hair, pointed ears and red eyes. A small, red fin protrudes from their chest and is part of their heart. When they become of age, they transform into a seraph.

Lapguis - a large serpent seemingly made of stone. Largely immune to most forms of firearms, these monsters are recommended to be engaged using a monster under the control of a hunter.

Fauna continued.:

Goblin - small, green humanoids. Primitive, they typically live in small tribes with an alpha male as their leader. Not much of a threat to any militiaman or hunter but can be more dangerous in large numbers.

Harpy - feminine, bird-like humanoids. Despite their human-like appearance in the torso and head, these creatures have no means to communicate beyond shrill screams. The attack using their razor-sharp talons and teeth.

Azure Dragon - a hammer-headed dragon with a long snout. They are blue in color, hence their name. They can bellow blue fire from their gut and are known for their extreme speeds. While they have wings, they are fairly small and cannot support flight beyond gliding.

Fauna continued.:

Seraph - the adult stage of a cherub's life. They have the appearance of an angel with blue hair and red eyes. They sprout feathered wings at their will or in combat. They have a red blade-like horn sticking from their chest, acting as part of their heart. Seraphs have massive mental powers, having the ability to sense emotions and control things with their mind alone. They also have the power to summon orbs of dark magic at will to attack with. Extreme threat to any human.

Mancubus - a large, blobby mass of fat with two, small stubby legs. These monsters are very slow and in the wild do not pose much of a threat but are commonly modified by necromancers to have fireball launchers in lieu of arms. In this configuration, this beast is a massive threat that can take a lot of firepower to take down.

Mythical Fauna:

Monarch - a mythical 'final' stage of a seraph's life. Legends say that a monarch has near-god-like powers and can banish beings to points between dimensions.

Mythical Fauna continued.:

Astreus - this titan is said to have created the heavens and its stars, giving Him the title of God of the stars. He takes the appearance of a serpentine dragon; whose length is immeasurable.

Guardian - it is said that only three exist in the entirety of Plataea. They have the appearance of a small feline with two tails. They are said to serve as the 'keys' to Aedurus and releasing Oionos.

Titan - legends say that the universe was created by three such beings. Oionos, Astreus and Gaea. Many thousands of years ago, Oionos battled his siblings for control of the universe, but was banished to Aedurus as punishment.

Oionos - a centipede-like titan with black dragon wings and massive pincers. He is the God of Death, and rules over Aedurus after being banished there for all eternity.

Mythical Fauna continued.:

Mother Gaea - a titan with the appearance of a white horse with blossoming flowers covering Her abdomen. She is said to have created all life, giving her the title of Bringer and Goddess of Life.

Basic Locations:

Plataea - the world in which the story takes place.

Avrush - one of the five provinces of Plataea, it is the largest province and home of the Order.

Krehaul - a small island province, located northwest of Avrush. Only one town is located there, protected by a tiny militia group.

Usora - the second-largest province on Plataea. This historically-rebellious and mountainous land is the homeland to Eric Hahn.

Aedurus - the underworld, serving as the realm of afterlife for all monsters. It also is known as Hell to humanity, serving as the place where the wicked go after death.

Basic Locations continued.:

Elysian Fields - a paradise, where only those deemed worthy go after death. There, anyone can live in peace for all eternity.